The Elite Crimes Unit works behind the scenes of Interpol—and employs some of the world's most talented criminal minds. Because as everyone knows, it takes a thief to catch a thief—or to seduce one . . .

The old farmhouse in the French countryside is a refuge for former jewel thief Josephine Deveraux. Admittedly, there aren't many men in the vicinity, but she has her cat to cuddle up with. It's a far cry from her former life, constantly running from the law, and she's enjoying her peace . . . until the intruder in the three-piece suit tackles her. He wants her back in the game, helping with a heist—and he's not above making threats to get his way.

Little does Josephine know that notorious—and notoriously charming—thief, Xavier Lambert, is after the very same 180-carat prize she's being blackmailed to steal. To his chagrin, he's doing it not as a free agent, but as a member of the Elite Crimes Unit—the team he was forced to join when his brilliant career came to a sudden end. And little does Xavier know that his comeback is about to include a stranger's kiss, a stinging slap, and a hunt for missing treasure—along with the infuriatingly sexy woman who's outfoxing him . . .

Books by Michele Hauf

The Elite Crimes Unit
The Thief

Published by Kensington Publishing Corporation

The Thief

The Elite Crimes Unit

Michele Hauf

LYRICAL PRESS
Kensington Publishing Corp.
www.kensingtonbooks.com

Lyrical Press books are published by
Kensington Publishing Corp. 119 West 40th Street New York, NY 10018

First Electronic Edition: April 2017
eISBN-13: 978-1-5161-0196-2
eISBN-10: 1-5161-0196-0

First Print Edition: April 2017
ISBN-13: 978-1-5161-0197-9
ISBN-10: 1-5161-0197-9

Printed in the United States of America

This one is for me. The Pink Panther *movie started it all. I have been in love with jewel thieves as heroes since then.*

Author's Note

I hope you enjoyed *The Thief.* Jewel thieves have always been a fascination of mine. Blame it on *The Pink Panther.* If I hadn't become a writer I'd probably be a jewel thief. I'm sure the diamond district is relieved about that choice. In this series I'm exploring the types of white collar crime that intrigue me. Watch for *The Forger*, coming to you in August 2017 from Lyrical Press!

Keep reading,
Michele Hauf

Chapter 1

Josephine Devereaux strode through the open front screen door into the kitchen. Creamy golden evening light spread quiet warmth across the aged hardwood floors. The old farmhouse had stood on this plot in the southern French countryside for centuries. She'd had the pleasure of owning it for two years.

Setting a clutch of fresh carrots pulled from the rain-damp garden into the sink, she spun at a tiny *meow*. Behind her, the two-and-a-half-year-old Devon Rex cat with soft, downy fur the color of faded charcoal batted at the hem of her long pink skirt.

"Do you want fish or chicken tonight, Chloe?"

She opened the refrigerator to find the only option was diced chicken, left over from last night's supper. Her neighbor, Jean-Hugues, had butchered a rooster yesterday morning and brought her half.

The cat went at the feast she'd placed on a saucer with big elf ears wiggling appreciatively. Chloe had come with the farmhouse. The couple moving out hadn't wanted to bring along a kitten on their overseas move to the United States. It had been love at first purr for Josephine.

She smiled at the quiet patter of rain. And then she frowned. "Mud," she muttered. And she hated housecleaning. She had never developed a domestic bone in her body and didn't expect to grow one.

She'd spend the evening inside, maybe finish up the thriller she'd found on Jean-Hugues's bookshelf. He always encouraged her to take what she wanted—she was a voracious reader of all topics—and she gave him vegetables from her garden in return.

Not that she was a master gardener. Jean-Hugues tended the garden, along with the few rows of vines that produced enough grapes for one big barrel of wine. Jean-Hughes was sixty, but he flirted with her in a non-confrontational, just-for-fun manner, which she appreciated probably more than a twenty-six-year-old woman should.

Living so far from Paris made it difficult to find dateable men, let alone a hook-up for a night of just-give-it-to-me-now-and-leave-before-the-sun-rises sex. But that's what grocery trips to the nearest village were for. If the mood struck, she'd leave in the evening for eggs, bread, and a booty call, and find her way out of bed and back home by morning.

Sighing, Josephine forgot about the dirty carrots in the sink and padded barefoot to the lumpy jacquard sofa that stretched before the massive paned window at the front of the cottage. The window overlooked a cobblestone patio, which stretched before the house and also served as a driveway, though no cars used it. She didn't own a car. And she never had visitors, save Jean-Hugues, and on occasion the neighbors who lived on the other side of him. They were newlyweds, Jean-Louis and Hollie, and they spent most of their time by themselves. And that was exactly how Josephine preferred it.

She picked up the book, and the creased spine flopped open to the last page she'd read.

An hour later, she had to squint to read because the sun had set. Splaying the book across her chest, she closed her eyes and breathed in the fragrance of rain on fieldstones. Chloe nestled near her foot, keeping her ankle warm. The screen door, still open, squeaked lightly with the breeze. Everything was....

Peaceful? Was that a word she was supposed to embrace? To somehow understand?

"I am embracing it. Life is good."

Or rather, more different than she could have ever imagined it would be.

She set the book down, but the sound she heard was not of a paperback book hitting the wood floor. Josephine closed her eyes to listen intently. The floor creaked carefully above her, where the bathroom was located. It did not indicate the aches and pains of an aging house. This house had settled long ago.

Curling her hand beneath the sofa, she gripped the cool bone handle of the bowie knife she'd tucked up into the torn fabric amongst the springs and pulled it out. Pointing the blade down, she took a deep breath and stood up. Moving sinuously, she crept around the end of the sofa. Her free hand skimmed over Chloe's body, comforting and promising she'd return. The cat purred but thankfully didn't follow.

Upstairs, it was silent. Josephine wasn't easily spooked by natural noises, but that had not been a natural noise. And she wasn't unnerved now. Just.... annoyed.

This was her sanctuary. No one knew where she had disappeared two years ago. Very few had known her location before that. But since then, she'd completely erased herself from the grid. Therefore, whoever was stupid enough to break in was looking to rob a random person. And they had to know she was home, which meant the intruder did not fear an altercation.

Tough luck for that idiot.

On the other hand, she had only herself to blame for leaving the ladder up against the north wall after knocking down a wasp nest this morning.

Approaching the stairway, which was worn in the center of the stone risers from decades of use, Josephine tugged up her maxi skirt and tucked in one side at the waist to keep from tangling her legs in the long, floaty fabric. The stairs were fashioned from limestone; no creaks would give away her position. Barefoot, she padded up six steps to a landing. Ahead, around a sharp right turn, rose another five steps to the second floor.

Hearing the creak of a leather sole, she realized the intruder had stepped onto the stairs. But where was he? Waiting for her to spin around the corner? He probably thought she was still downstairs relaxing on the couch.

Which gave her the advantage.

With her right arm thrust out, knife blade cutting the air, she rushed forward. As she turned the corner on the stairway, the intruder grabbed her wrist, forcing it upward to deflect the blade from stabbing his face.

Josephine yanked her arm back, causing the intruder to lose his balance. His weight crushed her against the plaster wall, and they struggled on the landing. Although it was dark in the stairway, she could see that he wasn't an average intruder—most tended to not wear three-piece suits. He was about her height and lean. She did not doubt she could take him out.

He managed a weak knee to her gut, but she didn't even wince. She rammed her head against his shoulder. He twisted his waist, knocking her off-balance. They spilled backward. Her hip landed his thigh as they slid down the stone stairs.

They landed on the kitchen floor, Josephine on her stomach, with the intruder on top of her. The knife flew out of her hand and skittered across the floor, landing before Chloe's toes. The cat bent to sniff the weapon.

"Chloe, no!" she shouted. The cat scampered under the sofa.

The intruder grabbed Josephine by the hair at her neck and lifted her head. Just when he would have smashed her face against the floor, she kicked him right between the legs. His fingers instantly released the pinching hold on her neck. He swore and dropped beside her.

Scrambling across the floor, she grabbed the knife and stood, flicking on the light switch on the wall, and moving to stand over the attacker.

"What the hell?" she gasped. "You?"

A man she knew well, and had trusted enough to let down her guard and actually date, offered her an imperious smile. He swore and rubbed his crotch. "Your aim has always been spot on, Jo-Jo. Ah fuck."

His head dropped. His eyes closed. Passed out from the pain?

Josephine inched closer and leaned over him. With the tip of the knife, she prodded him at the temple.

The man's hand whipped up and grabbed her long hair, jerking her off balance and swinging her to the floor. He slammed her knife hand on the floor so hard, she let go. Grabbing the knife, he pressed it against her left breast, right over her heart.

"I have a proposition for you, Jo-Jo."

No one had called her that in over two years. And hearing it now conjured up dread and regret. But along with those feelings, there was the sudden rush of adrenaline that always came with the game. She'd walked away from the game, and this man's world of larceny and lies. And she didn't intend to walk back into it—or be forced.

"Funny, your last proposition had me running for the hills." Away from the engagement ring he had offered like a tempting sweet. She wasn't that kind of girl. The domestic, let-a-man-own-you type. Her mother's horrible choice in men had taught her a few lessons. "Never thought I'd see you again."

He winced. "Your refusal wounded me, Jo-Jo. But I'm able to put past mistakes aside. I need you for a job."

A mistake? More so on her part than his. But with his narcissism, he'd never care that she did have feelings, and she could be hurt. Hell, it had taken her two years living alone in the French countryside to realize that herself.

She splayed out her arms and closed her eyes in surrender. "Just kill me, Lincoln. That's the only way this will ever happen."

"I assumed as much. You like living the hard way? Out here in the sticks? I'll give you that. But you owe me, Jo-Jo. For saying no."

"Seriously?" *Since when did a woman owe a man because she'd refused his marriage proposal?*

She closed her eyes, inhaling the cool, ocean scent of his skin as the knife's cool metal disappeared from her body. "What the hell could you possibly want from me?"

"There's a pretty bit of sparkle I need you to pick up for me. This Saturday. In Paris."

Lincoln was interested in the sparkly stuff? Since when? The man was into money laundering and securities fraud.

Did it matter? "Not interested."

The knife blade glinted from the light over the kitchen table. "One job and I'll never bother you again."

"Since when are you into jewel theft?"

"It's related to an offensive situation that could cast a black mark against my name. I'd like to remedy that. But since you know where my expertise is focused, you should also understand I have to bring in an expert for this particular heist."

The asshole could skim a million from a major stock as easily as gliding a knife over butter. It was that talent that had initially attracted her. He was Robin Hood, taking from the rich—but he'd never given to the poor. And that had been a sticking point for her, a woman who had always tried to give away some of her spoils to those in need.

An offensive situation? She couldn't imagine. And she didn't want to know.

"How'd you find me?" she asked.

"I've kept tabs on you since you went under. Did you actually think you could elude me, Jo-Jo?"

"Don't call me that."

"It's your name, Josephine." He straddled her hips, and his grip at her shoulder loosened. He let out a long, deep breath. It reminded too much of soft summer mornings spent lazing under the sheets against his warm skin. "You never did like this position," he said. "Me on top."

"You have a thing about being the one in control."

"And you don't?"

She was in no mood to discuss her preference in sexual positions, or even to converse with this man. But she remained still beneath him. The knife blade pointed away from her; he'd let down his guard. She had only to bide her time.

"You know I'm not in the trade anymore, Lincoln. If you need some sparklers, there are other options."

"Yes, but I require discretion and quality work. You're the only thief I know who can do this job. I'll even pay you."

She scoffed. "I know better. You are not a generous man. Leave."

He slapped her face. The smack rung in her ears, and Josephine's gasp burned in her throat. But she used the distraction to her advantage, jabbing her knee into the femoral artery in his thigh. Always a painful spot. The knife clanked on the stone floor. She twisted her body, slamming him onto the floor, and landed both knees onto his torso. Grabbing the knife, she lifted it above her head with both hands, aiming for his chest.

Lincoln chuckled. His dark eyes twinkled in the cool evening shadows. Yeah, that was a devastating twinkle, and he knew how to wield it. As he spread his arms out, and she felt his chest relax beneath her knees, he said, "If I know one thing about you, Jo-Jo, it's that you are not a killer."

She tilted her head and nodded. "Nope, I'm not so keen on taking life. But I don't mind causing a little pain now and then."

She slammed her hands down. The knife pierced Lincoln's Givenchy suit and nicked bone as it entered his shoulder. He growled as she stood up over him.

"Get the hell out of my home." She stepped back and glanced around the room. Chloe was still under the sofa. "Now!"

Gripping his shoulder but leaving the blade in, Lincoln stood up, staggered, yet managed a cool recovery. He swept a hand over his coal-black hair, slicked with pomade. "You will do this job for me. I will be back."

He turned and stalked out, leaving the screen door swinging out over the courtyard. Spots of blood dribbled on the floor and cobblestones in his wake.

As Josephine let out a long breath, she heard a car roll across the gravel drive. Lincoln must have had a driver park at the end of the half-mile drive. He had walked up and insinuated himself in her house as if he was a specter.

It didn't matter how he'd gained access. He'd crept back into her life. Not cool.

Josephine's instincts kicked into survival mode.

She ran up the stairs and pulled a duffel bag out from the bedroom closet. Stuffing it with shirts, pants, bras, and a Glock 42—a .380 automatic—she scrambled down the stairs, calling for Chloe. The cat scampered out from under the sofa.

"I'm sorry, sweetie, but my past just stopped by for a visit."

And she wasn't stupid enough to sit around and wait for that return visit he had promised. Because it would happen.

Ten minutes later, she'd pulled the rusty ten-speed bicycle she used for grocery trips out of the garage and pedaled up to Jean-Hugues's cottage. She handed him Chloe and bent to kiss the cat's downy-soft head. "I need you to watch her for a few days. I'm heading to Paris. I have some things to take care of."

Like finding a new place to live. The little apartment she owned in Paris's 8th arrondissement served as a safe house. It would provide cover until Dmitri, her go-to man, could relocate her.

"Is everything okay?" Jean-Hugues asked as he cuddled Chloe against his neck. He bent his head to allow the cat to nuzzle against his five-o'clock shadow. "You are not in trouble, Josephine?"

Her name always sounded whispery and sexy when he said it. Of course she'd let him flirt with her. She'd considered kissing him once—a deep and lingering taste from a wise and seasoned male—but had never gone beyond the thankful kiss to his forehead or cheek.

"No, not in trouble. Never."

She'd not told him why a young, single woman had suddenly moved out to the country to do nothing more than read and bike, and spend her evenings cooking meals straight from the garden alongside a sexy old Frenchman. He'd always accepted that she had some secrets, as did everyone.

"I'm going to pedal into town and catch a cab to Paris. I'll be back in a few days to pick up Chloe. Okay?"

"Of course, *mon petite chat* is always welcome. We will have chicken and eggs for breakfast, *oui*, Chloe?"

Josephine stroked the cat's head, then she leaned in to kiss Jean-Hugues's cheek. "*Merci*. I will not be long."

* * * *

Two days later, Josephine took a cab back to Jean-Hugues's place. She'd set up in the Paris safe house and had contacted Dmitri. It would take a week to relocate her to Berlin. She didn't look forward to that—she didn't speak German and the city was dismal—but it wasn't permanent. A quick layover that would provide much-needed misdirection. All that mattered was getting out of France and going under.

Again.

How Lincoln had managed to keep tabs on her was incredible. She'd been careful. Since moving to France with her mother when she was eight, she'd never been issued a driver's license or ID card. No internet presence, not even a credit card. The only phones she used were pre-paid burners. Of course, she should have expected Lincoln would not let her leave so easily. He'd been infatuated with her. So quickly. It had freaked the hell out of her. She'd refused his marriage proposal after dating only four weeks.

She wasn't the marrying type. Domesticity gave her the hives. Sharing her life with a man sounded so evasive. Since giving up thievery, she liked to keep her head down and her ass out of trouble. And Lincoln wanting her to step back onto the scene now was not keeping her head down.

She directed the cabbie to turn off the headlights so they didn't shine through her neighbor's bedroom window, then told him she'd be right out. She headed up the walkway, then stopped.

Michele Hauf

The front door was open. Instinctively, Josephine's hand went to the gun she'd tucked in the back of her leather pants. While she didn't like guns, sometimes they were necessary. She pulled out the small pistol she favored and held it pointed down near her thigh. She stepped over the cracked stone threshold.

"Jean-Hugues?"

A groan sounded from the living room. She hurried in to find the old man sitting on the wood floor before the smoldering fireplace. Blood dribbled from his forehead and had stained his upper lip. He smiled up at her, but then winced.

"Jean-Hugues, what happened? When did this happen?" It must have been Lincoln. Had to be. Had she passed him on the road coming here?

"They were here not too long ago. I am so sorry, Josephine. They took Chloe."

Heart dropping, she bent before Jean-Hugues and touched his forehead. He'd been punched, and probably cut with a ring. Not a deep cut, but it must hurt terribly.

"A man with dark hair asked for you. I told him I didn't know where you were. He had two thugs with him. Why did they take the cat?" he asked, spreading his hands. "I don't understand."

It was a means to force her to do the job. Lincoln was a ruthless bastard. Hurting an old man to get to her was beyond cruel.

"I'm sorry, Jean-Hugues. Let me get that first-aid kit out of your bathroom and we'll take care of you."

"No, I am fine. Just a cut and maybe a few bruised ribs."

"They beat you?" She stood and pressed the gun grip against her temple. "That bastard."

"Why do you have a gun, Josephine? Who were those men?"

Josephine clenched her jaw. "My past."

Chapter 2

Two days later...

The glamorous black tie ball charged five thousand dollars for entry and benefited the International Mission For More. Feeding hungry children was always a good cause, yet Xavier Lambert wondered what *more* meant. More money? Shouldn't charity eventually be able to achieve its goals? He'd made a point to give away seventy-five percent of his income throughout his career. Yet, did it ever really help?

If only the Elite Crimes Unit he had been forced to join could know how many charitable dollars had been removed from the system upon *his* removal from the system.

Didn't matter. He was doing well, and had become as close to a functioning normal person as the parameters of the ECU would allow. Or so, that is what his handlers had tried to drill into him over his past year of service. It would take a while to teach an old dog new tricks.

This new trick called "life now, like it or not" had made Xavier roll over, yet he would never beg. After a year incarcerated in an eastern Belgium prison, he appreciated the modicum of freedom he now had, granted by a digital chip embedded near the base of his skull that allowed the Unit to track him at will.

As Xavier strolled the marble-floored ballroom beneath a constellation of massive crystal chandeliers, he sipped sweet champagne and scanned every face in the room for about three seconds. That was enough time to fix them into his brain: male or female, rich or pretending, a player or a gentleman, a gold-digger or a trophy for one's arm.

He had identified the Countess de Maleaux earlier. She was wearing the diamond-strand necklace weighing a hundred and eighty carats. He intended to walk out the door in about twenty minutes with that prize tucked in his pocket.

Chanel No. 5 breezed by him. He closed his eyes and inhaled. The fragrance was common in the echelon of society he frequented. What startled him now was the scent of a natural oil like clove or lavender. Simple adornments were gauche amidst the champagne-and-caviar crowd.

Unfortunate. There were occasions where he preferred simple.

Xavier placed the empty tulip goblet on a passing waiter's silver tray and made his way along the edge of the black-and-white harlequin dance floor. Most of the waltzing couples were older; the women's faces hiked up with surgery and the men's hearts thundering from the Viagra they'd swallowed upon arrival.

He smirked at the thought. To live to be seen and admired seemed a sorry existence. He had always strived to walk the shadows, to never be seen or noticed. Growing up in a wealthy family, such social fanfare had once been integral to his existence. And yet the hundreds of carats of sparkling diamonds and colored stuff milling about the room beckoned all to observe, to admire. To invoke jealousy.

Perhaps even to lure one to take.

Because, in truth, those chunks of compressed carbon could serve a much better purpose fenced and sold for charity than resting in the wrinkled cleavage of Madame Chanel No. 5.

"How's the room look?"

Xavier tilted his head at the voice in his ear. He hadn't heard from Kierce since he'd entered the mansion and had almost forgotten his presence. Almost. The man was at headquarters, sitting before a computer system so complicated it boggled Xavier's mind. Yet Kierce Quinn could map out the floor plan of the building, access ventilation shafts and alarm codes, unlock windows, and even determine a person's temperature if Xavier touched someone with the tip of his forefinger, on which he wore a thermodynamic biometric slip.

But put the guy in a social situation—with real people instead of an online forum—and watch him quiver.

"The usual idle rich," Xavier answered quietly. He turned around to give the impression he was looking over the curved blue glass bar. He was careful never to allow others to suspect he was talking to himself. "I'm moving in soon."

"After you snatch the prize, take pictures with the cufflink camera," Kierce said. "It'll take me a few minutes to run an analysis, and I don't want to wait for your return to know what we're dealing with."

"I understand. No problem. Just the girdles?"

"Yes, the rims of the diamonds, if possible. Then I can verify authenticity. Depending on the setting, you may or may not have access. If not, do the best you can."

"They are in a prong setting." Xavier had noted the setting when he'd walked past the countess. "Girdles exposed, or at least a good portion."

"Excellent. I'm working on the access code for the garage. I've determined that's your best exit option. Should have it in five."

"Then we're on. Give me radio silence, will you?"

"They don't call it radio silence, old man. It's 'ten-four.'"

Kierce wasn't even twenty. And Xavier was not an old man. But there were days he felt it around the boy genius. He kept up on all the technology regarding safes, locks, and alarm systems. But it all moved so quickly. Had it been a good thing he'd been nabbed two years ago and taken off the streets?

He tried to convince himself of it, but always failed. Someone had narced on him and ended an illustrious fourteen-year thievery career. Revenge had never been his style, but should he learn who'd given him up? He'd consider changing that style.

One bodyguard shadowed the countess. Not a big man, but Xavier was sure that beneath his cheap suit, there were muscles trained to incapacitate with a few discreet, yet devastating, moves. The thug scanned the surroundings, and when the countess would speak to someone new, he'd home in his gaze on the conversation. If she lingered in the discussion for more than a few minutes, the bodyguard began his periphery scan over again.

So Xavier would have to chat more than a minute or two. Perhaps even entice her to give him a few private moments.

Moving across the dance floor, he deftly navigated the distance between him and the countess, whom he pinned at age sixty-two. Kierce had provided cursory research on her when he'd arrived at the party: married at seventeen; the count had died when she was fifty. She'd taken a new lover every year following until a devastating operation had left her scarred in a very personal location (botched plastic surgery was the speculation). She attended any and all events, Xavier guessed, because she was lonely. She had no children and favored private jets.

Her spangled blue gown dazzled as she delivered an air kiss to a woman in a green silk sheath and bid her thanks for something Xavier had missed. He stepped forward, bowing slightly, and took her hand before she could assess him. He kissed her warm skin, the sagging flesh spotted from sun exposure.

"*Enchanté*," he offered. "Countess, you dazzled me from across the room." He swept a hand to distract her attention across the busy ballroom and noticed the bodyguard's gaze also followed. Nice. "Might I beg the pleasure of your company for this waltz?"

The orchestra had launched into a Chopin waltz.

"*Mon cheri*, you flatter me, but I was thinking to find the little girl's room."

But his few minutes had not yet passed. "I understand." Xavier leaned in and touched the dangling chandelier earring, making sure to brush her skin ever so lightly. "Cartier?" he asked.

"Why, yes." She touched her neck where his finger had glided and he noticed the blush rise at her breasts. "How did you know?"

"I'm a jeweler," he lied. It was one of many roles he assumed on command. "Worked at Cartier a while back. Lovely place. The sapphires call attention to your eyes, but are certainly lacking in comparison."

Her body heat rose as his wrist brushed her shoulder. Kierce would get that reading as well. She was focused on him—his face, his voice, the compliments she surely received often and required like oxygen.

"I do love this composition. And the waltz is my favorite," she said.

"Then shall we?" He bowed again, grandly, charmingly. And when he looked up, the countess sighed and took both his hands.

"Just once around," she said as he guided her into a light and free stroll around the dance floor. "Oh, you are very light on your feet, *Monsieur...?*"

Ignoring her hint for his name, Xavier whisked her around, hugging the inner edge where dancers brushed shoulders and the swish of satins and silks harmonized with the orchestra.

A black moiré ribbon served as backing for the diamond strand, a throwback to eighteenth-century styling. Xavier considered it a bit of good fortune. No clasp to deal with, if he were lucky.

The duchess was also light on her feet, and they'd made it halfway around the dance floor when Xavier made to sweep back a loose strand of hair over her ear. It was a simple flick of his fingers to untie the ribbon necklace. As he did he leaned in to whisper in French, "I am bedazzled by you."

"Tell me your name, and I'll follow you home," she cooed.

"Uh, uh." He waggled a finger, while noting over her shoulder that the bodyguard had assumed a laser focus on him. "My wife would not appreciate the extra place setting."

The countess pouted. Xavier danced her back to her bodyguard. He waited with arms akimbo, as if to ready for a gunfight.

"*A revoir, ma jolie.*" Xavier lifted the countess's hand and kissed it. "*Merci, pour la danse.*"

The bodyguard stepped in. The brute's dull gray eyes narrowed. "So sorry," Xavier said to him. "I understand." He backed away, and turned to stride off, enfolding himself into the crowd.

Out of the ballroom, Xavier walked purposefully to the cloak room, which he had scoped out upon arrival. A long fluorescent light illuminated a row of purses—some worth as much as an economy car—top hats, and even canes. The pimply attendant talked to someone on his cell phone, likely a girlfriend for the purring tone he assumed. His back was to Xavier; the guy had not been instructed in effective security procedures.

Xavier pulled out the necklace, turned his back to the attendant some thirty feet away, and then used the camera Kierce had designed to look like a silver cuff link. Fitting the round aperture completely over the crown of the diamond, the ring-shaped lens was able to completely photograph the girdle. How such a thing worked, Xavier had no clue, but he liked it. Handy.

"Report," Kierce said in his ear.

"Have the prize. Snapping shots. Escape cleared?"

"Tell me when you need it four seconds in advance. I'll have the doors open."

"Ten-four."

Xavier snapped six diamonds before someone cleared their throat behind him and asked if he could help.

"*Non, merci.* Just needed a moment," Xavier said, adjusting his tie.

With a nod, he quickly walked out. Stupid excuse. But if he left quickly enough, the attendant would forget about it and get back to his girlfriend.

He strolled toward the ballroom. The outer hallway, which bordered the massive room, was segregated by marble columns spaced ten feet apart. It was lit only by LEDs around the bases of the columns, providing a quiet and dark aisle for escape from the bustle of the rich and famous, or even a illicit fondling session. Xavier scanned the crowd for the countess's blue spangled couture, but didn't spot her. She must have found the bathroom—

—the kiss came out of nowhere.

A woman's mouth landed on his with a firm and intentional connection. Xavier ran his hands up her back instinctively, feeling the curve of her waist under sleek silk fabric. She felt right. Comfortable. But he hadn't seen her face and had no clue who she was, so he gently pushed her away.

Even in the shadows, her aquamarine eyes flashed at him amidst lush black lashes. Dark hair was piled high on her head like Audrey Hepburn. No jewels about her neck or at her ears. Her bare red lips curved into a smirk.

"Aw, you don't remember me, Xavier?" she asked.

She nudged his nose with hers and glided a hand down the front of his suit. Again the kiss connected with his mouth and this time he let it happen. Because it was a crazy, weird thing.

She tasted like champagne and caviar. Her body fit against his as if they'd done this a thousand times before. And her heat had already given him an erection. He wished she'd slide closer, rub her hip against him to increase the intensity of his hard-on, but he wasn't about to break the kiss to give orders. Instead, he pulled her in tighter, silently indicating that he wanted this dive into the unknown.

She took the command, sliding a bent leg along his thigh and hugging her mons against his erection. Mm.... how he loved a beautiful, intricate woman who knew exactly what she wanted.

And yet. Had she....? She had called him "Xavier." So few knew him by name. And those who did? He knew in return.

Out in the ballroom, a woman shrieked. The attendees rushed to her, the commotion drowning the orchestra's rendition of the French national anthem.

When the women pulled away, she blinked at Xavier and purred. "I could never forget your kisses," she said. "I lose myself in them."

She stroked his cheek, and he noted tattoos of tiny...cats on her inner wrist. He would have remembered such tattoos had he met her before. He never would have forgotten such gorgeous gemstone eyes.

"I...uh...." If he confessed he didn't know her, he might lose the chance for another kiss.

Then again, what the hell was he doing? He didn't need this distraction. He was on a job. And the alarm had just sounded.

Damn it. She'd actually pulled him out of focus. That had been some kiss. But he had to get out of here. Whatever ruckus was exploding on the dance floor only grew louder.

"Sorry," he said curtly, and tugged at his tie. "I don't know you."

"What? How dare you!"

The slap stung his cheek but bruised his ego much more sharply. That was to be expected, but never accepted. On the other hand, now was not the time to admonish a stranger for a stolen kiss.

He needed to extricate himself before the thug scanning the crowd at the edge of the ballroom spied him.

"The kiss was great," he started, "but—"

"Yeah, whatever. Asshole." She turned and marched off, leaving him not so appreciative of her kiss after that rude oath. Women who swore like truckers never appealed to him.

"And a good evening to you, too," he said in her wake.

"Did some chick just kiss you?" Kierce asked through the earbuds.

"*Oui.* Happens more often than you can imagine."

"You live such a tough life, Lambert."

"Yes, well, you didn't hear that slap."

"I did, but I assumed you liked it rough."

No way Xavier was going to comment on that one.

"All but one of the photos came through clean," Kierce said. "I can read the code on the girdles. You headed toward the escape door?"

"Yes. And…"

The bodyguard who had been lurking over the countess charged around the marble column. He grabbed Xavier by the tie, and swung an uppercut to the underside of his jaw. Xavier wobbled, but maintained consciousness and, thankfully, his upright status.

"That did not sound like a slap," Kierce said.

"A new challenge has presented itself," Xavier muttered. He slammed an elbow into the bruiser's ribcage. "Give me a few minutes."

Chapter 3

The second punch hit Xavier squarely on the jaw. The thug's knuckles reverberated his skull.

"That sounded like another smart punch. Right under the jaw, yes?" Kierce asked. "Give him hell, Lambert. I know you got it in you."

He did not require the encouragement. Or the play-by-play.

Xavier punched the guy in his bicep and swung his left fist low for a direct kidney hit. For the moment, they were alone in the dark corridor, as the crowd grew around the countess halfway across the ballroom. They had to know she'd been robbed. And her bodyguard had a good idea who the culprit had been. If Xavier didn't finish this fast, soon the crowd would be upon them.

A knee landed in his gut. Xavier groaned as the thug's meaty paws grabbed him by the shoulders. He saw the head butt coming—

"Duck!" Kierce yelled.

Xavier twisted out of the bruiser's grip, forcing the bodyguard to smash his forehead against the marble column. He groaned and wobbled. Xavier ran off in the same direction the woman who had just kissed him had run. Fleeing the challenge? No, just smart enough to know when to run like hell.

He patted the inner suit pocket where he'd stashed the necklace. Something wasn't right. He didn't feel the reassuring hard edges of silver and diamonds. He shoved his hand in the pocket as he beat a quick path down the back hallway.

"You near the garage?" Kierce asked.

His fingers did not curl about the necklace. Xavier swore. He'd lost it? But how? He had only just walked away from the countess. This suit was fine, brand-new. There was no hole in the pocket, nor a slipped seam for easy transfer to another pocket. And if it had fallen out during the scuffle, both he and bodyguard would have noticed.

"That bitch," he muttered.

"What?"

"The necklace is gone."

"How the—" Kierce's sudden laughter did not influence Xavier to equal mirth. "She scammed you! She nabbed the necklace while you were kissing her."

"I did not kiss her. She kissed me." Though he realized how ridiculous that defense was now that he'd spoken it. "Can you get a video surveillance on the grounds? She wore red silk. Knee-length hem. Dark hair pulled up like a movie star. I need to find that woman."

"Yes, you do. Give me a minute. You at the garage?"

"Yes." He paused before the door labeled "Employee Access Only." The red light on the security panel suddenly blinked green. "Good to go?"

"You've got a minute to clear the underground garage. Go!"

* * * *

Josephine ran down the marble stairs before the mansion, feeling a bit like Cinderella, but knowing she wasn't about to lose one of the strappy shoes she'd practiced running in for hours.

The kiss had been necessary for distraction. And it had been hot. She had not expected to run into Le Renard at the party. And what a challenge he had presented. But an exhilarating challenge after two years hiding away from the world on her little farm in the countryside.

She had thought to never see that man again....

But no time to think of him now. Josephine tuned her senses to her surroundings as she veered around the garage. Crickets trilled in the fresh, sweet grass as she crossed the drive toward the main street. The late-summer breeze over her bare shoulder cooled her sweat-damp skin. Brakes squealed as valets maneuvered sports cars about the drive-up. And the satisfying weight of the diamond necklace nestled against her hip, where the waistband had been slit to contain the piece, thrilled her like nothing else.

The steal was like returning to an old and addictive drug.

However, she'd not anticipated fleeing from the party. Instead, she had planned to hail a cab to the meeting place Lincoln had designated. She hadn't expected another thief would go after the same piece she had targeted.

So she'd wing it. *Always expect the unexpected.* Those four words had kept her alive during futile situations.

In her periphery vision, she spied an elegant figure standing beside the valet station. The thief. Le Renard, which translated to The Fox. And foxy he was. Whew! That man knew how to kiss.

But enough swooning. She had to get him off her tail.

Josephine gripped the gate guard's forearm and sniffed as if she'd been crying. Real tears would be impossible; Josephine had bolted all her feelings into an emotional vault years ago.

She closed her eyes and imagined never holding Chloe in her arms again. A hard-earned tear dripped down her cheek.

"Please, he jilted me," she said, nodding toward the curb where valets strutted and the thief remained. "I must get away from that man."

Obviously put off by the female dramatics, the guard stepped back and gestured that she walk through and out of the mansion property. "*Bonsoir, Mademoiselle.* I will keep an eye on him."

"*Merci,*" she muttered.

Turning the corner, she walked along the hedgerow fronting the property. Noting the police car parked across the street, she forced herself not to pick up into a run. On second glance, she realized it was merely a private security car. Still, she'd play it cool.

Tilting her head to pick up sounds from the mansion, she eyed the upcoming cross street. She'd turn right and rush off.

The thief's voice alternated with the gate guard's. Then he called a thankful *au revoir.*

Really? That certainly wasn't what she'd call *keeping an eye on him.*

Knowing she'd been spotted by The Fox, Josephine dashed across the street, cursing her last-minute decision to wear a red dress. She should have worn black. She'd been out of the game too long. Thankfully, it was a moonless night, and while this street was busy, she only needed a few more strides before she found a narrow alleyway. She slipped down it, taking the ancient cobblestones in quiet clicks as she moved on the balls of her feet into a trot.

The art of the stealthy escape returned to her muscle memory. Swift, long strides. Minimal upper-body movement to avoid contact with walls, signs, anything that could move and make noise. Situational awareness was key. Head up and ears open to all sounds, especially those behind her. And eyes peeled in all directions, including over her shoulder.

He was gaining on her. With little concern for stealth, for his shoes chuffed the cobblestones that were currently hampering her balance as she tried to maintain a silent pace.

"Fuck it," she muttered, and picked up into a run, using her full foot now that silence was of no concern.

She cut to the left, unsure where she was. A scan of Google maps before heading out for tonight's job had noted all the nearby streets, turns, alleys, and dead-ends. But with panic flowing through her, she wasn't sure if another left turn would bring her back toward the mansion, or toward the river Seine, which was where the pickup had been scheduled.

A deep dip in one of the centuries-smoothened cobblestones caused her to miss a step. Her hip shifted and her body wobbled. She slapped the brick wall to prevent a stumble.

A warm hand caught her around the waist. Josephine cried out.

But the heroic rescue quickly turned painful when The Fox pushed her against the wall.

"Who are you?" he insisted, his fingers digging into her upper arms.

She lifted a knee, but he saw the move coming and slammed his body against hers before she could connect with any tender body parts. Her breath heaved out. His powerful muscles overwhelmed her. Her entire body was hyper-aware of the strength and dominance he exuded. He smelled exotic, like Moroccan spices warmed under the sun. Odd. Thieves normally did not wear scent.

"You have something that belongs to me," he said.

"Oh yeah? Finders keepers, buddy." She squirmed within his strong grip. "Now let go of me. I bruise easily."

His fingers tightened.

So Josephine relaxed. A different tactic was required. She took a deep breath, which lifted her breasts so that the red silk slipped over her hard nipples, but it did not draw his attention lower. If she had a knife or the Glock, she'd be long gone and he'd be on the ground bleeding. Now all she had was her wits. And those were still sharp, despite the leisurely country holiday.

"You don't know what you have," he said.

"I'm pretty sure I do. I thought you were retired?"

"Me? What? Who do you think I am?"

"Le Renard."

The moniker suited him well. Quick, agile, and always one step ahead of the authorities, this thief had alluded capture for over a decade, netting a multibillion-dollar spree of jewel heists. With stars in her eyes, Josephine had looked up to him and had modeled her career after his. Until the moment to take revenge had presented itself.

And yet, only a handful might connect the man she'd named Xavier with The Fox. Oops. She may have overplayed her hand.

He scoffed, and in the moment he looked aside, Josephine thrust her arms forcefully up and outward, breaking his hold on her. But she didn't dash away. He remained before her, hands splayed but not touching her.

"No deals," she said. "I don't work that way."

"Neither do I."

He gazed downward now and she inhaled, which again slid the silk across her breasts. But his eyes didn't linger there. Instead, they stopped at her waistline. Damn it. There was no way he could know the necklace was there, due to the billowy line of the skirt. But she felt the stones heavy against her skin, as if they were the only things she wore.

"Listen, I don't have much time." Lincoln was waiting to make the exchange. "I need this necklace. They...." *Yeah, it could work.* Josephine forced a shaky voice. "They've got Chloe. They'll kill her if I don't hand over the jewels."

"Chloe?"

She nodded, but was unable to manufacture another tear. She'd depleted her paltry emotional stores with the gate guard.

"She's all I have," she said. Then, daring to move, she touched his chest, right over his heart. Not enough pressure to feel his heartbeat beneath the suave black suit and smartly pressed shirt, but it did cause him to startle. Good. She had to keep him wondering and off his game. "I love her."

He blinked and sucked in the corner of his upper lip, revealing teeth. A tense move. An indecisive moment.

She thrust up her right fist, connecting with his jaw and snapping his head back sharply. She had landed the uppercut perfectly and he staggered backward, his shoulders hitting the wall. She didn't take the time to see if he would go down and out.

Josephine dashed toward the Seine.

* * * *

He didn't quite black out, but that punch had knocked the wind out of him. Surprising, coming from a woman. But then, Xavier had been in scuffles with his share of women over the years. He never took them for granted. That was an idiot move. And really, he was still aching from being accosted in the ballroom. At the moment, his reaction time wasn't top-notch. That was the only reason the woman had gotten the upper hand on him.

By the time he sorted his senses and headed down the alley after her, he'd lost the thief in red. So, standing at the intersection where the alley met a dark, quiet street, he closed his eyes and listened. She'd worn heels that had clicked loudly when she'd run. Nothing now. And he could pick up no discernible perfume trail. Smart woman.

He veered right. The street headed away from the busy section of the city and toward the river. If she were going to meet for a drop-off, it could go either way. A quiet corner, or a busy, tourist-cluttered street.

Who was Chloe? And why did he care? He didn't care. But for a moment he had wondered if it could be a sister or friend. *She's all I have.* Maybe she was a lover?

When had he become such a softie? Her problems didn't matter. He had to get that necklace.

"The first analysis of the girdle markings are in," Kierce said in his ear. "You want me to pretend I didn't just hear a chick take you out?"

"Yes, please. And she did not take me out." Xavier hurried down the street, following his instincts at the turn. "The analysis?"

"As we suspected, it is a recipe list for a biological weapon."

Greed was not the reason he'd been sent to obtain the necklace. Each stone in the strand had an ingredient laser-etched onto the girdle. When combined, those ingredients would produce a biological weapon. The necklace was a clever way to deliver the recipe to a Turkish terrorist who had been exiled from his country. The man was suspected to have ties to ISIL. After Europol intercepted the coded communications, the Elite Crimes Unit had been brought in due to the highly sophisticated situation. To obtain the recipe and end the threat, they'd needed an expert on jewel heists.

Intel had determined the Countess de Maleaux was unaware of such underhanded dealings. She'd likely thought the necklace was merely a gift from an admirer. But she had been scheduled to meet the Turk tonight for a drink after the charity ball.

As well, the female thief could have no idea what she had in hand. Unless the Turk had sent his own thief to ensure the necklace was taken for him? Covering all his bases in case he was unable to procure it directly from the Countess?

"You listening, Lambert?"

"Loud and clear. Continue. I'm tracking the thief."

"Right. Chloe. That's going on record, you know."

Yes, yes, so his moment of weakness would likely get him double the visits with the ECU shrink now. He hated those monthly sessions. A requirement for his pseudo-freedom and to avoid a return to prison. But really? He was a thief because he had the talent and the wherewithal to take what no one else could, not because of anything his entitled asshole of a father had or hadn't done for him.

"I'm still pixelating and refining the last shot you sent us," Kierce said. "I'll have more info soon. Do not lose that necklace."

"On it."

By some sort of luck, he walked into the Tuileries, a vast city park that was crisscrossed with aisles of lime trees. There were no tourists on this moonless night, though here and there the homeless slept on salvaged pieces of cardboard. One dozing form sprawled on a full-size, stained mattress. Industrious fellow, carting that about the city. Xavier smirked to imagine such machinations.

His reason for feeling lucky stood at the end of an aisle of wide-leaved lime trees, silhouetted before the stone balustrade that hugged the Seine. A cage or carrier of some sort sat at her feet. Down the street, a black limo rolled away.

Xavier's heart dropped. She'd already made the exchange. To run after the limo or her?

"The limo," he decided. But not before he ensured he could find her again.

Sliding a hand inside an inner pocket of his suit coat, he brushed his finger over the clear tracker sticker he always carried on a job. He ran up to the woman. She turned as he grabbed her by the shoulders, his fingers slipping into her hair. As she raised an arm in defense, he pushed his fingers up against her scalp, ensuring the tracker was embedded.

"Where are they headed?" he asked. He shook her roughly. "Tell me!"

At their feet a cat meowed from within what he now saw was a pet carrier. "What is that?"

"That..." She crossed her arms and smiled widely at him. "...is Chloe."

"A cat? You did this for—"

His throat closed up. He didn't know what to say. He'd lost the necklace because of a cat?

Chapter 4

"You're kidding me!"

Josephine laughed at the man's utter dismay over discovering Chloe was her cat. Poor thing. The cat, not the man. She had to get her home and give her some tender loving care.

As for the man...

"If you run, you might catch them." She nodded toward the black Audi that drove toward the bridge, signaling for a turn. "I'd say it's been fun, but any man who forgets my kisses is not worth lying to. So long."

She picked up Chloe's carrier and spun to walk away, expecting that he would not let her go so easily. With a swing of her shoulder, she cast an unobtrusive look back at the man. And...he wasn't following her.

Frowning, she quickened her pace along the river and toward the 8th arrondissement, where the safe house she'd owned for six years was located.

"*I* remember the time we kissed," she muttered. Coffee and a kiss. A sweet, yet unknowing kiss-off for both of them. "Jerk." Of course, he'd been on a job. Focused. As she had been.

Xavier's heels echoed quickly away from her as he tracked the Audi. He'd never catch it on foot. And why would he go after the car when he could have tried to squeeze—maybe torture—the details out of her? The kiss in the ballroom hadn't been *that* awful. Not nearly as long or sensual as their first—shared under the moonlight—but it sparked a desirous memory in her.

So she'd gotten one over on The Fox this evening. Again. Hadn't even planned it. It had just happened. After watching him abscond with the countess's jewels, she'd been forced to react. But that was her forte, thinking on her feet. And now she was free and clear. Lincoln had returned Chloe. And she could look toward starting over.

Again.

How she loathed the exercise of getting lost and going dark. Leaving the grid. Apparently, though, she had not done it properly the first time, if Lincoln had known where to find her. She'd have to take exemplary precautions this time. Maybe Dmitri was not the man she should trust with her relocation since he had failed the last time?

"What do you think, Chloe?"

The cat mewled softly. It had been two days. She hoped Lincoln had not kept her in the cage the whole time. There was actual cat food in her tiny steel bowl.

"I'm so sorry. This won't happen again. It can't. You're all I have."

Because, much as she craved connection with another human being, a cat was the only living thing she could trust with her life, her secrets, her future.

* * * *

Water from a shower in a bathroom down the hall pattered against porcelain tiles. Xavier carefully closed the front door and, at sight of a cat with strangely short fur and freakishly large ears, he paused to see how it would react to him.

Chloe, eh?

The thing looked like a sorry rat. Make that an elf rat, thanks to the ears. And yet, it wandered up to him, sniffed at his shoe, and then strode away as if she couldn't be bothered to even meow at him.

"Not so pleased to meet you either," he muttered. Especially when he'd thought Chloe would be a person.

He scanned the room. It was dark, yet dappled with a hazy illumination from an outside streetlight. There were no curtains on the windows, and a couple of them were open, allowing in the summer breeze.

The open windows might have provided a sneakier entrance than picking the lock—a standard five-pin tumbler lock that hadn't required much more than raking the pins—but the place was on the fourth floor. He'd assessed the fire escape, which hugged the side of the building, yet whenever the stairs were possible, Xavier took the easy route. Besides, climbing the side of the building risked unwanted attention.

He brushed his fingers over the bare white mantel above a fireplace that emitted the faintest scent of smoke. A single gray velvet armchair sat in the center of the room beside two cardboard boxes that were opened but looked unpacked. So this was not her home, or maybe a new place, or even a safe house. Couldn't have been occupied for more than a day or two at most. When he peeked around to check out the narrow kitchen, he didn't smell traces of cooked food. Everything was pristine and bare of personal touches.

Sitting in the living room chair, it creaked as he settled onto the low cushion. He gripped the arms to stop the creak, but then relaxed. The shower still pattered about twenty feet down a hallway and to the right. And Chloe had taken up a perch on a windowsill, her nose wiggling to inhale the night scents of burned sugar and some flower he couldn't name.

He'd tracked the black Audi for less than a quarter mile. As soon as the car had turned onto the bridge, it had picked up speed and disappeared into the 6th arrondissement faster than his slick-heeled shoes could carry him across the uneven cobblestoned streets. It would have been fruitless to follow any further. So he'd tapped into the GPS tracking app via Kierce, and now here he sat.

Just as he touched the earbud, Kierce spoke. "Xavier, I know you're in her place. Tracked you there. I'll talk. You listen."

"Fine," he said quietly. The shower had stopped.

"So we figured the recipe was for a biological weapon, and the few ingredients you snapped a shot of proves that. Yet one of the stones names a specific location order."

He was about to ask for an explanation, but Kierce continued. "I need the entire strand to verify and be sure what we actually have. But there could also be a time frame we have to work against."

Xavier exhaled heavily.

"Get that necklace," Kierce said.

"Ten-four," Xavier replied. "Going silent now."

"Dude, no—"

He tapped the device twice to turn it off. He'd reconnect when he left, but his focus had to be on his next move. What that was, he had no idea. To force the woman, or utilize a more tried-and-true method involving seduction?

A naked female derriere strolled past the open bedroom doorway. It gave him a few ideas.

Chapter 5

Josephine pulled on a long white T-shirt that hung loosely to her thighs. She normally slept in the nude, but the apartment was chilly, probably because she'd left the bedroom window open before heading out to the ball. No bugs buzzed about inside, though. She loved the inner city's lack of insects.

She smiled, picturing The Fox's expression when he had realized that Chloe was a cat. She almost felt sorry for him. Almost. She'd gotten her cat back. Her slate was clean with Lincoln now that he had the diamond necklace in hand. Back to life as she assumed the normal people tried to live it.

Sighing, she lifted her shoulders and nodded resolutely. Normal? Yeah, whatever. It was the life for her. The only life. She preferred the jail of going underground again over the prospect of real cell bars. Too bad the country house hadn't worked out. She had been getting into gardening. And she would most certainly miss late nights spent chatting with Jean-Hugues over a glass of wine and a few slices of hard cheese.

But she'd felt it when skulking around the mansion's hedges with the necklace hugging her hip. The thrill of the steal. It was a delicious drug. She'd be smart to kick the habit for good.

Chloe meowed from the living room.

"Here, Chloe," Josephine called out. "Come here, girl." The cat did not come scampering in.

"Must be mad at me for this crazy adventure." Or annoyed at the confining apartment after having the big country house to explore. "I promise to pick up the premium cat food tomorrow as an apology, Chloe." She strolled out in search of her disgruntled companion and spied her on the living room windowsill.

A hand grabbed her around the waist; another slapped across her mouth. Stunned, Josephine forced all her weight backward, trying to knock her attacker off balance. Other than the chair across the room, there wasn't any furniture to work with. She reached back and clawed her hand across what felt like a suit jacket.

"It's me," a familiar voice warned. "I'm going to take my hands off you, but only if you promise to be nice to me like Chloe has been. She rubbed her head against my ankle."

Released, Josephine spun away from the bastard and backed toward the window. Chloe meowed and ran off toward the bedroom. "You are an asshole."

"So you've previously told me."

"I thought you went after the necklace?"

"I did. They were too fast. You, on the other hand, were an easy find."

"Fuck that. I covered my tracks." How had he… "This place has been secure for years." The only way he could have… She clenched a fist and stomped her bare foot onto the floor. "Where is it? You hugged me in the ballroom. Then you grabbed my head when I was standing by the river."

He'd gripped her by the hair; he could have put a tracker on her. She ran her fingers up through her wet hair, gliding them over her scalp, checking for anything out of the ordinary.

"It's gone now." Xavier gestured down the hallway. "You most likely washed it out in the shower."

He strolled to the chair and plopped down like he owned the place, leaning back with a satisfied smirk.

Being caught unaware was not cool, and her heart still raced. Folding her hands into fists, Josephine stalked into the kitchen. First, she downed half the bottle of water in the fridge. Then she grabbed the bowie knife she kept in the silverware drawer.

When she returned to the living room, Xavier was not in the chair. She dashed to the open window. It wasn't open wide, but enough for a quick escape. A glance to the front door confirmed it was closed. And the hinges creaked on purpose. She would have heard if anyone entered or left.

Something clattered in the kitchen. She veered back around.

Asking how a master thief had managed to elude her within the minimal square footage of her tiny Paris apartment would get her nowhere. He wasn't called The Fox for no reason.

He tilted her half-empty water bottle at her. "Do you mind? I've had a busy evening. A bit parched after all the to-do."

"You are impossible, Fox."

"Please, my name is Xavier. As you, apparently, know." His brows furrowed. "How do you know that?" He put up a palm. "Doesn't matter. I'm not the Fox anymore."

"Yeah? You could have fooled me when I saw you slip that strand of sparklers from around the countess's neck right in the middle of the crowded ballroom. Masterful. Oh, by the way, thanks for doing the hard work for me tonight."

He set the empty water bottle on the counter and approached her. Fingers still firmly wrapped about the knife hilt, Josephine waited to see what he would do. The only light from the bathroom gleamed out into the bedroom and barely lit the kitchen, so she couldn't tell if his eyes were gray or some pale color. He smelled too freaking good. Unlike most men, his scent was sublimely faint and teasing, with a hint of something rich and valuable.

"I'd ask how you know my identity, but there's a more urgent topic that requires utmost focus," he said calmly. "We need to discuss your helping me get that necklace back."

He stood four inches from her. His gaze did not waver. Using eye contact to soften her defenses would never work. She could win a stare-down against the baddest of the bad. "I didn't go to the charity ball this evening with the intention of leaving empty-handed. So now that you've saved your precious pussycat, let's focus on my needs, shall we?"

Josephine blew out a breath. "Typical male. Always so needy."

His hand glided up her wrist, just above where the knife blade angled toward his thigh. She wasn't surprised by the move; what was surprising was how the hair on her arm stood upright in anticipation of just how far he would dare move.

"I need..." His hand traced her elbow and up higher to her shoulder, slipping along the t-shirt sleeve and then following that curve along her back. "...your compliance."

When his other hand braced across her back and he pulled her tight against his chest, she knew the kiss was coming. A split-second decision— stab him or pull him closer?

Josephine held the knife away from their embrace as his mouth crushed against hers. He took his time, lips moving gently, until finally his tongue teased open her lips and dashed against her teeth. He tasted like champagne. A giddy pleasure bubbled through her system.

She murmured a pleased tone into his mouth and hitched a leg up, hooking at the knee and hugging his thigh. Easing a hand over her hip, he coaxed her closer as the connection between them grew even more intense. The funny thing about men was that it took them a few times to learn their lesson. Their first embrace had been—no, she wouldn't think of it. Heartache wasn't hers. She was better than that. And she'd done something to assuage that horrible ache. But apparently that something hadn't stuck.

Their second embrace, earlier this evening, had resulted in him losing the sparklers to her.

Time for lesson number three.

Xavier slapped a hand onto Josephine's wrist just as she twisted the knife blade against his thigh. She forced her hand, but he held her with a seeming ease. Their noses almost touching, she couldn't see the laugh in his eyes, but felt it in his relaxed smile that brushed her lips.

"I will never trust you," he whispered.

Score one for The Fox. He was finally firing on all cylinders. "Smart thief."

"I will tell you something about me," he said. His mouth moved slowly over her skin until a tilt of his head allowed him to tongue her earlobe. Josephine's nipples tightened, yet she kept back a sigh. "A secret."

"Secrets mean nothing to me," she said. And that was truth. So many ways to ruin a person with a secret. Been there, done that. Some regrets? Of course.

"It's about who I work for—"

Glass shattered in the living room. At the sudden sound, Xavier pressed his thumb into her radial nerve at the wrist, producing a piercing twinge that shot up through her palm. He secured the blade as Josephine twisted toward the sound. Shards of glass skittered across the living room floor toward the arm chair.

He pushed her toward the front door. "Time to go!"

Slamming her hands against the door frame, Josephine turned to see the crouched figure, dressed in a black suit, who had just crashed through her open fourth-floor window. The force of entry must have broken the window, which hung inward. He wasn't lying flat, and she didn't see much blood. As soon as he got his wind back, he'd be on them within seconds.

Xavier pulled open the door and shoved her into the hallway. "Go!" he insisted. She stood frozen, wondering what to do next.

Who had followed her home? She'd only been in town two days. Or had it been someone who had followed Xavier? The Fox wasn't normally so messy. Or was he was working with someone else to blackmail her?

He gestured toward the stairway with the bowie knife. "What's wrong with you?"

Shaking her head, she sucked in a breath and nodded. "Right." She turned to follow Xavier, then paused on the top step. "Oh, no!"

Rushing back inside the apartment, she dodged the charging behemoth as he shook off the glass shards from his shoulders and headed toward the bedroom.

"What the hell?" Xavier called.

"I'm not leaving Chloe again!"

The thief swore and said something about a crazy cat lady, then she heard him take a punch with a lung-crunching *ouff.* The cat was out of sight. Josephine lunged to the floor and scanned under the bed, thankful for hardwood floors and nearly a foot of crawl space. Chloe meowed. Josephine reached, but the soft ball of paws and ears was just out of reach.

What sounded like her only chair breaking echoed out from the living room.

"Please, Chloe? I promise you the best kitty toys if you'll come out. We've got to go. There's a bad man here who doesn't like kitties."

Chloe's meow didn't disguise the sound of a chair leg connecting with the sheetrock. She had bought that yesterday morning at the antique shop down the street. She hadn't been able to finagle a deal from the owner, despite complimenting her green buzz cut.

Pushing forward with her toes, she grabbed Chloe and rolled out from under the bed with the cat clutched to her chest. The warm little critter nuzzled her head against Josephine's neck. "I'm so sorry. You've been through more than one cat should have to experience."

The cat carrier sat next to the wall, but the sound of wood slamming against the living room wall freaked Chloe. She jumped, but Josephine managed to keep her in her grasp, even as claws dug into her arm.

With a little shove from Josephine, Chloe scrambled into the carrier. Josephine secured the door and picked it up. Shuffling her feet into a pair of ballet slippers, she decided not to pull on pants. If they didn't get moving, Xavier would be reduced to mush on the floor.

"I'm ready!" she called as she rushed down the hallway and out the front door. "Are you coming, darling? Really loved that chair. Hate you!"

A thud announced the end of the battle. Not looking to see who had been the victor, Josephine dashed down the stairs to the third floor. Behind her, a huffing-and-swearing someone followed. When he caught up to her, she recognized his scent. She fought the urge to elbow him as he sideswiped her and took the lead toward the first floor. She could smell blood and sweat. And anger.

Pausing on the first-floor landing, he stopped her before the final set of stairs. "We can't take the cat with us. We need to move fast. Whoever that is up there followed us from the charity ball. And he's not going to stay down long."

"I came out of retirement and stole a freaking diamond necklace for this cat. I am not going to leave her behind now."

"Just for—" He wiped a smear of blood from his nose and gestured helplessly. "What about the concierge? I said *bonsoir* to her on the way in when I explained we were lovers and I'd forgotten my key. She looks like she'd be a fine cat sitter."

Madame DaCosta had swooned when Josephine had mentioned she would be moving her cat in today. The concierge had wondered why Josephine had been gone for years, but then asked about Chloe. Was she really a Devon Rex? That was her favorite breed. She'd been without her beloved Charles for a year and so wanted to get another cat.

The Fox was right. She couldn't tote the cat around while on the run. And circumstances required she run.

Lovers, eh? Had the man been privy to her fantasies? Oh, the irony.

Xavier started down the stairs, and Josephine followed, feeling as if she were marching the accused toward the gallows. Poor Chloe. "I don't know."

"We're not arguing about this." He stopped before the concierge's door and rang the bell repeatedly. Eyeing her with extreme annoyance, he raked back his loose dark hair over his ear. It was a devastating move that tugged at Josephine's sense of propriety. And teased her nipples to harden. Yet beyond the distraction of his brutal sensuality, she also saw the corner of his left eye had started to bruise.

It was well after midnight, but Madame DaCosta answered within five seconds, in full makeup and a lushly ruffled pink robe.

She swept her long silver hair over a shoulder. "Oh, Josephine, I knew this handsome man was for you when he stopped in earlier."

"Josephine, eh?" Xavier winked at her.

He'd gotten that one as a freebie.

He turned to the concierge. "Yes, and I'm terribly allergic to cats. I wonder, if you might look after the kitty for a day? We've...er...a previous engagement."

The concierge exchanged knowing looks with Josephine. The kind of look that oozed romantic desperation. And much as she wanted to deliver a roundhouse to the thief's head and march out of the lobby with Chloe firmly in hand, Josephine surrendered to necessity. Because she heard glass shards clink from above.

"If it's not a problem?" she asked as Xavier grabbed the cat carrier and set it inside the concierge's foyer.

"It's not a problem," he said quickly and grabbed her hand. "So sorry, but we must be rude and dash," he called to the old woman. "Lock your door and don't open it for anyone else tonight. She'll be back tomorrow!"

"But, mademoiselle, your clothes!" Madame DaCosta called after them. "Oh, bother." They heard the concierge's door close and the lock slide into place.

"That was rude," Josephine said as they strode the sidewalk along the front of the building. "I didn't leave any food."

"Madame looked like she could manage caring for one small animal. The cat will be okay."

"She's been kidnapped and shuffled around for the past few days. She will not be okay!"

Xavier shoved her against the wall, and this time his kiss was forceful and deep. He pinned her wrists. The rough brick abraded her skin, but she didn't fight his aggression. She wanted to see how he would play this out. He was diving into the deep. But she suspected the man had no clue just how deep she could take him.

She had the upper hand with this one. And intended to keep it.

When he ended the kiss, he peered up at her wrist, "Two cats?" He narrowed his brows in thought.

Was he running through his memory? Trying to place the tattoo? The second cat had been an addition before she'd moved to the country. He couldn't possibly remember.

He kissed the tip of her nose. "I'll figure it out. Come on. We need to get out of sight and find you some pants."

He grabbed her hand, and they crossed the street on a red light. No cars drove through the neighborhood. Nor were there any late-night wanderers taking in the sights or shuffling home from the all-night wine shop. No excessive noise, just the rustle of leaves from the chestnut tree canopy.

So when the bullet took out a chunk of brick a foot away from Josephine's shoulder, she heard it before she felt the spray of brick hit her arm.

Chapter 6

Once again, Xavier shoved Josephine up against the wall, but this time it was to shield her from any more bullets coming from behind.

"Shoot him," Josephine commanded.

"Really?" He waggled the bowie knife before her; the only weapon he had. In his line of work, his body was the only weapon he'd needed. But his martial arts skills were worthless against a sniper.

"That's mine." She snatched the knife, but when she started to shove it at her waist—where she should have been wearing pants—she let out a frustrated sigh. "Hold this for me, will you?"

Smirking, he took the weapon. The blade was eight inches long, and he didn't have a leather holster to protect *his* eight inches from damage. There was no way that thing was going in his waistband.

"Who is that guy?" she asked as Xavier dared another look around the building corner.

The shooter had followed them from Josephine's apartment. "We should leave. He's on the run."

Pushing her onward, they headed down an alley. He wasn't sure of the direction they were headed, but he wanted to keep moving. He let her lead, thinking she must know the neighborhood.

"He's the countess's bodyguard," he said behind her. "I can't imagine he followed me from the charity ball."

"Yeah? Well, he didn't follow me. Nice. Bringing the party along with you. I didn't ask for this, Monsieur Renard."

"My name is not—"

Argument was futile. He'd make proper introductions later. If he deemed her worthy of such information. He'd not expected to become so entangled with this woman. This heist had become a literal fiasco.

"Maybe we should split up?" She stopped at an intersection of two alleys, a small cross of darkness that didn't capture any of the thin moonlight. Yet her white shirt called attention to them. If the fact she wore no pants did not.

Static crackled in Xavier's ear, reminding him he'd turned off the earpiece while waiting for the woman.

"Just give me a minute." He waved the knife, hoping the idle threat would be enough incentive for her to cool her jets.

He tapped the device in his ear. Kierce's voice whispered so rapidly, he missed the first few words. "…weapon is bigger than we'd expected. There is a compound of quadnite that takes a simple biological weapon that could endanger a dozen, perhaps cause a minor airborne emergency, and explodes that danger to massive proportions. If that recipe gets made and the weapon is released, it won't simply take out a few people, it could flatten the entire 8th arrondissement. That's the location I read on one of the girdles. We need to bring you in and reassess the mission plan, botched as it is."

"Can't do that at the moment. We're being pursued by the countess's bodyguard. He's got a gun and he's not afraid to use it."

A few seconds passed and Kierce confirmed. "Right. You're in the 8th. Don't risk going to your place. There's a safe house close."

"How did you—?"

"You haven't figured out by now you're always on my radar?"

So sometimes he forgot about the tracker he wore.

"Is the female thief with you?"

"She is." He eyed Josephine. She tapped her fingers impatiently against her wrist where she wore no watch, but instead, cats. He had seen that tattoo before. Where and when? But it had been slightly different. Only one cat then. Maybe? "Get us to the safe house and from there we'll regroup."

"Take a left on Rue Beaujon."

"Come on." Xavier grabbed Josephine's arm, but she struggled out of his grasp. He put up his hands placatingly. "Fine." Bowing low as if she were the countess in the ballroom, he entreated, "If you would be so kind as to accompany me, there's a safe house close by."

The thump of heavy-soled shoes pounded closer. Josephine bit her lower lip. Xavier could imagine the scenarios running through her thoughts. None of them were favorable. A thief forced to trust another thief? While being pursued by a maniac with a gun?

With a decisive nod, she rushed ahead of him. "Let's get moving!"

* * * *

They managed to elude the gunman and arrived at the safe house. Josephine watched Xavier enter the digital code on the door—3275; she could never not look. She was exhausted. It had been a long day. She had just run across an entire Parisian neighborhood in nothing but a t-shirt and some silky white undies. And she was seriously worried that Chloe might never forgive her for the antics she'd been imposing on the poor feline's life lately.

She wasn't a crazy cat lady. It was just that cats were the best companions, and if you respected them, they returned the respect and unconditional love. The only creature she dared accept love from was a cat. Men were too fickle. And assholes. And if one wasn't shooting at you, another was dragging you across the city in your underwear.

"Voila!" Xavier opened the door and allowed her to walk in first.

Glad to be any place that offered refuge and possibly a comfy piece of furniture, Josephine let out a deep breath and looked around. The third-floor apartment was spare of furniture and decoration, and everything was beige. There was only one window, behind the sofa. She guessed that down the hallway she'd find a bathroom, and a bedroom with at least another window or two.

The door closed behind her. Tapping his earpiece again, Xavier said, "Lock us in until seven a.m., Kierce."

Bolts on the doors clicked into place. Josephine turned to see that the windows were now barred with steel rods. "What the—?"

"I can't risk losing you after I've fallen asleep. We have a business deal to discuss."

"Yeah? And what about when the fire burns us alive because we can't escape?"

"Are you planning on roasting marshmallows?"

She had mastered the condemning glare.

He laughed dismissively. "There is an emergency switch. Naturally, I won't be revealing its location. Now, you've already showered, so I believe I'll have first go at the bathroom. You may take the bedroom down the hall, if you wish."

"I thought we were going to talk?" She plopped onto the sofa. Oh, man, it felt good to settle onto the deep foam cushion. A blanket thrown across the back settled onto her shoulder, and she pulled it forward over her arm and lap. "Not that it will matter. I'm not working with you. No matter what. And don't even think about threatening my cat."

Michele Hauf

He handed her the bowie knife. "I'm not much for harming small animals. Or women, for that matter. It is a pressing matter, though."

"You were going to tell me about who you really work for."

"Yes, that. Uh...." He glanced down the hallway. "Shower first. Then, if you're not too tired, we'll talk."

"Tired? I could go dancing right now. Just watch me."

"Keep the ruckus down, will you?" Xavier slipped off his shoes, then padded down the hallway and into the bathroom.

The door closed. Josephine leapt up and leaned over the back of the sofa. She tested the bars. They were steel and slick and likely fit a good six-to-eight inches down into the wall frame. Damn, it was like a high-security prison. She really did not want to know what kind of organization the man worked for.

She checked the hallway. Beside the bathroom—in which she already heard the shower running—the only other room was a bedroom. Bars secured against escape in that room as well.

She walked in and checked out the closet. It offered dark, featureless clothing for both men and women. She entertained the idea of slipping on some pants, but her exhausted body had other ideas.

Yawning, she wandered out to the sofa and collapsed, face first and arms by her sides. Curling into the fetal position, she tucked the blanket under her head into a comfortable nest. She'd feign sleep when he came out of the bathroom, then wield the bowie knife and force him to let her out.

* * * *

The delicate flower of a jewel thief was sawing logs when Xavier strolled out with a towel wrapped about his hips. Must have danced herself to exhaustion. He whispered her name, but she didn't respond. He touched her bare foot—gave it a good, solid nudge—but again no response.

He knew the feeling. The night had grown long and frustrating. He couldn't wait to hit the sheets. But before he did that....

He walked into the bedroom and took a folded chenille blanket from the closet. Back at the sofa, he covered Josephine to the shoulders. For a moment, he considered kissing her on the forehead, but then thought better of it when the gleam of the bowie knife, loosely clutched in her hand, caught his eye.

"Sleep well," he muttered. "I wouldn't be doing this unless I had to. Kidnapping is not my style."

He stood back. Neither was running from a gunman.

Tonight's job had been botched beyond belief. He cringed to consider how this would reflect on his perfect record. Much as he had always been a one-man operation, now that he worked for the Elite Crimes Unit he continued to take pride in doing the job well. Time off for good behavior? That was his greatest hope. For he was indebted to work with the ECU for the length of his prison sentence—another eight years. And much as he did appreciate the pseudo-freedom, he would never fool himself that it was anything but slave labor.

As he wandered into the bedroom, he sorted through the night's events. He had successfully removed the necklace from the hands of the Turkish terrorist. No word on whether or not the man's meeting with the countess had been cancelled. Likely it had been. Now he had the countess's bodyguard on his ass. Yet the diamonds were in the hands of a nameless, and unexpected, third party. And he had been forced to play nice with a cocky jewel thief who had an inordinate love for a strange cat named Chloe.

He landed on the bed, back first, arms splayed out. "And I know her. Somehow…"

Because those cats tattooed on her wrist were familiar. He just couldn't place a finger to why. She'd mentioned they had kissed before. He'd kissed many women in his lifetime. Was a man expected to remember them all?

Reaching to remove the earpiece, he paused, then tapped the device. "Kierce, you still with me?"

A yawn on the other end. "What up?"

"I've got plate numbers for you. A black Audi. Whoever owns that car is the one the woman handed the necklace off to." He gave Kierce the numbers he had memorized. It was second nature to note the license plate numbers of suspicious cars. "Full report by morning, yes?"

"Will do. The Boss wants you to report in as quickly as possible."

"I'm dead on my feet. He knows where I am. I'll check in when I wake up."

"Sounds like a plan. Good thing I like sleeping on a cot. Night, buddy."

"Good night, Kierce."

He tugged out the earpiece and set it on the nightstand. The kid wasn't fooling anyone. He rarely left ECU headquarters. That cot was his bedroom. One of these days, Xavier would have to bring him out on the town. A guy couldn't survive on computer code and microwave meals forever.

Nor could a normal, healthy man who hadn't had a real date in years sleep peacefully with a sexy woman twenty feet down the hall. That woman was going to try his every bit of patience and fortitude. He was sure of it.

Chapter 7

Josephine sniffed the air. Eyes closed, she smiled. That smell. It had been a long time since she'd enjoyed the familiar savory scent. It was something the gods must have quested for and sacked small villages to obtain. She sat up on the sofa and rubbed the sleep from her eyes. In the kitchen, The Fox stood before the stove, his back to her, tending the gods' quest in the frying pan. A pitcher of orange juice sat on the counter next to him.

"Bacon," she cooed. Mercy, but she needed that in her mouth.

Said food of the gods was being prepared by a man wearing only pants. His broad back exhibited steely muscles that bulged and flexed with his every movement, a symphony of sinuous sensuality. Mmmm.... Now that looked tasty, too.

"Morning," he called over his shoulder. He scooped up the bacon and deposited it on a plate, beside what looked like eggs over-easy. "Thought you'd be hungry." He set the plate on the counter, then poured two glasses of orange juice.

Indulging in a leisurely eye-stroll over man flesh or...devouring bacon? The answer to that question was ridiculously easy.

Unconcerned for her lack of pants, Josephine took three long strides and plopped on a stool before the kitchen counter. She picked up the fork and inhaled the lush aroma as he set the plate before her. No time for words; her mouth had better tasks to accomplish. As she crunched the first bite, salty sweet savory goodness spread across her taste buds.

When she finally noticed Xavier sitting beside her, a forkload of eggs suspended before him, she stopped chewing. Why was he staring at her instead of eating? His face crinkled in the cutest smirk. And what was with the sexy lines that creased at the corner of his eyes? Did she want to trace them? *No. Yes. No!*

"What? Can't a girl worship bacon?" She crunched another divine bite. "It's better than a sugar habit. Am I right?"

"I don't think I've ever seen a slice of bacon enjoyed so thoroughly."

"Pay attention to your own food. As soon as I'm done refueling, I am out of here."

"The doors are still bolted. And you're not wearing pants."

Was it really that early? Since living in the country, she'd grown to enjoy a leisurely awakening well after seven a.m.

"A bolted door has never stopped me before." If given enough time, she could pick any lock, even one in a fortified safe house. "Nor has lack of pants."

"You didn't take that challenge in the middle of the night."

Yeah, so she had slept like the dead. The past few days had been stress-loaded and crazy. And they weren't over with yet, because she was a pseudo-hostage in this not-so-safe safe house. Though she wouldn't pass up the prison food. Hell, no.

The eggs went ignored as she bit into another slice of heaven. Not too much grease, yet just the right amount. The man did know how to fry up a pig.

"You have a phone I can use?" She spoke with her mouth full. Yeah, she had no shame.

"Why? You want to make your one promised call?"

"Are you kidding me?"

He smirked and shook his head. "I have a cell, but all calls are tracked and traced."

"Seriously? Forget it. I wanted to call Madame DaCosta and check on Chloe. We left so quickly. And I'm pretty sure the intruder didn't sweep up and close my apartment door behind him when he left. The concierge is going to freak when she sees the mess."

"Kierce ordered a clean-up team sent over immediately in our wake last night. There's no evidence to be found, surely."

"Kierce?"

"Yes."

Sensing he wasn't about to expound, Josephine tried the eggs. They contained the perfect ratio of whites to slightly runny yokes. But she was starving.

So The Fox was working with another, and she had fled a maniacal thug with a gun. And for the second time she'd abandoned Chloe. What nightmare had she stepped into?

After a few bites she noticed Xavier, head tilted, staring at the tattoo she had written along her left forearm.

"Go ahead, underestimate me," he read the words.

"You got it."

"I will try my best not to. We are going to discuss things this morning," Xavier announced. "The clock is ticking. Please do not make the mistake of believing you've time for argument or escape."

"Says the guy holding the key. Whatever you want from me, there is not enough bacon in the world to buy it."

"Actually, you owe me."

He was making the ridiculous presumption that she cared what he thought. No matter what happened between them, she would never owe a man anything. *Been there, done that.* Not making that mistake ever again. She was not her mother.

Josephine set down her fork and eyed the front door. Without professional picks, it would take some time to jimmy the bolts. Doubtful the bathroom would reveal a forgotten hairpin, either. And in that time, Xavier would probably ramble on about all that she owed him. Her kingdom for some chloroform to knock him out for a few hours. Not to mention a pair of pants.

The only other option? Play along. Learn what she could about the mess she found herself in while he was in a chatty mood.

"First, tell me what you know about me," she said.

"That's easy. Not a thing. Until you attacked me with the kiss in the ballroom, I had thought this was a one-man operation. Thanks to the concierge, I know your name is Josephine. Though I've got someone working on your background right now."

"Kierce?"

"Yes. We got a clear shot of you from the security cameras at the ball. That was sloppy on your part. I expect results on the background check soon. But apparently, you know much more about me than I you. If we've kissed previous to last night's adventure?"

Josephine pushed her plate aside. Yeah, that first kiss. Infatuation had always been a weakness of hers. Admiration for the bad boys. The suave, cool criminal who could slip into a person's home and steal their entire life away with a wink and a smile.

Would she ever get over that ridiculous desire for validation from one so obviously wrong for both her heart and her existence?

"I used to look up to you," she finally said. "You were once a master thief, unrivaled by any other. What the hell happened? You know in this game of snatch–and–grab that it's winner take all. You took it. Then I took it. If you want it back, you'll have to take it again."

"Exactly. I need to take it from the man you've handed the necklace over to. What was his name again?"

"I don't think I mentioned a name." Despite not being a fan of Lincoln Blackwell, she wasn't prepared to give The Fox any more details on him until she knew who Xavier was working for and just exactly what his game was.

His jaw tensed.

"You know him, yes?" he asked. "Are the two of you close? Allies? Lovers?"

She turned back to her eggs. She could manage some more protein. She needed to keep up her strength when the time came to fight her way out of this situation.

"No answer? Fine. My guess is you know him well," Xavier continued. "Lovers? Maybe."

She would not give him a clue. Josephine shoveled in the eggs to keep him from sensing any small flinch in her facial muscles or flicker of recognition in her eyes.

"So," he continued, "I'm placing bets that you have been inside his home and can provide me with a layout."

"You've a wild imagination, Fox. I'll grant you that. It does come in handy for plotting heists."

"Please call me Xavier. And do tell me there was nothing going on between you and the man who stole your cat?"

"Why? You jealous?"

He exhaled and shook his head in frustration. "If I'm working with a two-timing thief right now, I'd like to know."

Josephine dropped her fork with a clatter. She wasn't hungry anymore. And she was in no mood to expound on her failed romance with the larcenist bastard Blackwell. Most especially to a man who currently activated all her lust buttons. He was too sexy sitting there without a shirt, pushing his eggs around on the plate like he meant to eat. His pectorals pulsed each time he moved his arm. Yeah, she noticed. The man may have been off the scene for a few years, but he'd certainly kept the machine in shape. But more so than his muscles, she sensed his mind was moving, the gears turning and shifting.

Which meant she had to stay a gear-turn ahead of him at all times. Appealing to a thief's weakness? Easy as pie.

"Fine." She picked up the glass of orange juice and tilted it back. Oh, yes, that tasted fresh. The man squeezed his own juice? Her lust levels rocketed up another notch. "His name is Lincoln Blackwell. I have been in his place. And yes, I know exactly where he would store the necklace. He's very proud of his Zeus 5000 safe."

"The Zeus." He sat up straighter. Details on a safe? Totally hooked. "Ten million possible combinations. That's a tough crack."

"But you've done it before." She didn't have to be told.

"It concerns me you know so much about my skills."

Far too much to ever reveal. Until the time was right. And that time may or may not ever arrive.

"Will you draw me a floor plan? That's all I ask, Josephine. You can walk out of here and need not worry I'll follow if you'll just give me that. It is a desperate situation—"

"Sure." She cut him off before he could concoct a sob story that might actually pluck at her emotions. She wasn't that stupid. And seriously? She'd served her part. Handed the necklace over to Lincoln. Whatever happened to it now wasn't her concern. "But first, I need a shower. The trip across Paris without pants was not one of my finer moments. I'll draw you a plan when I've washed off the city. Deal?"

She held out her hand for him to shake, and he eyed it with that same curiously bemused smirk that had been activating her lust meter. When he didn't offer his own, she pointed her thumb and index finger in the shooting gesture. "Got it. No trust among thieves. Wouldn't have it any other way. I'm going to grab some clothes from the bedroom closet."

"Help yourself. That's what they're there for."

In the bedroom, she tugged out a black t-shirt and pair of black leggings. An assortment of sneakers in gray and black lined the wall, and she found a pair of gray Chuck Taylors that might actually fit her size sixes.

With a glance down the hallway, where the sound of clanking dishes in the sink assured her he was an odd man indeed—cooking *and* cleaning?—she headed into the bathroom and turned on the shower.

Fortunately, the bathroom looked out onto an inner courtyard. A one-foot-by-three-foot transom window was set over the shower. Nary a steel bar to be seen, either. Her morning had just improved one hundred percent.

Chapter 8

As expected, the thief's hand appeared on the edge of the rooftop, groping for a good hold on the rough-edged slate tiles. From his observation point, rain spattered Xavier's cheeks and nose. It was just a drizzle, but enough to thwart any determined climber ascending the inner stucco wall of a courtyard apartment building to the roof. So when she hoisted herself up and rolled to her back, he silently gave her extra credit for the accomplishment.

Still unaware of his presence, a satisfied sigh escaped her lips.

He had to smile at that. Escape. That feeling of accomplishment. Of achieving something few others could. Of pulling the wool over someone's eyes. The rush of the game. It was worth the sigh and the little chuckle that followed.

That was one hell of a sexy chuckle. And he immediately imagined hearing it in his bed, as she lay alongside him, sweaty and thoroughly pleased after a night of wicked, mind-exploding sex.

Now Xavier chuckled, and gave himself away. He heard her startle and sit up, so he swung around the side of the chimney vent against which he'd been resting and slid down to sit beside her. He hooked the heels of his rubber shoes into the metal transom for a sure hold.

"*Canard*," she muttered.

He thought she didn't speak French, judging by her obvious American accent. Being called an asshole, even in his own language? How lacking in originality.

"You performed to my expectations," he said. "Wouldn't have thought you'd actually stick around and cooperate."

"My cat is waiting for me."

"Yes, dear sweet, Chloe. The poor thing barely has any fur. How does she stay warm?" He paused, but knew better to expect an answer. "You think it's safe to return to your apartment?"

"I don't intend to stay. Chloe and I have another place waiting."

"Your starting-over place?"

"Maybe."

Angry birds chirped behind them. Xavier guessed there might be a nest in the nearby vent cap.

"In exchange for the shower and the new clothes," he said, "I'll take that diagram of Blackwell's home layout. As promised."

"If I push you off the roof, I won't have to worry about straining my drawing muscles."

Enough. He didn't have the patience for this. Swinging up the bowie knife that she'd forgotten under the sofa cushion, Xavier slammed her against the roof, blade to her throat. Reflexively, she kicked at him, then decided better when the blade cut flesh.

"Dude, chill, will you? You are not a person who hurts people."

How could she know whether or not he hurt people? Didn't matter. What did matter was getting that necklace in hand.

"I work for an organization that is very concerned about recovering the diamond necklace," he said.

Rules were that the agents did not reveal their ties to the ECU unless it was necessary. He felt it very necessary to appeal to this woman's lacking sense of fairness, but he could do that without giving up certain information. However, she would need some impetus to cooperate. She was like him. Every man for himself. Unless that man possessed a modicum of heart. Which he did. The jury was still out on whether or not she possessed any empathy.

"I was supposed to nab the necklace to ensure the Turkish terrorist who had plans to meet the countess after the ball did not get it." When she squirmed, he pressed the blade harder. A pearl of blood spilled down the curve of her neck. She was right. He never hurt a person without good reason. "There is a recipe for a biological weapon lasered onto the diamond girdles. It could prove fatal to innocents."

"Shit," she muttered.

"We originally thought the weapon could be contained, a small threat. But evidence taken from a few shots of the girdles while I had the necklace in hand now suggests the weapon is much more dangerous."

"How dangerous?" she whispered.

"In the wrong hands? It could take out the entire 8th arrondissement of Paris."

He released her and turned to sit, facing the open space that framed the inner courtyard. The scent of oregano from the nearby Italian restaurant carried on the air. Knife in hand, wrists propped on his bent knees, he waited to see if the sacrifice of information would serve him.

Josephine sat up, but didn't say anything. He'd give her a moment to process the information. When a person worked only for themself, it took a while to grasp the "help others" concept. It hadn't been difficult for him. It was something he'd strived to accomplish all his life, despite his entitled upbringing. A man should never take without giving back.

"What did you say was the name of the place you work for?"

Curiosity was a good sign. "I don't think I mentioned that."

"Secret organization, huh? Tell me more."

"The facts are given on a need-to-know basis."

"Then I'm out of here."

He grabbed her by the upper arm and this time didn't allow her to struggle free. The woman was strong, but he had a much bigger problem to contend with than any bruises she might sustain.

"The entire city of Paris relies on you helping me out, Josephine. And I'll remind you that the area of target includes your precious Chloe."

She pressed her lips together. Her gaze flittered to the side and down, in the direction from which she had climbed three stories to attempt her failed escape.

Xavier had taken the staircase.

The rain continued, and they were both soaked. He didn't want to screw up this mission any more than he already had. There were consequences.

"I care about Chloe," she finally said, "I meant it when I said she was all I had."

"Come on. No friends?"

"You're in the same line of work as I am. You tell me. How many friends do you have, thief?"

"Touché."

"That said, ultimately I am concerned with preserving human life. I need more. Why would you, a professional thief, now work with some... group? And how? You were in prison."

How she knew that fact was beyond him. Then again, she seemed to know things about him. His conviction and incarceration had been kept out of the media. Only now did he realize that had been a carefully orchestrated forethought by the ECU. But surely there were police records. Any information was obtainable with the right motivation and determination. Had she been following his career?

While that should disturb him, he couldn't help but enjoy some satisfaction over the idea of having a fan girl. He wasn't entirely without his pride. And after the past few years he'd experienced, the feeling was like welcoming back an old and much-needed friend.

"I served a year for a crime I had thought never made the news." He cast her a searching gaze, but she wouldn't take the bait and provide him more intel. "On day number three hundred sixty-five of my incarceration, I was taken from my cell and brought to an undisclosed location. I was offered a position with the...shall we call it...organization. I was also shown a picture of my tombstone, if I choose to decide against taking their offer."

"That's so *La Femme Nikita*."

"Is it?" He had seen that movie, so long ago. Couldn't recall much of it, despite spending his free time in movie theaters. If not occupied with his next heist, he liked to lose himself in other worlds on the silver screen. "So I agreed, because I value my freedom and breathing. But if I screw up? It's the tombstone for me."

"Looks like you've screwed up this mission. Big time."

Stating the obvious wouldn't earn her any points. "There's still an opportunity to save it."

"You mean save your ass?"

"How about the asses of the entire 8th arrondissement? And one small cat derriere?"

"Why must every man who comes into my life insist on threatening my cat?" She stood confidently on the slippery roof tiles. The gray sneakers she'd borrowed sported rubber soles. "That is so not cool."

"I'm sorry. That was crass. You seem to...." *Bring out the worst in him?* Never had he allowed a woman to get under his skin so quickly and easily.

Then again, a woman had never foiled what should have been a slick and easy heist.

"It's that I know this weapon," he continued, "if created from the recipe on those diamond girdles, can harm so many. Even I, a man who has always acted for himself, would never wish to see that happen. And if I can prevent it, I will."

"So now you've become some kind of legitimate hero? Former jewel thief who once took from the rich and gave to the poor like Robin Hood now pulls on the cape and leaps tall buildings in a single bound?"

He gaped at her. How could she know he had given away so much of his booty? She had to have been following him, tracking him by some means. Who *was* this woman?

She sat against the chimney vent and looked down at him. Xavier laid back, tilting his head to match her gaze. They were at an impasse. She unwilling to provide information he'd love to have, but which wasn't necessary to this mission. And he was unwilling to lower himself any further and beg for her help.

On the other hand, her decision could mean the difference between certain freedom or the tombstone for him.

He'd never asked for a favor before. Never wanted or needed one. If she only knew how hard this was for him.

"Forget it," he decided. He'd figure things out on his own. He climbed to the spine of the roof and walked to the access door. Just as he grabbed the rain-slick doorknob, Josephine called out.

"If there's more bacon," she said, "I'll draw you that damn building layout."

Opening the door, he grinned. There was no more bacon. "I'll see what I can do."

* * * *

Josephine took pride in her drawing that detailed the layout of Lincoln Blackwell's mansion. She'd been inside half a dozen times. Mostly his bedroom, but she hadn't labeled that room on the schematic. The home sported infrared sensors along the perimeter of the property, precision locks with seismic sensors, and security cameras in most rooms. The most important information was the side garage window, and the windows along the back and north side and the roof tower. Yes, the man had a security tower on the roof of his mansion. Made sense. He was worth hundreds of millions.

"You said the safe is a Zeus 5000?" Xavier asked. He sat beside her at the kitchen counter, watching intently as her sketch grew.

Bacon was sadly missing from the scenario.

But she was giving him a pass because he smelled like a man and that smell she had missed of late. Rugged yet sensual. She bet his skin was warm and his fingertips were sensitive to any and all movement. Like, for instance, a woman's body gliding beneath his touch.

"Huh?" She yanked herself from the distracting fantasy.

"A Zeus 5000?" he repeated.

Right. He wanted her to confirm facts. Not touch his hot abs. "I'm not giving more than the building layout," she said. "The rest is up to you, buddy."

"I'm not your buddy. I'm not your friend. You hate me. I dislike you, despite your appeal. So let's work with that a moment and just drop the ego bit. It's not going to hurt you to give me a few more details."

"Nice bedside manner. That work for you?"

"What? My bedside— You want me to *seduce* the information out of you?"

"Doubt that would work. You didn't even like my kiss."

"I never said that. The kisses last night were exemplary."

Oh, mercy, yes, they had been. And he thought she appealed to him? He had said it. After the dislike part. The man needed to polish up his seduction skills.

"And I do remember it from before."

She stopped drawing, but didn't look at him. "It?"

"The previous kiss you alluded to? Our first one that occurred well before this whole adventure began last night?"

Years ago. And her hair had been shorter and probably dyed blue at the time. Or no, she'd worn a blond wig that night. Going for the vixen look. "Is that so?"

He tapped her wrist, right over the tattoos. Two tiny black cats. In memoriam. She hoped it would be a long time before she'd have to add a third.

"There was only one then. But to be honest, I don't recall when or where we've met before," he said. "I know I haven't fucked you. I would remember that."

Because he fucked so few, or because—what was she doing? She didn't care about the man's sex life. And she knew what *he* was doing. Trying to get more details from her by being softer, keeping the conversation going. The room still smelled of bacon, yet he hadn't dragged out the frying pan since their return from the roof. He'd lied to her about having more.

But when had she ever told him the truth?

Well, there was that part about Chloe being everything to her.

"So my kisses are not so memorable. Way to make a woman feel special, Fox."

"Don't call me that."

She tapped the tiny symbol she'd drawn at the upper corner of the page. A simple diamond topped by ears. The Fox's calling card. "Aren't you proud of Le Renard's legacy?"

"I am. Who would not be?" She could feel him straighten beside her. "I am the best. But I am so because I do not advertise it or put it out there on all that social media."

"All that social media? You sound like such a geezer. But as for not advertising...you always left your calling card at your jobs."

He eyed the drawing of the fox. He gave her one of those classic Frenchman shrugs that said yes, of course, but at the same time brushed off the importance of the topic.

"Your secret is safe with me," she offered. "You are a pro, and pros work alone and don't shine in any spotlights. The best do their work in the dark."

He waggled his brows. Should she take that as some kind of seductive suggestion? Well, she did, and she inhaled and wiggled on the seat to reset her relaxing muscles, which only wanted to melt up against the man and see how quickly she could make him remember the power of her kisses.

"I've been following your jobs. Learning from you," she confessed. "You know I used your 'hairspray on the heat sensors' method to snag a nice string of sparklers from the Venetian Art Fair?"

"That was you? I read about it in Le Monde. I thought the method seemed familiar. That was quite the take. How much did you walk away with?"

"Never as little as is reported. You should know that."

He nodded. "Most often the offended party reports much less. Too embarrassed to admit how much one thief actually walked away with."

"Yep." She rolled the pencil under her forefingers over the schematic drawing. "I give most of it away."

The touch of his hand to hers, covering her fingers and curling over to clasp, was so startling she sucked in a breath. She jerked her gaze to his eyes. Hazel green. Not vivid but interestingly flecked with emerald against the lighter iris. This was the first time she'd actually looked into them for more than a fleeting moment.

She shouldn't have done it. Her heart thundered. Josephine quickly tugged away from his touch. She didn't want him to read the rise in her body temperature as a sign of weakness.

"I do the same," he said. "Or I did. I can only shake my head when I consider how putting me in prison took so many charity dollars out of the system."

She had known that about him. Which had provided the catalyst for her doing the same. Just because she'd hated the guy hadn't meant she couldn't use his best tricks and spread the charity even farther. She appreciated that he wasn't in it all for himself. Not an asshole. He was a cad. There was a difference between the two. Cads were bad boys. The kind that made her heart pump and her fantasies take to flame.

"It's not like a person needs much more than a couple hundred thousand to keep them in clothes and food, eh?"

"I live a spare lifestyle," he agreed. "Albeit, in upscale homes. Or I used to. As an agent with the...uh, people I work for...we are given a place to stay and a budget."

"Wow. So you've moved from one prison to another?"

"You could say that. But much as it's different from when I was free, I am still doing some good."

"By chasing those who do the same thing you once did? I bet you like that, putting away the competition. So what are your plans for me?"

"I have no plans. Well, no, I shouldn't say that. I have developed a plan just now, actually." He tapped the building layout and pulled it before him to look it over.

Josephine sat there, waiting for him to reveal his marvelous plan. But he didn't. Instead his eyes wandered the sketch, moving down hallways and around corners. She could sense the gears in his brain moving. It was a high to plot out the heist. No caffeine, drugs or—yeah, even sex—could match it. And the final payoff? Bliss.

Finally, he stood, folded the plan, and tucked it in an inner suit coat pocket.

"So?" she prompted.

"What?"

"You were going to reveal your plans for me."

"Did I say that?"

Much as he frustrated her, she had to give him points for tossing the snark right back at her.

Finally he asked, "You sure you want to know?"

She took a moment to consider his teasing proposal. Whatever the plans were—arrest her, turn her over, let her go—they'd have a condition and a lie attached. So she shrugged. "Dazzle me."

"I can do that."

He slid his hand along her jaw and his fingers wove through her hair as his head bent and his mouth found hers. The kiss was intense, firm, and commanding. He sensed her internal struggle, and his fingers curved against her scalp, claiming her, defying her to make it end.

She didn't need this to end. This kiss was well worth the hit to her emotional stronghold. She inhaled his subtle yet compelling scent and drowned in the heat of his expertise. He opened her mouth and traced her inner lip with his tongue. Mercy, that sent delicious shivers throughout her body, all the way down to her toes.

Josephine gripped the front of his crisp white shirt and tugged him closer. His hair, still moist from the rain, smelled like her country home. Freedom and lack of worry. Kissing this thief was wrong. *So wrong.* But when had she ever wanted what was right?

Never. Always she had sought that which had been just out of her reach. Whatever would toss up a challenge and a wicked punishment should she not succeed. She had always succeeded. And when it came to bad boys? Sign her up.

It was that *screaming no* feeling she got when she knew she should run, screaming no, no, no, and never look back. That damned feeling always meant she wanted in.

She hated not knowing the plan, but she had to admit she did like following Xavier. Because the challenge of such a man? Much more fulfilling than the escape.

He pulled away and strode to the front door, leaving her with her mouth gaping and eyes closed. "Let's go, Josephine. We've a lot to do before tonight."

Chapter 9

Victor Katirci stood between two steel support columns that framed a window overlooking the Seine. The building in the 13th arrondissement, set a stone's throw from the *peripherique*, was under construction. Before him, Alex Toyo shrank from his glare. He'd given the man a simple task: shadow the Countess de Maleaux at the charity ball. All he had to do was stay close and keep an eye on the diamond-strand necklace. Then, after the ball, escort the countess to a quiet tête-à-tête with Victor without letting her know something was up.

The countess had known only that Victor was a friend of her former lover, who went by the mysterious name, Ashwood. He had gifted the countess the necklace. She'd thought it a selfless gift. Ashwood had a beef with the police, who had arrested his cousin for making terroristic threats and who wanted to make a political statement to the police. Victor had intended to pull a switch so the countess would have left with a fake and he the diamonds that contained the ingredient list. The list supposedly included the location and a payment stone, which contained a code to access a bank transfer for five million euros.

That, along with the necklace—comprised of lesser stones, but still worth a hundred thousand—would have made Victor a very happy man.

The meeting with the countess had not occurred because someone had stolen the necklace. Right from under his man's watchful eye.

Toyo had explained there had been two thieves present in the ballroom working together.

Victor approached the man. Arms crossed high over his chest, he held his Ruger .9mm pointed behind him and toward the floor. "What did the thieves look like, eh?"

"The first was tall, had dark loose hair. Dressed well. He had pale green eyes."

Victor lifted a brow. That sort of description would get him nowhere. He needed weight, distinctive marks, tattoos, accent and—why the hell not a selfie inadvertently showing the unsuspecting thief standing behind his man's shoulder? The current trends in social media made gathering intel so much easier. The veil of privacy had been smashed by collective acceptance.

"The woman looked like that movie star from the Tiffany's show."

A woman? Victor sniffed and stretched out his arms, waving the gun before him. He knew how to use his imposing six feet, six inches and smirked as Toyo's color grew pale at sight of his flexing biceps.

"Are you telling me you could not keep a valuable diamond necklace safe from a *female* thief?"

The idiot put up his hands in defense, noticeably shaking. As he should be. "I followed the man to an apartment in the 8th. It was hers. There was a cat."

"What?"

"I can give you the address!"

Victor tugged out his cell phone, scrolled to his contact list, and handed it to him. "Enter it."

Toyo typed as his hands shook madly, then handed back the phone. Victor checked the map app, which zoomed in on a point in the 8th, about six blocks north of the Champs Elysees.

"You said you shot at them?"

The idiot nodded.

"You missed. What? Was there a cat in your way?"

Toyo actually chuckled, then instantly sobered as Victor's condemning stare found its mark. "No. I didn't want to draw attention, shooting in the street."

"Yet you had no problem whatsoever with breaking a window?"

"I went through an open window. I guess I must have been rough when entering. The window just broke."

"You *guess* you were too rough." Enough. He'd gotten all he could from this one, and with an address, he had somewhere to start. That's what he got for sending idiots to do a job he should have tended. "You are dismissed."

Victor swung up his arm. Pressing the pistol barrel to the man's forehead, he pulled the trigger.

* * * *

The Blackwell mansion was situated in the 6th arrondissement, a neighborhood of old money. It was the most suburban area Josephine had found on the inside of the *peripherique* freeway that surrounded Paris and separated it from the suburbs. While most homes were mansions, each had a neat green lawn and statuary surrounded by the requisite wrought-iron fence sporting decades-old ivy climbing the bars and obscuring views.

Xavier's plans had required her to go along with him tonight, and after initially balking—because she couldn't appear too eager—she'd agreed. Because not only was this her first opportunity to accompany The Fox on a real heist, but as well…ah, she was trying *not* to think about the attraction she felt toward the man. And if he insisted on kissing her at every moment when she least expected it, that attraction would not cease. The man was just so…bad. And talented. And smart. And sexy. And she had admired his work for years.

While also hating him.

So there was *that* to keep her from jumping him when her lust levels breeched code orange. Also, she did possess a modicum of self-control. She wasn't a teenage girl; moreover, she'd never even had the obligatory teenage crush. At the time, she'd been too busy simply surviving.

But to think back, perhaps The Fox had been her first real crush.

A phone call to Madame DaCosta had been greeted with a happy squeal. She and Chloe were getting along famously, and if Josephine couldn't pick her up for another day—or a month—she'd be just fine.

A day it was, then. Josephine wasn't about to let some crazy cat lady move in on her cat.

"This reminds me of *Gone in 60 Seconds*," she said, putting her ballet-flat-clad feet on the dashboard of Xavier's 1995 Megane Renault and spreading her knees. An unladylike position, but it was comfortable, and it kept her from nervously tapping the floor. She looked through Xavier's night-vision binoculars. The lights were still on inside Blackwell's mansion, but she knew the peripheral lights were a constant. When the living room lights when out, that would be their signal for "all's clear."

Xavier sipped the coffee he'd gotten at the McDonalds on the Champs Elysees. The man always drank coffee before his heists. "You like American movies?"

He hadn't come right out and asked if she was American, though it should be obvious. Displaced from Iowa at the age of eight. Toted overseas with her mother, who had followed the baddest of the bad boys to Paris. She'd landed in the *banlieue*. Not all the Parisian suburbs were idyllic and quaint. Points to The Fox for not wasting breath on stupid questions.

"I like any and all heist movies," she said, dropping the binoculars onto her chest. "Jewels, gold, cars. It's all good, Becky."

"Becky?"

"*The Italian Job.* Becky was the dupe. Good stuff. So, we've got the place staked out. Let's talk."

"Like the couple in the movie? Which movie are we on now?"

"Back to *Gone in 60 Seconds.*"

"Didn't they start making out?"

"So you have seen it." Josephine waggled her brows at him. It wasn't an invitation, more a tease.

She'd spent the afternoon trailing Xavier as he prepared for tonight's heist, every moment in awe of his style, finesse, and attention to detail. She'd even learned a few things. He never kept any information on his phone. Always aware of digital theft. All handwritten notes were burned. (He'd burned her drawing of Blackwell's home.) He preferred to shop at mom-and-pop hardware stores. And he must have a budget, because he'd bought the cheapest pair of binoculars.

Still. She was trailing the master. And this time, not in secret.

But she had turned her life around. Had begun anew and had been doing quite well at it. The life of a thief was no longer for her. After tonight, she would pick up Chloe and head to Berlin. Dmitri had secured an interim place for her that he promised she would find suitable, safe, and plunked right in the middle of suburbia.

Joy.

Thankfully, it was only for a few weeks until a more permanent residence could be located. She hoped for a beach, but would probably end up in Iceland. She'd have to tell Dmitri no cold climes.

"What's your favorite heist movie?" Xavier asked. He looked calm and relaxed, with his wrist on the top of the steering wheel and head tilted back. Yet his eyes took in everything in their periphery. "If we're talking American films, mine is *The Score.*"

"Love that one," she said. "Robert de Niro as the old and experienced thief. And Edward Norton was amazing. Have you ever pulled on a character for one of your jobs?" Norton had pretended to be a mentally challenged janitor to learn the layout of the hit by gaining the trust of those working there.

"Never so extreme as taking on a whole new personality," he said. "But I can affect a convincing British accent when need be, love." His accent was, indeed, excellent. "I'm also quite good with Italian. I can change my gait, my manner, wear a disguise. Some thick-rimmed glasses tend to change my whole face. It's all part of the job."

"I love playing dress up," she agreed. "Wigs are my thing. And high heels."

"Heels?"

"Distraction." She winked at him.

"I get that. The female grifter always has the advantage when it comes to using sex appeal to distract."

"I'm sure your powers of distraction are fierce."

He rubbed the back of his knuckles against his chest and lowered his eyes in a look she mentally dubbed I-dare-you-eyes. "Not too shabby, if I do say so myself. So, what's your favorite heist movie?"

"The aforementioned *The Italian Job*. The newest version starring Mark Wahlberg. I've never been able to get into the original with Michael Caine."

"That was a gold heist. Clever use of the Minis, though."

"I almost bought a Mini Cooper because of that flick. I always look in the safe when I open it. Don't you?"

"There's no other reason to crack open a safe than to look in it."

"True. So, let's see. Discussion topics... Favorite color is stupid. Do you have a favorite sport?"

"I once swam competitively," he told her.

"Nice. In an Ivy League school?"

"I'm from Marseilles. We call them *grandes* écoles."

"But you did grow up in a rich family."

"You're making an assumption."

"I am. But I'm right."

He gave no signal of agreement, but Josephine didn't need it. The suits, the élan, the way he walked as if he owned the world, yet knew its value and would never take it for granted...all clues of a man who had been brought up with a silver spoon.

"You know, this is our first job together."

He took a heavy breath and stopped rapping his thumb on the steering wheel. "I'm not The Fox anymore."

"I'm starting to figure that out. Who *do* you work for?"

"An organization you'd do well to stay as far away from as possible."

"Really? Because it seems every chance you get you keep pulling me back, closer to your mystery organization. Is Kierce here with us?"

"Uh..."

"He's in your ear, isn't he?"

"I'm radio silent at the moment, but he will be online once we get started."

"I'm not even going to ask. Must suck to have a babysitter."

"I—"

"We've got movement." Josephine put down her feet and hunched into the car seat low enough so no one could see her. Xavier, too, slid down.

The iron gates before the Blackwell estate swung open to emit a black sedan, likely an Audi. It had to be Lincoln in that car. It was a Friday night. He never sat home on weekends and tended to occupy the best private seats in the hottest nightclubs or restaurants.

"Does he have a driver?" Xavier asked as the Audi turned two blocks ahead of them.

"Yes, and minimal staff. Two security guards that remain on site. They take shifts, so one may be sleeping. A chef comes a few times a week."

"Maid?"

"You mean his latest fuck?"

Xavier glanced at her reflection in the rearview mirror. It was angled so they could see the corner of one another's faces. "You two *did* have a thing."

"*Thing* is as good a word as any for it."

His fingers curled tightly about the steering wheel. "Care to enlighten me as to what I'm sticking my neck into tonight?"

"Do I sense reluctance? From the greatest thief known?"

He tilted his head sharply, as if to wrench out a kink, but didn't reply.

"If you're worried about the *thing*...don't. It was over two years ago. And I'm over it."

"Apparently, he is still the *thing* to have yanked you out of retirement."

"We need to get our feet on the ground while the getting is good. Leave the personal stuff for the tabloids. Business now. Got it?"

"I would normally agree, but I have to protect myself." He grabbed her wrist as she started to open the car door. "If you set me up, you'll have powers greater than you can imagine on your ass."

"The only thing I want on my ass is a cool breeze and a hot summer sun. You can never trust me, Xavier. And vice versa. But I promise, the last thing I want to do tonight is rock the boat. We're in. We're out. You get the sparklers. I'm gone. Good?"

He nodded and released her wrist. "Good."

They left the car and strode down the dark street. Both were dressed in black and wore soft-soled shoes. No weapons. That was gauche. No streetlight on this section of the road. Lincoln had carefully chosen the location for that missing safety feature. And the houses were mansions; their inhabitants the idle rich. It was August, and most were away on holiday, so the neighborhood was relatively dark, save for a few lights in windows here and there.

"What's the voltage on the fence?" Xavier asked as they approached Blackwell's ivy-coated fence. He tapped his ear twice.

He must be signaling Kierce. "Zero," Josephine said. "The only outer security is motion detectors at the front, in the garage, and out back."

"Security cameras?"

"Yes, but the guards are generally watching porn this time of night."

He looked surprised and somewhat impressed. Josephine chuckled softly. "It is my job to know as much as I can about everything I see. Right?"

"Indeed."

"There's a window on the side of the garage. The cameras on that side of the house only take wide shots, and the bushes don't have thorns. It's our best bet."

Xavier led the way, hugging the side of the garage, until he reached the window. A basic garage-style window, it was about two feet wide and one foot high, and open a crack. He glanced at Josephine and nodded at it, pointing out the blatant security breech.

Josephine shrugged and stepped forward. Lincoln spent the money on security, but he left it to his employees to tend. Which is why she knew this break-in would go smoothly.

She put her fingers into the crack and gently jiggled the window. The motion engaged the crank handle on the inside, slowly turning it and opening the window wider. She hadn't been able to convince Lincoln that infrared motion sensors would be a good buy for the garage. His indifference surprised her; the garage boasted four car stalls containing his Audi, the Mercedes, and a couple of Ducati motorcycles. He never rode the bikes because his balance sucked.

Once the window was open about ten inches, she stuck her head inside. Without asking, Xavier offered her a boost by holding her foot against his knee. Arms before her as if she were flying, Josephine glided inward into the dark, cool garage and angled slowly toward the floor.

"Let go."

He released her to land the last eight inches on her palms, like an expert gymnast. Before her body weight could transfer to her wrists, she tucked her head and rolled forward. She came up to a stand beside an Audi. A Mercedes was parked on its other side. Lincoln must have bought another car.

Josephine turned to the window and cranked it up the rest of the way. Xavier climbed inside, then rolled the window back to the original two-inch gap.

A door clicked open.

Xavier grabbed her hand. They ducked behind the Audi, backs to the car, ears open to the action.

The garage light flicked on.

Chapter 10

"I'm taking the Audi," a male voice said. "So what if it's black? Sweetie, come on. You know I love driving the Audi. I haven't got much time while the boss is out. If you want me to come over there and—"

A pair of leather shoes stopped on the opposite side of the car where they crouched. Josephine eyed Xavier's hand, which had balled into a fist. She nudged her knee to his thigh. He tilted his head toward the speaker's shoes. She wasn't sure what he was planning, but she hoped he would sit tight.

"Seriously? I hate the Mercedes. It's old and smells like *pomme frites*. Sweetie. Come on. Really? You'll let me do you in the back seat? Okay, I'll drive the Mercedes. But only for you, lover baby sweetie."

Josephine rolled her eyes and caught Xavier's smirk.

One car away from them, the engine revved. They froze in position as the garage door opened and the Mercedes backed out. The door slid shut. After thirty seconds the overhead light blinked out.

Josephine swung around the front of the Audi and swiftly crossed the concrete to the entry door. Behind her, Xavier pulled on a latex glove, and gripped the knob, jiggling it gently. It was locked. A keypad glowed on the wall near the door. Xavier patted his thigh pocket, which carried all the tools he'd need for the job.

"I got this," she whispered. "Hand me your phone."

Xavier gave it to her. Josephine tapped into the mobile phone network she'd often used to access the lock on Lincoln's door. She had always forgotten her own key.

"SS7?" Xavier asked, an ear to the garage door.

It was an international mobile phone network that average consumers didn't know about, but hackers did.

"He changes his cell number every month, but he increases the end digits by eight each time. Easy for him to remember. And for me. And...I'm in."

The access app for the house locks popped up on the phone. She knew that code got changed often as well, but it was on a rotating list of about half a dozen numbers. She only had one chance. Not bothering with gloves because her fingerprints were already in the house, she tapped in Lincoln's favorite password: CASH.

The door clicked open, and Xavier pushed it inside. They waited two long, breathless seconds. No alarm.

"Nice," he commented.

The breathy comment in her ear sent shivers right to Josephine's core. She felt it hum as if the man had whispered a sweet nothing and touched her clit.

Whew! She shook her head. Not the time to become a victim of accidental seduction.

Of course, the man would never accidentally seduce. If he turned on the I-want-to-fuck-you smolder, he would mean it. And that was the real danger.

Slipping in quietly and closing the door behind them, Josephine tapped him on the shoulder as she slinked by. They wouldn't speak much now, and she would take the lead. Xavier knew the layout, and they hadn't actually discussed her taking charge, but the adrenaline rushing through her wouldn't allow her to stand back and follow the master. She'd been here before—both in the mansion, and in the moment, when getting to the place where the prize waited was the biggest challenge.

Excitement shivered across her skin and tingled in her fingers. She shook her hands, finding her calm, then took long, quiet strides to the end of a dark hallway. Security cameras were mounted around the right turn. They worked on a thirty-second sweep.

The office was down the hall and to the right. The lock on the door could be picked, but that gave them only thirty seconds to clear the hallway, pick the lock, get inside, and close the door. She eyed Xavier.

He held up a torque wrench and a rake pick. The pick worked by bumping up the pins with some fancy yet precise finagling. If the thief got lucky, the lock would fall quickly.

Josephine glanced around the corner and eyed the camera. It was up high, at the crease between the wall and ceiling, and faced away from them. It was so dark, she couldn't quite make out when it would swing back—

She jerked back behind the wall at sight of the flashing green LED. Caught on camera? She prayed not. But she'd wasted four seconds already, so she put up her palm to stay Xavier and began to count. At thirty, she looked again. The camera swept back toward her.

She spun around the corner and raced underneath the camera. Xavier, beside her, hugged up close. They hadn't much clearance, or the camera would pick them up. He smelled like coffee and sex again.

Wait. She hadn't thought before that he smelled like sex. Sex didn't really have a smell. Well, it did during the act—

A nudge from Xavier knocked her out of her possibly fatal musings. The camera had already swept too far to the left, and they'd lost valuable seconds while she had been considering The Fox's sex appeal.

"You got this?" His whisper sounded worried.

"Yep. Next sweep. Promise." She watched and counted, and this time when the camera swept overhead, she lunged toward the office door, Xavier behind her.

Xavier slid the pick in and out of the lock, over and over as he zipped the pins. She pressed her fingertips to the door and eyed the camera. About ten seconds until they were featured on *Paris's Most Wanted....*

The lock clicked, and he pushed the door open. He pulled her into the office and closed the door just as she counted "ten."

"Shit, that was close," she said as they stood in the dark, backs against the door.

"Perfectly timed," he said quietly. "As always. Safe to the right?"

"Yes, behind the fake Monet."

He crept over to the wall. After making sure that the painting was not connected to a security switch, Xavier removed it and set it on the floor. And blew out a breath. "That's...not the Zeus 5000."

Josephine peered over his shoulder. He had put on a pair of magnifying glasses that sported tiny LED lights at each temple. And the illumination beamed on the money-green brushed steel surface of...not a Zeus 5000.

He narrowed his eyes at her, and in that gaze she felt his chastising waggle of finger rather than saw it. Lincoln had installed a different safe. Because of her? Or, as with cars, women, and stereo systems, because he always liked the bigger, better, newer models? She should have foreseen this.

"What kind is it?" she whispered.

"Not sure." He stretched his latex-sheathed fingers before him in preparation. He traced the surface of the safe, then spun the combination dial, his eyes closing as he listened.

Josephine swallowed. She may have just compromised the heist with inaccurate information. Shit. And she'd wanted to impress him.

"Not a problem," he finally said. "Give me room. I can figure this one out."

Because he was a pro, and nothing could crack his icy cool. And she had once been as cool and unflappable when facing sure failure. Leave it to a master to teach through example. Smoothing her hair over her shoulder, Josephine backed up to the office chair and let him work.

Ten long, excruciating minutes passed.

Josephine stood up and began to pace. He'd been working on the safe too long. Well, not too long. If he'd never touched this brand of safe before, he was doing well. But the security guard in the garage was only out for a quickie in the backseat. She hoped he had problems getting it up.

The security guard, not the thief. She suspected Xavier handled a woman as precisely and practiced as he did a safe dial. She imagined his fingers circling her bare nipple. Oh, so slowly, pausing…then pinching firmly to loosen her defenses. She gasped.

Xavier glanced over a shoulder at her.

Shit. She had to get out of here before she jumped the guy in her ex-boyfriend's office.

Leaning over his shoulder, she said, "I'm going to pee."

"What? No."

"The bedrooms are down the hall. When the call of nature commands, I listen."

"And I insist you stay here."

"Seriously? You think I'm going to ditch you? Set off the alarm on the way out? That's a clever plan, but nope. I just have to pee. I'll be back in a few. Time enough for you to have this monster open, eh?"

She didn't wait for his further protest. If it were her in his position, she'd have said the same. And she didn't have to relieve herself. What good jewel thief, in the middle of a job, had to take a potty break?

The man should be suspicious.

Chapter 11

Xavier checked his watch. Seven minutes remained on his pre-set twenty-minute schedule. He wasn't sure he'd get this safe open. He'd already run into three false notches, but he did have four of the five wheels cracked. It was proving a bitch. Time spent arguing with Josephine had taken valuable minutes from his schedule. And now his focus was torn between the wheels and her absence.

If she were smart, she'd already be out of here. And, he hoped, without alerting the security guards or setting off any alarms.

He shouldn't have taken her with him. He'd succumbed to base desires this afternoon, thinking it would be a kick to take a beautiful woman along for a job. Teach her a few things. Show her what he was really made of. Never mind that she had been inside before and knew the layout.

Except he hadn't cracked a safe of this caliber in over two years. And he was rusty. He had no qualms about working with a woman. They could be just as talented as a man. Not that he'd met any with such talent, but still. Josephine had the talk, but he wasn't sure she could perform the walk.

He'd prefer her prone and under him, if truth were told. The sinuous glide of her body through the garage window had set his thoughts wandering. He'd gripped her firmly by the thigh, and then the knee and ankles, but he'd seriously wanted to lean forward and bite that tight ass before it had disappeared through the window frame.

Cocky and secretive, she was everything he did not favor in a lover. Perhaps a one-night fling? Was it worth the risk?

Wasn't as if he had taken a vow of chastity since signing on with the ECU. His private life was…there. Somewhere. He could have relationships if he chose to. Yet he knew the wisest option was hookups or flings. He didn't want any woman getting too close to him, learning things. Asking questions. Getting caught in the ECU's all-reaching surveillance net. Becoming a suspect, or worse, a victim.

He bowed his forehead once again to the safe door. It was warm from his body heat; he'd had his forehead pressed to it for nearly fifteen minutes as he'd listened to the inner movement of the wheel-pack mechanism. One more number to go and....

A low whistle sounded behind him, and he flinched as someone touched his shoulder. How had he not heard—?

Xavier let out a shaky breath as Josephine's ballet flats came into view. Sneaky woman. He refocused on the combination. One number left, but it could take another ten minutes. And he'd just lost two of those precious minutes by considering his partner's assets and whether it would be worthwhile to explore them further.

Partner? No, this thief always worked alone. In theory.

"Want me to take a stab at it?" she asked. She stood so close, he felt the heat of her thigh seeping against his shoulder. "Since your stabbing isn't quite up to par?"

"I stab quite well, thank you very much. No one has complained yet."

"I prefer a nice smooth glide myself. Much more romantic."

Were they actually having this inane conversation? Yet, why did his cock suddenly pulse and remind him of what he'd been thinking about her?

"Almost in." He winced, thinking how she would take that one.

"Good boy. Nice and slow is the way to win her heart." She tapped the safe to indicate the *her.* "You bring along your chalk?"

"I don't do that anymore." He'd always drawn a chalk fox on the safe, wall, or floor at the scene of his heists. A few simple lines formed a diamond-shaped fox head with triangles for ears. His ego could not allow him to simply walk away without claiming credit. "Like I said, I'm no longer the Fox."

"If you say so. But I think we should leave while the getting is good."

"We are not leaving without the necklace." He closed his eyes and listened for another notch to click into place.

"Oh, you mean this?"

The clatter of gemstones against the safe door was a distinct sound Xavier could recognize from across a crowded ballroom. He tilted his head. The tiny light beam emitting from his glasses caught the dazzler hanging from her crooked finger and flashing brilliantly.

He reached to grab the necklace, but she snatched it away.

"I remembered Lincoln had a stash safe behind an ugly Warhol painting in his bedroom. Thought I'd give it a look."

"You could have mentioned that before we entered the premises. It would have been first on our list."

She shrugged. "Just remembered it. While I was peeing."

She winked, then flicked him the necklace. He grabbed its end and gave it a cursory once-over. The moiré ribbon had alternating smooth and rough textures under his gloved fingertips, and the silver settings clung to the fabric with prongs that could be easily dislodged with a bit of jiggling.

"This is it," he said. "Remind me never to do a job with you again."

"What's that?" She turned her ear toward him. "Why, thank you, Josephine, for finding the valuable jewels that might cause an entire Parisian neighborhood to turn into zombies."

"I don't think I said anything about zombies."

She bowed grandly. "You are very welcome for the necklace, Monsieur Renard. Happy to have been the one who—"

"Yes, yes." He grabbed her upper arm. "We need to leave. Through the same window we entered."

They slipped from the room and down the hall before the camera swept back on its silent watch. As Xavier slid around the corner, a shadow moved toward the end of the hallway before the garage door. He froze. Josephine ran right into his back.

She swore under her breath. "What is it?"

"Someone's down there. The guard from the tower? Or the Mercedes returned from the quickie?"

"We're going to need a distraction," she said. "But he'll recognize me."

The last thing he needed was for this job to escalate to violence and endanger an innocent.

"I got it," he said.

Against his better judgment, Xavier reached into his pocket and pulled out the keys to his Renault. "You slip out and pick me up at the curb two houses to the east. Can you handle that?"

"Drive your car? Uh...."

He turned and eyed her fiercely. Though it was dark, he heard her swallow and nod. *Now* she would let fear take over? Bad timing.

"I don't trust you," he said as she took the keys. "But I'd rather see you out of here first than myself. Never leave a man behind."

"Is that some kind of self-righteous bullshit you tell yourself to make it all better?"

"Have I mentioned how women who swear turn me off?"

"Fuck no."

He sighed. "Follow me. And don't move until I've engaged the guard."

"Sure thing, boss."

She clutched his hips and leaned up to kiss him. *Was it a peck for luck, or a stolen moment of romance?*

"What are you up to?" he asked.

"Just trying to stay ahead of the game."

She slipped the necklace out of his pocket, then glided down the hallway. As the guard approached, she pressed her back up against the wall.

Just like a woman. Leaving the rough stuff to the menfolk. Xavier sighed and stepped into full view of the guard. He lifted a hand and made a beckoning gesture.

The guard obliged.

* * * *

It had been easy to slip by Xavier and the guard as they'd exchanged punches. Josephine left the garage window open wide, assuming Xavier would be battered and bruised and would appreciate any helpful access she left for him.

She got the car running and rolled down the street toward the Blackwell mansion. As she hunted for the turn signal, the passenger door opened and Xavier jumped inside.

"Move it," he ordered as he pulled on his seatbelt.

Josephine looked down at hers. She hadn't even thought of putting it on. No time now. She shifted her focus to *moving it* and stomped on the middle pedal. The car slammed to an abrupt, head-jerking halt.

"What the hell? The guard has a nine millimeter. And I don't think he'll stay down for long."

As if to punctuate Xavier's words, a bullet zinged the front left headlight. Panicking, Josephine stamped on the right pedal. The car peeled away from the curb and down a dark street, right toward a parked car. She jerked the wheel to the right, just in time to avoid a collision.

"That was a close one!" Adrenaline coursed through her, along with a weird excitement. She palmed the wheel with both hands and glanced in the rearview mirror. The mansion receded quickly.

Another bullet struck and transformed the back window into a spider's web of shattered glass, and lodged in the rearview mirror. Josephine whipped her attention between the shadow of a man standing down the street behind them and—

The garbage can on a street corner jumped out at the car and landed the right headlight with a loud crash.

"Shit. Oops, sorry!" She steered abruptly left and again stepped hard on the accelerator. With bullets behind her and menacing garbage cans attacking her, it was like being in a video game. And she could play a video game. "Eyes ahead and fingers on the buttons."

"What? Turn left!"

The car's tires squealed and the trunk fishtailed. Xavier grabbed the steering wheel and spun them out of the skid. When he released the wheel to her, she took off straight and fast.

He slapped the dashboard. "Do you know how to drive?"

"Was that a requirement?"

"What? I thought you said you almost bought a Mini?"

"I did! But then I didn't because I don't know how to drive. So, you know, not much need for a car."

"Why didn't you say something when I handed you the keys?"

"You signed on for the distracting part. That was the tough job. I figured 'getaway driver' was the least I could do." She swerved sharply to avoid a stop sign. The front tire nicked the curb, and an oncoming car honked gruffly. "I'm getting the hang of it! And I think we lost him."

"There's still another car in the garage. He'll be on us in seconds. Pull over and let me drive!"

Josephine turned toward the curb—and collided with an oncoming car in a spectacular crash.

Chapter 12

Xavier scrambled out of the car, spat blood onto the grass, and rushed around the trunk and to the driver's side. They'd hit a parked car; something to be thankful for. That meant no innocents had been injured.

He'd trusted a woman who didn't even know how to drive to man the getaway car. He was slipping. Or was it that he'd allowed the infatuation over some pretty blue eyes and an irresistible mouth to curtail his better judgment?

Had to be the case.

He opened the door and pushed Josephine's head back. She'd been knocked out upon impact. He quickly inspected her body, running his hands over her head and shoulder and down her chest and there at her hip—he felt the diamond necklace—then he gave a cursory glance all over for blood. None to be seen.

And no seat belt on, either. Why hadn't the airbags deployed? She had been lucky.

He scanned the neighborhood, but other than the hissing from the engine, everything was quiet. Residents obviously weren't concerned someone had just crashed into a parked car...unless they were calling emergency He didn't see any movement. But that didn't mean someone inside a house wasn't calling for an emergency vehicle right now. Or that their tail had somehow miraculously lost them. It was only a matter of minutes before the security guard located them.

He jostled her. "Josephine?"

She didn't respond, but there was no time to waste. Grabbing her shoulder and wrapping his other arm across her back, he pulled her out. The movement startled her back to consciousness, kicking and flailing. When her leg connected with the door, it propelled them both to the ground. He landed on his back with her back on top of him, almost spooning.

"That's not exactly how I planned that daring escape," he said. "But it'll work. You okay?"

She lay still, and he could feel every bit of her body against his. It was an odd moment to have to caution his body from going full erection mode.

She touched her forehead and nodded. "Yeah. Just a bit discombobulated. Why am I lying on you? Is this some weird sex position?"

He chuckled. "I prefer to look into my lover's eyes when making love. But no. I was trying to get you out of the car. We really should get up and go."

"Right." She rolled off him, landing on her hands and knees. She glanced down his chest and torso, stopping at his crotch. He didn't think she could see his erection, but hell, she'd probably felt it.

She pointed at his mouth. "You're bleeding."

He swiped a thumb over the blood on his lower lip. "Must have bit my tongue when we impacted."

"Right. That way." She nodded, then took off in a runner's dash.

Xavier sat up, considered the car for a few seconds—it was a junker; he could requisition for a new one... a new junker—and took off after her.

Tires squealed at the end of the block. Josephine dodged into a shrub-lined yard. She sprinted across the lawn in light steps. Xavier watched her, relieved she wasn't hurt from the crash.

Trekking through an adjacent yard, he kept an eye out for security cameras or guard dogs. Most dogs in this neighborhood were purse poodles, though. Probably asleep at the foot of their mistress's beds in a fancy, gold-trimmed cradle.

They ran through three yards, a gated courtyard that opened into a covered alley, and out onto a retail area. As the shops had closed hours earlier, it was dark and deserted. Across the river, the spinning neon lights on the Ferris wheel tucked at the edge of the Tuileries blinked over the tops of the lime tree canopy.

"Stop." Josephine slipped between a parked SUV and a storefront, where it was darker and more secluded than the narrow cobblestoned street. "We're finished."

Xavier was panting far more than she was from that short dash. Not cool. He put back his shoulders and nodded. "We are."

"You got what you wanted."

He patted his pants pocket. "That I did."

"Ah shit, really?" She patted her hip. "When did you nab— Fine. It already served my purpose, now it'll serve yours. You happy?"

"Immensely. You?"

"I would have been a hell of a lot happier had I never ran into you."

She had to be lying. Why should it matter? They were finished, as she'd said. He had the prize. Time to move onward. Back to the ECU with his head held high. On to the next job.

So why was he finding it so difficult to simply turn and walk away from the woman who had bested him at his own game? It couldn't be because her eyes seemed to seek the same unspoken reassurance from him, could it?

"You can't return to your apartment," he noted.

"Don't plan to. I'll pick up Chloe, and we're off to...uh, wherever we plan to go." She toed the SUV's back wheel.

It was good she was getting out of the city and away from Lincoln Blackwell.

"If you need anything..." he started.

She laughed and slapped a hand onto his shoulder. "Really? We don't have to do this formal goodbye thing. In fact, this is how it's going down."

And then she kissed him, her body crashing against his so that his back slammed against the vehicle. Her thudding heartbeats played timpani against his. The woman knew what she wanted, and that was to make him lose track of what he had been doing, where he was headed, and even why.

Answering her wanting kiss with a greedy desire of his own, Xavier turned her around and pushed her up against the truck. Her leg slid up along his leg. He clutched her thigh, holding her there. He slid a palm up under her shirt and across her back, coaxing her to tilt forward and crush her breasts against him. Mmm, she was warm and supple, and her mouth was hot and seeking. He could get used to this. He could get used to this woman.

"Damn, your mouth is like a drug." She pushed him away. "I gotta get away before I don't want to leave. Thanks for the tricks, X."

She wandered down the street, a bounce to her step. As she arrived at the corner, she looked over her shoulder. Waving, she kissed her fingertips and blew that teasing morsel his way. As he considered grasping the invisible treat, she stepped out of view.

"Tricks," Xavier muttered. He patted his pocket to ensure the necklace was still there. He'd forgotten about it when she'd kissed him. But yes, it was there. She'd given him the win this time.

So why did he suspect the next time their paths crossed, she'd fight to the finish?

"Never going to cross again," he said. He turned in the opposite direction and walked off.

* * * *

The headquarters for the Elite Crimes Unit was situated in an undisclosed location. A private car had picked up Xavier at his apartment in the 1st arrondissement. The windows were blacked against the sun so he couldn't see out, but he never bothered to look. He could see through the sky-roof blinders, and they always passed under plenty of tree cover. And he did have a sense of direction even if he couldn't visualize it. If he were to guess, he'd place the headquarters somewhere near the southwestern edge of the Bois de Boulogne, a massive park that edged western Paris.

After the driver announced their arrival, Xavier stepped out into the dimly lit underground garage. He'd never seen the place from the street. He'd always been delivered directly into the garage. The entry ramp seemed to twist and wind for a good half-mile. He had no desire to walk out to try to pinpoint where he'd gone underground, either. Didn't matter. It was better not knowing some things.

He thanked the driver and grabbed the attaché containing the necklace. He hadn't handcuffed it to his wrist. Too blatant. The briefcase appeared a simple black leather businessman's carry-on, yet the interior was titanium and he'd challenge anyone to attempt the nine-key digital code and biometric verification.

The elevator interior was lined with red LEDs near the floor. He took it down three levels and walked out into the air-conditioned animosity of a marshmallow white hallway. Heels clicking, he checked his cell phone. Five a.m. The ECU never rested.

But he would have the day off to rehash the wrong step he'd taken and how to avoid it happening again. Of course, there was a chance he'd be assigned a new mission. Or not. He seemed to average one a month; some took a few days, others required more intense research, and actually insinuating himself into a suspect's world could require weeks.

He enjoyed this work. To a degree. He was never free. That was evident in the tracker chip embedded at the base of his skull, close enough to the brain stem to keep him from digging for it. That chip had been a condition for his release from the Belgium prison.

He'd never been one for making bargains to save his ass. But after spending a year behind bars, a man adjusted his standards to include freedom. At any cost.

Turning abruptly right, he faced a door set seamlessly into the stainless steel wall. A biometric scanner read his heartbeats and a 3-D sensor confirmed his facial structure. He waited for the audio prompt, then spoke his name clearly.

Kierce could override the security checks and simply open the door, but that rarely happened.

Two seconds passed. The door slid open to reveal a small room completely walled in brick. The floors were limestone. It was a jarring contrast; the cold white hallway, and a small office that looked like a long-lost hideout in a decades-old bunker. What kept it from being quaint were the computer monitors on streamlined blue resin desks and the overhead screens that lined the far wall, featuring world maps where ECU operatives were stationed. A ticker tape of current events ran in red LEDs above it all.

Generally there were not many stationed at the desks, and being early, Xavier saw that only one chair was occupied. He nodded when Kierce Quinn looked up. Young, pimpled, and still not acquainted with the virtues of a comb, the operative tugged his headset off his dirty blond hair and jumped up to shake his hand.

"You got it?"

Xavier handed over the attaché. "It's all yours."

"It was a tough grab, eh?"

Xavier winced at the reference to his failure to walk away with the necklace that first night at the ball.

"Define tough?"

Kierce smirked. "You went radio silent more than usual. Did that have anything to do with the sexy young ingénue you were working with?"

Xavier raised an eyebrow.

"Maybe I'd better keep those comments to myself."

"Wise man."

"The boss wants to talk to you. He's in the Paris office for the week." Kierce nodded over his shoulder. "I'll get this processed." He sat and pulled something out of a drawer and attached it to the digital lock. A code breaker. He could have asked Xavier to open it, but the kid liked to use his gadgets.

The boss, eh?

Suppressing a nervous sigh, Xavier strolled toward the back of the room, where a narrow aisle led down a hallway to the armory and storage room where all nature of high-tech gadgets were kept. It was Kierce's domain, but, when he had the chance, Xavier liked to browse and see what he recognized. Figure out what could be cracked, and what would give him a headache merely trying to figure out how to turn it on.

He wasn't old. He was just...set in using the tried-and-true methods. Touch, sound, and intuition continued to work marvels above digital high-tech gadgetry any day. But that didn't stop him from keeping up with changing security measures. It had been necessary after losing a year in prison. Technology moved swiftly. A good thief kept up with the times or would be stuck targeting only the old safes, which harbored nothing more than moldy estate papers and granny's fake pearls.

Putting off the gadgets room for later, Xavier stopped at an office door. Before he could knock, he heard someone call for him to enter. Of course, there were cameras all over. Dixon had known the moment the limo escort had arrived, and had probably watched him talking with Kierce.

Hunter Dixon was a grizzled man who carried his emotions in his jaw. It tensed and relaxed as the conversation went on. Graying brown hair slicked away from his face, and his beard made him look like General Custer. Xavier always thought the man might be just as comfortable herding mustangs on a Wyoming ranch as he would in a three-piece suit, guarding the pope as he cruised by in the Popemobile. Xavier knew little about the man's history, though he would place bets Dixon hadn't been plucked out of a prison to head this motley crew.

"How's it going, Lambert?"

And most definitely American. Again, images of the man riding horses and herding cows popped into Xavier's mind.

"It's going well." Xavier took a seat in the chair before Dixon's desk. Dixon pushed a little silver tray with wrapped sweets toward him, but Xavier shook his head politely. "I handed over the necklace to Kierce. Sorry about the cock-up. I hadn't anticipated another thief being on the scene at the ball."

"Seems she managed to snag the prize from you with relative ease."

Xavier stopped a protest with a tight jaw. "I got it back. It's now safely in our hands."

"Right. You talk to Walters lately?"

"Three weeks ago?"

Michael Walters was the psychologist on staff. Monthly visits with the shrink were required of all the agents, either in person or via Skype. Xavier didn't mind. But he wasn't about to strip himself bare and start talking about his daddy issues. He didn't have any. Really. He'd left the entitled old bastard in his past where he belonged.

"Is there a problem?"

"Not at all." Dixon pulled a black file in front of him and opened it. "I have a new assignment for you. I know you like to keep busy. You're about the only one who can handle this one."

"What's that, Monsieur?"

Dixon tapped the file. "It's a recruitment."

"I've never done that before. I thought that was your thing." After all, Dixon had been the one to visit him in that secret compound away from his jail cell and lay out the conditions of accepting the position with the Elite Crimes Unit.

"I believe you can be trusted to handle this one. We will occasionally use the most persuasive methods possible when luring in a recruit."

"This person is not incarcerated?"

"No. But we've enough evidence to warrant leverage."

Leverage. Indeed, those details of crimes that were used to create the illusion of a rock-solid case against a person. As well as the perceived threat that they could be put away forever. Euphemisms aside, it was dirty business. But Xavier was not above employing leverage. He was rather pleased he was being trusted with such an assignment.

Dixon closed the file and turned it toward him. The phone rang. The director picked up the rotary phone receiver, and Xavier heard Kierce's voice on the other line until Dixon turned away from him and pressed the receiver tightly to his ear.

"You're sure?" he asked. He flicked a steely glance toward Xavier.

Xavier breathed through his nose, knowing they were discussing something related to him. It would never do well to worry. He'd get the info in a few moments. But he couldn't find the interest to look over the file while he waited.

Dixon's fingers curled into a fist and he pressed it against the desk edge. "Thanks, Quinn. We're almost finished in here. Uh…arrange a conference room, will you, please?"

The director of the Elite Crimes Unit hung up and eyed Xavier carefully. "There's a diamond missing from the necklace. Care to tell me about that one?"

Chapter 13

Victor Katirci had no compunctions about deleting the bodyguard he had hired to shadow the Countess de Maleaux. He could not abide incompetency. A thief had grabbed the necklace and still the bodyguard had returned empty-handed? Victor had extracted all the necessary information about the thief's identity and his route the night of the charity ball before the deletion.

Now he stood in the lobby of an apartment complex in the 8th arrondissement staring at the door marked "Concierge." Apparently the thief had followed a woman to an apartment on the fourth floor, which Victor would search after he'd gotten what he could from the concierge. He could shake down the man without having to use his blade—or with. Didn't matter to him.

When the door opened to reveal a smiling elderly woman with lush silver hair spilling over one shoulder, Victor decided to cool his anger—until the door was closed and he stood inside.

He slammed his hand up under the woman's neck, pinning her to the wall. She struggled but couldn't scream. Her fingernails clawed at his hand, but the cuts were nothing more than a nuisance.

"There was a man here one night ago. Fine suit. He left with a woman who had long brown hair."

The woman nodded, tears streaming from her eyes.

"What is his name? The woman's name? Do they both live here?"

She shook her head, so he loosened his grip. She gasped and slid down, so he pinned her shoulders to the wall. She sagged against him, but he wasn't about to let her slump or faint.

"I... I don't have his name." Her voice shook. "Who are you?"

"A friend of the family." Victor smirked at his joke. "I need to locate the man."

"I didn't know the man. I only…"

"What?"

"I…the woman. She owns the apartment. But she's never here. A week every few years. She's gone again. With her cat."

What did a cat have to do with anything? Toyo had mentioned the same. Victor sneered and leaned in until he smelled the woman's salty fear. "Her name?"

"Chloe," she managed, and wiped a teardrop.

"Chloe what?"

"Just Chloe. Cats don't generally have surnames."

The cat? Yeesh. This was going to be a tough nut to crack.

He glanced down the sunlit hallway and sniffed. "Do I smell tea?"

She nodded. "M-mint."

"I would like a cup. If you please."

* * * *

Sitting before the boss's desk, Xavier shook his head as the details of the past night dodged about in his brain. He tallied the few things he knew about Josephine—hell, he didn't even know her last name! She was a thief. She was in it for herself. Supposedly she was out of the game. Yet she still did jobs to save her cat.

Had to be more to that. Cats were great, but really? It had to be something deeper. Most likely involving Lincoln Blackwell. Was there more going on than she had let on?

No matter. He should have expected the dirty move from her. Slipping a diamond out of the necklace when she had the chance? That would give her control over him. Not that he could imagine why she would need it—what did she have against him?—but it had been a wise move on her part. Never be the victim. Always play the upper hand. And always keep three steps ahead of everyone else. It's what had kept him alive and free until… someone had matched his steps and turned him in.

"Lambert?"

"Uh, right. I mean, sorry. There's a stone missing? Perhaps Lincoln Blackwell removed it when he had it in hand? It could have fallen out during the scuffle after we removed it from Blackwell's home. There was—"

"A collision, I know. You've the battle wounds to back up your story."

Xavier had forgotten about his eye. The skin around the edge was swollen and maroon. His lower lip still hurt from when he'd bitten it during impact.

Toss in a few bruises from his fisticuffs with the mansion guard? Prison had proven much less painful than real life.

"Or..." Dixon leaned forward. "...Josephine Devereaux could have removed the stone from the necklace."

Josephine Devereaux. So the background check had been completed. Knowing her full name didn't deepen his appreciation for her thievery skills.

"Very possible." He hated to admit such a thing could have happened on his watch. "Has Kierce finished compiling the code from the other stones in the necklace, or does the missing stone hinge on interpreting the entire thing?"

"Not sure yet. Kierce just noticed it. He's not finished photographing the other stones. We'll have to perform a routine search of your home, Lambert. As well as the safe house you occupied last night. Standard procedure."

Xavier nodded. "Of course."

He had nothing to hide in that miserable little shack they called a home. Unless Josephine had planted the diamond in the safe house? Didn't make sense to him. She had no clue whom he worked for or how devastating such a move would prove to him. And—no, the necklace had already been out of their hands by then. Had she removed a stone the night of the ball?

No, her window of opportunity had occurred in the time she had left Blackwell's mansion, retrieved his car, and had picked him up last night.

The tattoo on her forearm niggled at him now. *Go ahead, underestimate me.* Indeed, he had.

"I'm sorry," Xavier felt compelled to offer. "I feel as though I've failed this mission."

"You have." Dixon crossed his arms over his chest. The man's eyes were close together. Predator eyes. They didn't miss his flinch. "But the recruitment assignment remains. I believe you can handle that. In fact, you are the only one who can." He nodded toward the black file. "Take it and learn it. We'll dispatch you on the recruitment in a day or two after we've gathered our ducks."

"Ducks, monsieur?"

Dixon waved away the comment. "For now, head into the conference room. Doctor Walters will be in any moment."

They'd called in the shrink? But he hadn't taken the diamond! Hell, this felt like the night of his arrest all over again. His heart beat quickly. Accusations, while not stated, had certainly been assumed. Handcuffs weren't necessary. The building's security would keep him locked inside, nice and secure. "Yes, of course."

He stood, clasping the file to his chest, and nodded to Dixon. As he walked out, Xavier couldn't help but wonder why he hadn't been sacked. Or maybe the sacking was yet to come? Get one last job out of him with the recruitment and then, so long, Lambert. Which meant only one thing: the tombstone.

Closing the office door behind him, Xavier pressed a thumb to his brow. His skin was clammy, and he hadn't felt so unnerved in years. It took a lot to set him off kilter. Whatever had happened to that stone, he'd find out. He had to clear his name.

Kierce sat up from his hunched position before a computer monitor and nodded. "Sorry, man. I just noticed the missing stone. I had to report it." The diamond necklace lay before him, the black moiré ribbon curled about the end of his forefinger.

"Don't worry about it. That's your job."

"The search team has been dispatched to your apartment and the safe house."

"I have nothing to hide." He hoped. He leaned over the desk and tapped the ribbon, avoiding the diamonds. "Can you give me a size and cut on the missing stone, any details that will help me identify it when I do find it?"

"Sure, but is the boss putting you on the hunt?"

Right. He hadn't been told to go after the stone. He'd only been directed to speak to a psychiatrist. But he would not give up on this. His pride demanded he locate the diamond.

"Whatever happens," Kierce said, "I'm rooting for you, dude. The missing stone was here…" He moved the piece and pointed to six tiny holes in the ribbon. "…the first on the left side of the necklace. It should be a match to the stone opposite it on the strand." He slid the necklace out of Xavier's reach. "I'll get carats and cut for you as well. Give me a few minutes?"

Xavier pressed his palm to his chest, a pacifying move that kept him from snatching for the thing. "Not a problem. I've a meeting in the conference room."

"And a recruitment assignment, eh?"

"How do you know that?"

Kierce flicked the corner of the file Xavier held. "Recruitment files are black. Who is it?"

"Haven't had time to glance at it." And at the moment he had more monumental worries to consider. Another man strolled in from the outer hallway, tugging at his tightly knotted Windsor. "There's the shrink now." Xavier sighed heavily. "I hate these damned head trips."

"I kind of like them."

Xavier almost commented that the loner who spent all his time at the office—yes, even through the night—hadn't anything more exciting to look forward to, but he kept his mouth shut. He liked Kierce.

Doctor Michael Walters gestured he follow as he strode down the hallway toward the conference room. Xavier dutifully followed.

* * * *

Victor Katirci wandered the living room of the female thief's apartment. Madame DaCosta had told him her name was Josephine Devereaux, but hadn't been able to produce any records of rental agreements because she didn't take care of the building's paperwork. Mademoiselle Devereaux had only stayed in the apartment two days recently, though she'd owned the place for years. And then the other night she'd frantically handed the concierge her cat and told her she'd be back.

That was the night Alex Toyo had broken in, Victor determined, inspecting the living room windows. None were broken. Had the concierge time to replace the glass? It hadn't seemed that she'd been aware of the altercation that had occurred in this apartment, and he hadn't wanted to mention it. The less she knew, the better.

There was only the one chair, broken to splinters and placed in an empty cardboard box sitting near the front door, as if in wait of removal. In the kitchen, one place setting sat in the cupboard. In the fridge he found a half-eaten, foil-wrapped ham-and-cheese baguette. Smelled edible. Victor took a bite. Passable.

Striding into the bedroom with the sandwich in hand, he smelled citrus wafting out from the bathroom. Girlie smells. He ran his tattooed fingertips over the rumpled bed sheets. Not a stray hair left behind. A few dresser drawers had been left open. A quick leave, then. The concierge said Devereaux had returned for the cat earlier today and hadn't gone upstairs to her apartment. She'd simply returned to the waiting cab.

Tossing the crumpled foil onto the bed, he checked inside the closet. Few items of clothing remained, and on the floor sat an open bag of cat food. Victor lifted the bag, checking behind it, then squatting to press the wall for secret—

"Ahahaha." He chuckled as the wall panel gave, and he pushed it inward to reveal a hollowed-out cubby.

He pulled out a U.S. passport for "Leda Stone," some American money, a German passport in the same name, and euros.

"America or Germany?" he asked himself. "With a cat."

The answer was obvious.

Chapter 14

Oddly, Xavier always fell into an ease with the shrink in a matter of minutes. Maybe it was the man's quiet Welsh accent. Perhaps it was the calm atmosphere of the conference room, which sported leather chairs so huge, even a large man could get lost in them. While normally he would sit up straight and face the door (never put your back to the door), with Walters he melted into the chair.

They spent the first few minutes discussing Xavier's getting along with the Elite Crimes Unit and his living conditions, as usual. Xavier mentioned he'd need a new car, but he knew the shrink wasn't the man to whom he should report an acquisition request.

And then the slam, as Xavier always thought of Doctor Walters' sudden and firm move to the tough questions.

"How are you feeling about the person responsible for turning you in when you had just walked out of the Hortensia heist?"

That's what he always called it. Xavier had taken Marie Antoinette's Hortensia diamond from the storage room in the National Art Museum in Bucharest. On a stop during its cross-country European tour, it had been scheduled for public display two days later. Of Indian origin, the peachy pink diamond weighed in at over twenty carats and had been purchased by King Louis XIV. Pink diamonds were incredibly rare. The stone was rumored to have a crack in it, but Xavier hadn't the opportunity to look it over before he was apprehended by the *politia Romana*. He hadn't even considered running. The idea of being caught red-handed always occurred to him, but he'd never thought it could happen. He'd been too cocky. Because, yes, he'd always signed his jobs with that little chalk fox drawing. "Stunned" was putting it lightly as the handcuffs had clutched about his wrists.

"I haven't given it another thought." Xavier rubbed his jaw and eyed the shrink.

Walters' brow rose in that infuriating I-know-you're-lying-but-do-*you* manner.

"You're telling me if I had a file that named your accuser, you wouldn't have any desire to read it? I could simply burn it?"

"Do you have such a file?"

Doctor Walters smirked and set aside his notepad. He rose and poured himself another cup of coffee. "It's early." He gestured toward an empty mug on the table, but Xavier shook his head. "Suit yourself."

Coffee would have pumped adrenaline through his system. He only drank it when headed toward a job.

"Tell me about Josephine Devereaux."

Xavier rubbed a hand along his thigh. The shrink probably knew as much as he did about the woman. But that was how this mind-trip stuff worked, so he went with it.

"She's a thief. Lincoln Blackwell yanked her out of retirement to steal the same diamond strand the ECU sent me after. She managed to extract the necklace from me. I then used her to get it back."

"Is she pretty?" Walters sat across the massive conference table and sipped his coffee while eyeing him over the mug rim.

"Gorgeous."

"Did you have sex with her?"

Xavier shook his head and planted both palms and forearms on the table. "No. There wasn't time."

"But you would have, if there had been time?"

To answer that one truthfully or not? He was damned if he did and damned if he did not, so... "The thought crossed my mind. Relationships are not easy when in the ECU. A man has to work within the playing field he's been placed on."

"I understand. But do you believe she may have detoured you from focus on your job?"

"No. It's obvious she knew what she was doing when she initially nabbed the necklace from me. I'm sure that's all on digital record, thanks to Kierce. But I never took my focus off the goal, I can assure you."

"You are detail-oriented. Can handle more than a few scenarios at once. Always thinking two steps ahead of everyone else. I tend to marvel over the mind of a thief. Your work is singular and challenging."

"I prefer working on my own."

"Unlike, say…working with a family member?"

Xavier exhaled and leaned back in the chair. This again? The man never failed to bring up the topic, and after a year of these sessions, he was beginning to tire of it.

"No," he replied automatically. "I have not contacted my father, nor do I intend to. Next question."

"That the question always tends to rile you gives me some concern." Walters scribbled something on his notepad using what Xavier recognized as a tactical pen. So the man was prepared to defend himself? Against the world, or just his patients?

Xavier leaned forward and splayed out a hand. "A tailor's life is dull and monotonous. While I enjoy a bespoke suit, I never have taken a shine to its creation. And much as my father would have had me believe the family business was all paperwork and marketing, I could never stand the visits to the weaver's factory. The labor was never treated well; abused even."

"You could have changed that," Walters suggested.

Xavier shook his head in frustration. "I work alone, Doc. Always have. Always will."

"You work quite well with the Elite Crimes Unit."

"Thank you. I'm doing something I am good at, something at which I excel, and take great pride in accomplishing."

The doctor took a long sip, then pushed aside his notepad, indicating he was finished with the tough questions. Or so, that was the standard MO Xavier had come to learn about him. "Dixon tells me you've been assigned a recruitment?"

Xavier nodded and glanced to the file he'd set aside on the table. "Tell me that's not my last job before I'm tossed behind bars again?"

"Why would you assume that?"

Rubbing the back of his head, Xavier had had enough of the tossing of questions back at him. "I don't know. I fucked up the job."

"Then prove your worth by bringing in the recruit. I suspect you'll have a breakthrough with this one. See you in a month. Or sooner, if need be."

* * * *

Hunter Dixon met Xavier after his chat with the shrink and slapped him across the back. "You're still on this case, Lambert. I've given it some thought, and you are close to the subjects of interest and have the skills to get back the missing stone. You good with that?"

"I wouldn't have it any other way."

"Review the file." Dixon snapped the black folder with his fingers. "Keep it on a side burner. I'll give you the go-ahead when you can step into that job. Stay in contact with Kierce at all times. We'll feed you what we can find on Blackwell, and you fill us in on the Devereaux woman."

"Will do. Thanks."

As he left headquarters and strolled through the cool concrete hallows of the underground parking lot, Xavier ran through all the sources he could tap to help him locate the missing diamond. Depending on who had it, he had various options. Blackwell could have fenced it. There were half a dozen fences in Paris Xavier knew of. But one single diamond?

Kierce had caught him on the way out and reported it was a small five-carat round cut. Color rating was H, which meant it had some color but wouldn't be noticed in the silver setting. And yet, it was riddled with flaws. It wouldn't be worth the trouble fencing, because the value had to be minimal.

Which meant Blackwell—if he had the stone—was probably holding on to it, and when he learned the necklace had been stolen, he'd step forward with whatever devious plans he had to get it back. Could he know there was sensitive information laser-etched onto the girdle? He certainly would check. A man who operated in white-collar crime wouldn't miss something like that, even if his forte was in another realm.

If Josephine had the missing diamond, she wouldn't keep it. Thieves did not hang onto the merchandise. They didn't steal for the sparkle and admiration of a pretty piece; they stole for money. Or the challenge. And the satisfaction a man received when handing over a big chunk to charity.

If she had taken the diamond as a challenge to him, Xavier had to applaud her bold move. She might even still have it; a means to flaunt her obvious talent before him. On the other hand, if she were living the hard way, she could simply need the cash and had likely sold or fenced it by now. But she had said she gave her stolen money to charity. Was she telling the truth?

Either way, he would start with the fences. It would be a tedious, touchy job, for most knew him. Yet they knew him as a thief, not a man who could put their asses away for decades. The ECU worked with the city police, Interpol, and Europol. Granted, a workable option, but...no. He had to approach this investigation from a standpoint from which they were comfortable. Yet he had to watch his back as well.

Reaching the underground carport, Xavier tugged out his cell phone. He scrolled through the few Elite Crimes Unit contact numbers he had. One he had a reasonably friendly rapport with, and the man would provide the muscle he required to walk in to a fence's domain and wrangle out some information.

A waiting driver signaled him with a flick of the headlights. Tossing him a nod, Xavier walked over and slid into the silver Peugeot's backseat and tossed the black file to the side.

Pressing 'call' on the phone, he leaned over and opened the file. The photo stapled to the front page hit him like a fist to his gut.

"Damn."

"Eh?" the man on the other line answered.

"Gentleman Jack." Yet his attention was focused on the file photo. Really? *That* was whom they wanted him to recruit? The shrink's suggestion that this mission would serve him a breakthrough resounded now. Seriously?

This mission had turned into a cluster-fuck.

"Lambert. Speak," the heavily-accented man on the phone said. "I don't have time to listen to your heavy breathing."

Right. He'd worry about the delicate alliances and absolute fuckery such an assignment presented soon enough. "I'm in need of your services."

Chapter 15

"I thought he was gone, out of my life," Josephine told Chloe, who batted at the crunchy blue foil ball on the sofa. "And suddenly I'm forced back into the game. I put on a fancy dress for a charity ball and there he stood. Like he had never left my life. And he didn't remember me. Which was a good thing at the time. But now...?" She scratched Chloe's back just above her tail; the cat's favorite spot. "I want him to remember. I think. Oh, I don't know!"

Josephine stood up and looked out the window. In the yard below the apartment complex, a swing set caught the rain on its rusted metal poles. She'd specifically requested not to live near children, but she had yet to see any little ones outside on the thing, nor had she heard children in the hallways, so she hoped it was a relic. It couldn't be safe, judging by all the rust.

Not that it mattered. She wouldn't be here much longer. Her options were Belize, Iceland, or Romania. She was leaning toward Belize. Sun and surf sounded too good to resist. It was either that or icebergs—or vampires. Not that she believed in vampires, but hadn't Dracula lived in Romania? She'd been to Romania once. Memories of that visit haunted her.

The night was cool, yet she opened a window to let in the scent of rain on grass. Sounds from the street were minimal, even though there were a few businesses in her semi-residential area. The night shivered through her thin t-shirt. Josephine let out a deep breath, closed her eyes, and imagined that instead of the cotton fabric gliding against her skin, it was a man's fingers. *Xavier's skilled fingers.*

She hadn't been able to get him out of her mind since leaving Paris. Kisses were all she had to remember him.

Not enough. She needed more.

Yes, even from that man.

But she was a smart woman, and she had every intention of once again abandoning her life of crime. The best way to do that was to forget about the sexy thief who had stolen into her thoughts like a skilled safecracker.

Which left only her and her vibrator. And that particular self-care item had not been packed in her rush to leave the French countryside. She would never return for the few things she'd left behind. She was reluctant to sell the property. It had been so beautiful there. But as long as Lincoln Blackwell knew that she had once occupied the place, it could never be safe.

"I'll have to rip off the Band-Aid." She sighed. She would miss Jean-Hugues, and she hated that the last time they had been together, he had been bleeding and frantic.

Leaning against the window frame and hiking up a leg onto the sill, she patted her lap to encourage Chloe to jump up. The cat leaped gracefully and curled onto her legs, finding comfort even in an awkward position. Josephine stroked her head and massaged the base of her big wide ears.

If this was going to work—the hard way—a girl should probably get a job. That was how one survived in normal society. Not that she needed the money. She had enough tucked away in Swiss accounts to live comfortably. But without a job to occupy her time, what to do? Did she need a hobby? She wasn't artistic and really didn't want to become domestic and start decorating her home, or baking, or even meeting with girlfriends to gossip about makeup and shoes or, ugg, baby formula.

Her place in the French countryside had kept her happy, and leisurely busy with the simple gardening, walks through the lavender fields, and the friendship she'd developed with the sexy senior.

The idea of striking up a friendship with anyone who lived in a suburban apartment building such as this one did not appeal to her. Maybe she could travel for a while before settling down? No, she couldn't tote Chloe along. The cat traveled well enough on short trips, but to make it a habit? The feline fur would fly.

"What do you think, Chloe? Am I being honest with myself? Why does it call to me so strongly?"

"It" being the life she'd once had. The dangerous-yet-provocative lifestyle of a thief who lived under the radar and could take whatever she wanted whenever she wanted. The taste she'd had last week had whetted her appetite. And much as she knew it could only lead to disaster, she also knew she would never disown her soul's need for that delicious danger.

"What if I like stealing the sparkly stuff? Huh? What do you think about that?"

The universe didn't reply, save for the deep warm stirring Josephine felt in her core. Because yes, she was a good thief. A *great* thief. And weren't people always seeking those jobs that they enjoyed and did well? Nine-to-five was not her thing. She was quite sure she had no employable skills, and the mere thought of listening to angry customers complain about not enough ketchup on their burgers made her want to stab something. Multiple times.

The Fox would never find himself flipping burgers. That man had style, class, and—whom did he work for? Some underground crime organization? He seemed to be helping the good guys. Who else would seek to stop a biological weapon from being released in Paris? So was he Interpol? Europol? Some kind of black ops?

How could Xavier have found himself working for the cops?

They showed me my tombstone.

That may have convinced any criminal rotting in prison to give the good guys a try.

She couldn't imagine getting involved with someone who worked for the law. But she could imagine all the things she and Xavier could involve themselves in together. Without clothes. And for hours on end. And again and again.

Josephine exhaled and let her body bow forward over Chloe, forehead meeting the window frame.

Apparently, she'd gone too long without sex.

But there was nothing wrong with fantasizing about having sex with a handsome man who challenged her physically and mentally. They could understand one another.

If she was honest with herself, she needed Xavier. The only time she'd ever been truly happy was when he had followed his calling as a thief and she had followed him. If he had given up on the Fox, then what use was it for her to aspire to such thievery?

They belonged together in a way she couldn't quite formulate. Only she felt something real when they were together. Connection.

She placed a hand over her heart and nodded as she realized what was really missing from her life. "Him."

* * * *

Jack Angelo followed Xavier down the alley that led to the fence's shop. Known in the ECU as "The Thug" for his prior hobbies of extortion, smuggling, and even running the occasional bank heist, Angelo had never pulled his punches. Xavier had a healthy respect for the Irish/Italian's cool demeanor. He knew it hid a quick temper that usually resulted in the other guy bleeding.

Those in the know called him "Gentleman Jack" because he always wore a suit. Not Armani or Zegna, as Xavier preferred, but a clean, pressed, black suit with white dress shirt and yellow tie. Xavier considered the yellow a warning sign. *Slow down, back off, if you're wise.* Jack's uniform was standard, as was the temper. And he was so much a gentleman that his MO was to apologize before smashing your nasal bones into your brain.

Anyone could respect such politeness.

"I know this fence," Jack offered as they stopped before the plain black metal door set into a graffiti-covered brick building. No sign, not even a door pull. The only way to enter was to stand and stare up at the security camera, and hope for mercy. "He's a right idiot."

"Let the idiot breathe long enough to give us an address," Xavier said. "He's the one who relocated the subject."

"The subject. Heh." Jack shrugged his massive shoulders forward and jeered at Xavier. "Kierce Quinn filled me in. Your subject is also your lover, oi?"

"What? No."

"My man Quinn said she took you for a ride."

Xavier exhaled. "It wasn't that kind of ride. More like..."

"Oi? She double-cross the great and powerful jewel thief then? Ha!"

Much as he wanted to go a few rounds with the man, Xavier resisted the urge to curl his fingers into fists. "Keep your enemies close," was a rule he'd always abided. And while Jack wasn't officially an enemy, he certainly didn't fall into the friend category. Not many did.

The door buzzer rang and the lock mechanism clicked, signaling they'd been granted access. Xavier was glad to leave the annoying conversation out in the alley.

They walked down a dark hallway into a vast, dimly lit garage. Shoulders swaying as his bulk moved forward, Jack took the lead. Xavier didn't mind. He could play the cool cop if need be. The only light bled from inside a cage at the far end, which surrounded the office. The air smelled strongly of gasoline, and cars in various degrees of dismantle sat in dark bays. The shop was greasy with decades of neglect, just as it should be.

The fence stood behind a barred door watching them approach. The chain-link cage was coated in black rubber, which obscured what was behind it, so Xavier couldn't read the guy's expression. He'd used him in the past to fence jewels, but he'd never spoken to him directly. Most good thieves used a liaison for the fence, such as Jack, so the man wouldn't recognize him and shouldn't expect to. He knew how the game worked.

The intel Kierce had provided on Dmitri Rostonovich had been sparse. He'd been fencing for eight years, give or take. Before that, he'd been a skip tracer, relocating high-profile executives fleeing tax evasion. An all-around swell kind of guy, depending on which side of the law you lived.

"Jack Angelo," Jack said as they stopped before the cage. Xavier's thug assumed his role with ease and authority. "This here is my associate, Joe."

Joe? He was the furthest from a Joe. Standing against the chain-link, Xavier could see the doubt in the fence's crimped brow line. Then again, doubt was a necessity in his line of work. Trust was an asset that was hard to come by, so a man had to take his chances or never make a buck.

"You men have a vehicle in need of work?" A distinctive Russian accent flavored his speech.

"Does it look like it?" Jack asked.

The Russian's eyes slowly moved over them. He wore a beard and his brown hair tugged back in a messy man bun. Add to that the cardigan sweater, band logo T-shirt, and lack of visible tattoos, he looked more like a hipster than a low-life. But Xavier was always leery of the Russians.

"What do you have?" the fence asked.

Jack looked over his shoulder to Xavier. They needed to get into the cage. And now it was Xavier's show.

"Diamonds," Xavier offered casually. "Unset, twelve flawless stones, nothing less than five carats." Which had a street value from half a million, all the way up to five, if the right buyer could be found.

A buzzer sounded again, and the cage door opened to emit Xavier and Jack. Once inside, the fence introduced himself. "I am Dmitri Rostonovich. Pleased to make your acquaintances. I am familiar with Gentleman Jack here."

"Good." Jack stepped up to the man. He stiffened in response. "Then you'll know what I'm capable of, should you refuse to answer Joe's questions."

"I don't understand?"

Jack cracked his knuckles. "Sorry about this, but a little loosening up is always a necessity." And he unleashed an upper cut under Dmitri's ribcage, likely connecting knuckles to kidney.

Xavier winced as Dmitri's face went pale and his jaw dropped open to emit an ugly groan.

Jack landed his opposite kidney, bringing the guy to his knees. But Xavier had to give it to the fence; he didn't whine or plead for mercy.

Instead he shook his head and asked, "What do you want? I will guess there are no diamonds?"

"Good guess," Xavier said. "We know you helped relocate Josephine Devereaux."

"Never heard that name before—"

Jack's knee stopped the man's protest. Blood spattered the office desk, which was littered with random papers and bills.

"Maybe." Dmitri spat onto the floor. "Brown hair? Sexy. And a cat?"

"Very good." Xavier drew his gaze over the papers on the desk. Amongst the blood spatters, he didn't see anything that could implicate the man in a crime. Not that he'd leave such information out for anyone to stumble upon. "Where is she?"

"Come on, I like that woman."

"We do as well," Xavier said calmly. "We're concerned for her safety, which is why we need to locate her."

"Lies," the Russian spat. Then he croaked as Jack's fist landed his throat. He gestured frantically as he swallowed to find his voice, and then said, "Berlin. That is all I know!"

"You know more than that," Xavier said. "You found her a new place to live. You have the address."

"No, I do not keep addresses. It is always a blind move."

Jack pulled up the man's head with a jerk of his man bun. "Explain."

"I have a realtor contact who handles the details. Berlin is temporary, anyway. I don't know the ultimate address!"

A temporary move? Smart. The misinformation would set skip tracers and other ugly sorts on her tail *off* the trail of breadcrumbs. If Berlin was a stopover before Josephine moved on to her final destination, they had to move fast.

Xavier hiked a thigh up onto the desk corner. "Give us the realtor's name."

"She is off the grid. I don't have a name."

"Then you have a contact number."

The fence winced as Jack tightened his hold on his hair.

"Have at it, Jack." Xavier stood and walked to the cage doorway. He never stuck around for the bloody work. He stepped down and strolled toward a lipstick-red BMW 5 Series, which was up on struts.

Behind him, a heartfelt apology preceded the crunch of bones. The sound made Xavier shiver. Of course the fence was trusted for the very reason he wouldn't give up information on pain of death. But Gentleman Jack could prove very convincing. Xavier would give him another thirty seconds.

The bright yellow Jaguar next to the Bimmer had been gouged in along the back quarter panel by what looked like some kind of forklift. How to fix that? The man must be a genius. Too bad he wouldn't be using his hands for weeks, possibly even months. Probably had employees to do the real front work here.

Silence suddenly sounded louder than the thud of Xavier's heart. He checked his cell phone. It had taken forty-five seconds. So he didn't know Jack as well as he thought.

The cage door clattered and Jack strolled out, tugging down his sleeve and adjusting his tie.

Xavier motioned to his cheek, and Jack swiped off a spot of blood. He tugged out a slip of torn paper from his pocket and handed it to Xavier. "It's a burner," he said of the phone number. "Better act fast with that one. You need me for anything else?"

"Can you come along to talk to the realtor?"

"Oi. You know I have a date in a couple hours." Jack strolled alongside Xavier toward the dark hallway.

"We'll make it fast," Xavier offered.

* * * *

An hour later, Gentleman Jack strolled away from Xavier without a look back. He hadn't even had to lift a fist to the realtor. She'd squealed, or rather, with surprising calmness, had written an address on a piece of paper and handed it to Xavier. She was out of the digital loop. No one would be able to trace her if they wanted to, so she had nothing to fear.

Standing curbside and watching Jack hail a cab, Xavier called Kierce and gave him the address.

"You heading to Berlin?" Kierce asked. "I can get you the red-eye, which leaves in an hour."

"It'll take me forty minutes to get to the airport."

"Nope. I'll send Wheels to pick you up. She's in the area." The phone clicked off. Kierce could track down his location with the GPS in his skull so all Xavier had to do was stand around and wait.

"Wheels," he muttered.

This was not going to be a pleasant ride.

Ten minutes later, a black Mustang with gray racing stripes on the hood pulled up to the curb with a screeching halt. Xavier opened the passenger door and slid inside. The car took off before he'd even closed the door.

"Good to see you too, Al," he said to the gorgeous brunette behind the wheel.

If she didn't have her hands on the wheel of a sports car, she'd be right at home modeling designer clothing on the runway. "Gorgeous" was putting her appearance mildly. Mirrored Ray-Ban sunglasses hid her lush green eyes, but not her knowing smirk. "You want to make the airport in twenty minutes?" she asked.

That was about how much time he'd need if he wanted to make it to the gate without sprinting faster than Usain Bolt. "Yes."

"Then buckle up, bitch."

Chapter 16

The Mustang pulled up to the curb at Charles de Gaulle airport. Xavier had never gotten queasy during fast rides, turbulent flights, or even rappelling down the side of a fifty-story glass-walled building. But Alliance McKenzie had a manner of driving that lifted his stomach to his throat. It wasn't that she was unsafe. The woman was a marvel behind the wheel and had dodged and woven through traffic like a snake on crack.

"The boss said to give you this." She tossed him a small black leather attaché that resembled a passport wallet.

Xavier tucked it in an inner pocket of his suit coat. "*Merci.*"

She smirked, and a curl of lush hair spilled over her t-shirt, calling attention to her hard nipples. "You're looking a little blue around the gills, thief. What's wrong? I thought you liked it fast and furious with me."

Yes, but with her behind the wheel? That would take some getting used to.

"It was good to see you, Al," he said, opening the door. "Stay fast."

"I will!" she called as he got out. "You keep that tight little ass safe!"

He shut the door, then took a moment to steady himself from the lingering effects of the harrowing ride. Xavier then stepped into the receiving area of the airport and made a beeline for the private jets.

* * * *

Josephine leaped to avoid a puddle and landed in a smaller one that splashed up her bare ankle. Never should have worn sandals on a rainy day. It was taking some getting used to, this city dwelling. It wasn't the lush and wide-open French countryside, that was for sure. Yet she'd grown up in a big city, Des Moines, and had thrived after moving to Paris with her mother when she was eight. Just proved that some old habits should be left in the past.

As for old skills? She was struggling with that decision.

Streetlights glistened in streaks across the wet sidewalk. She took some joy in the fact she was out shopping for groceries, just a few blocks away from her interim place. The neighborhood sat at the edge of a boisterous nightclub district. Ahead, down the block, neon bar signs beckoned.

She wasn't much for drinking and partying. Wasn't even sure how it worked. She'd led a disciplined life since being forced to adapt after her mother had dropped her at the foster home when she was fourteen. Yeah, that had been a crusher. No one adopts fourteen-year-olds. Especially American fourteen-year-olds in France. And what teenager wanted to be absorbed into a new family, even if her mother had been a drug addict who had given her up because her boyfriend had told her to?

Despite that blow, Josephine had never turned to drugs or alcohol. Who had the patience for the idiocy of drinking when there were so many better ways to spend one's time? Such as cracking a lock or practicing scaling a concrete security wall. As for the dating scene, she had never been an expert on that, either. Tinder, Snapchat, and sexting? It was easier to hook up with the stranger in the produce section and walk away the next morning. No emotion involved.

Yet her personal truths screamed loudly from within. She wasn't as cold-hearted as she preferred her image of Josephine Devereaux to be. Or Leda Stone, her oft-used alias. Never like her cold-to-the-bone mother. She wanted. She desired. She had needs that required fulfillment.

And right now she needed yogurt and nuts, and some cat food for Chloe. It did not take much to satisfy her basic needs for sustenance.

It was the need for connection that was really messing with her head, now that the solution to that need had taken on an actual persona.

"Don't think about him," she muttered, and turned into the shop mart.

She blinked at the bright fluorescent lights. It was after ten in the evening, but she'd hoped the store would be quiet. Not so. It bustled with energy. A family of six argued over watermelon and peaches. Stock trolleys loaded with food clogged the aisles. Older women pushed carts laden with wine and broccoli.

Is that what she had to look forward to? Hunched shoulders and comfortable shoes made palatable with cheap supermarket wine and bland-yet-fibrous veggies?

Josephine sighed and aimed toward the organic aisle, thankful that such a section existed. Almond milk was necessary for the smoothies she enjoyed. She grabbed bags of pistachios and brazil nuts, wishing she'd picked up a basket at the front of the store. Turning, she slammed right into a tall man.

"Oh, sorry—what?"

Grinning like the Cheshire Cat, Xavier Lambert stood before her, wearing a three-piece suit, hair slicked over his ears, and hazel eyes gleefully arrowed onto hers.

Josephine's heart dropped, while her anger rose.

"No. This is not happening." She shoved around him, but he grabbed her by the upper arm. She almost dropped the almond milk. "Let go of me! How are you here? In some no-name little market in the big city of Berlin, and you just happen to run into me?"

"It's a marvel, isn't it?"

"You've been following me."

"No." He held up placating hands. "I just stopped in for something to microwave because I'm starving."

"Is that so?" She slammed the bag of pistachios onto a shelf. "You're not that impressive a liar."

"I haven't been following you. Tonight. I have tracked you because we need to talk."

"You always want to talk! You got everything you needed from me in Paris. Diamonds. Action. Adventure. And too many kisses. We're through."

She grabbed the pistachios, and this time turned too fast for him to nab her. Marching to the registers, she realized she'd have to wait in line to pay. Bastard! She wouldn't give him the satisfaction of wandering up and watching her annoyance level explode. Leaving the food behind, Josephine scurried out of the store and swiftly marched down the sidewalk.

The rain had grown heavier. She looked around for a taxi, and cursed when there was none nearby. And…she was walking the wrong way. Her apartment was in the opposite direction. But she could hardly turn and go home. Xavier would follow her. She wasn't going to look over a shoulder. He was behind her. A smart secret agent would be.

Was he a secret agent? He had to be. No one else would have the means and curiosity to follow her.

What the hell did he want her for now? They needed to talk? Oh, no, no, no. She was out. Totally. For good. And for as much as Lincoln and Xavier might try, they would not lure her back in.

Well, maybe not.

Clenching her fists, Josephine cursed her subconscious wavering. She was a big girl. She could live the life she chose. But she would not be forced to it by any man. The only way she'd turn back to thievery was on her own terms, thank you very much.

The screech of tires rounding a corner broke up the chatter from the crowd spilling out of the nightclub. Josephine twisted at the waist and glimpsed Xavier striding up behind her. She knew it! Picking up her pace, she splashed through a puddle painted blue by a neon club sign. And then she felt something burn the back of the neck. It pierced deeply and....

Had he— She slapped a palm over her shoulder, unable to reach... It stung. And it was not an insect. Instinctually, she knew she'd been hit by... something. Not...a bullet....

Xavier's arm wrapped around her waist.

"Don't stop," he said. "You've got about five seconds before you lose the ability to move your legs."

As he hurried her down the sidewalk, Josephine opened her mouth to protest. Then everything went black.

Chapter 17

Xavier walked with the slumping Josephine clutched at his side. He gripped her across the back and under her armpit, but what he'd suspected was a tranquilizer dart stuck at the back of her neck had taken action. He'd been watching the dark SUV since she had raced out of the supermarket. He'd thought to shout after her, but hadn't wanted to draw attention.

He was thankful for the triple-wide line of people outside the nightclub. He insinuated himself into it, dragging Josephine. Perfume and marijuana smoke dizzied his senses. He heard a couple comments about his date "starting early."

"She's a lightweight," he commented in French, knowing a few would understand.

Pausing, sure he was surrounded by people—the SUV had to have slowed upon seeing him grab their target—he quickly hefted Josephine over his shoulder, then ducked down the alley behind the nightclub. It was alive with people drinking, smoking weed, and dancing to the tunes that echoed out from an open backstage door.

He approached the door, but the bouncer crossed his arms.

"I need to set her down and let her catch her breath," he said in German. "*Bitte*?" Now Josephine was completely out, and he made show of struggling to hold her upright.

The bouncer remained stoic.

Xavier pulled out a fifty-euro note from his pants pocket. The bouncer snatched the cash, then stepped aside, allowing Xavier access into the dayglow-lit hallway that pulsed with a techno beat so intense it throbbed in his veins. He didn't want to go into the main club area, just hide out until he could be sure those who had tranqued her were gone. Finding a narrow, dark hallway, he stopped and set the unconscious woman on the floor.

Crouching over her, he pushed the hair from Josephine's face. He found the dart still in her neck and carefully pulled it out. He didn't touch the tip, but thought he should hold onto it for analysis, so he tugged out his handkerchief, wrapped it up and tucked it in a pocket, making sure the tip pointed downward.

"Kierce, find me a way out of here," he said.

"Uh, what's up?"

He looked over Josephine's sprawled body. "Being tracked by a suspicious vehicle. A black SUV. License plate B KL three two eight five."

"On it. And... I'll send a cab your way."

"*Merci.*"

He sat against a wall that was plastered with tattered concert posters and pulled Josephine up to rest her head against his chest, placing a hand firmly below her breasts to keep her upright. He couldn't know how long she would be out, but she needed protection from whomever had done this to her.

And who was that? For what reason? Was she involved in things he wasn't aware of? Beyond the Maleaux necklace heist? Whomever had darted her certainly couldn't have been targeting him. The dart had landed her neck, exactly where it needed to go. Likely her attackers hadn't been aware of Xavier. Or maybe they had been. It was never wise to rule out any scenario. Could it have been the countess's bodyguard, who had followed them to Josephine's apartment? But he had been after Xavier.

Someone had put two and two together and now Josephine was on their list. A list Xavier was already on.

He never wanted it to go down this way. But she was involved in a hell of a lot more than he even dared confess to her. If she'd never kissed him that night at the ballroom and absconded with the necklace, would they even be here right now? Could she have been safe?

"Your life will never again be the same," he muttered to the woman whose chest rose and fell slowly in a deep slumber.

Could she forgive him for that?

She'd answer all his questions soon enough.

Settling against the wall with the heavy warmth of her back and head tucked against his shoulder and arm, Xavier tugged out his cell phone with his free hand. He scrolled to the information the Russian fence's realtor had given him.

The apartment building name had been more than enough info. Xavier entered the address into his phone's GPS. The app showed it wasn't far from here. It was in the opposite direction that Josephine had walked out of the grocery store. He must have rattled her. But the SUV might have followed her from her home. She could have been aware of the tail and attempting diversion.

To return to her place or not? And with an unconscious woman in his arms? That was no way to be stealthy.

"Six minutes," Kierce reported. "I told the driver you would come out the alley door. I've a bead on the van. Sent in a driver to distract them."

A driver, such as Al, but someone stationed here in Berlin. An agent of the ECU, someone who lived and breathed behind the wheel and who drove the vehicle both offensively and defensively.

Bowing his head to Josephine's, he inhaled all of her. Soft hair and salty skin. Rain tinted her with a fresh, ozone smell. No perfumes, not in her hair or on her skin. A wise thief never left a scent trail. Xavier never wore cologne, unless he thought it could aid in seducing an aging countess. But a wise thief always kept one eye over her shoulder, too. Had she really been living the hard life and Lincoln Blackwell had pulled her back in, rusty and lacking the finesse she'd once possessed?

Xavier had read Josephine's rap sheet in the dossier that Al had handed to him. It had been updated from the black file the boss had given him. There was only one heist for which Europol listed her as a possible suspect. In Phoenix four years ago, a fifty-carat ruby had been stolen from a traveling jewelry show. They'd never pursued her because they'd had bigger names ranked above hers. So basically the ECU had nothing on her. Why was she so important to them?

Yet, she'd alluded to following his career for years. And the one heist she'd confessed to him had not been small time. Had she emulated his style and walked away with millions in sparklers and colored stuff? Xavier's own rap sheet had only shown two possible connections to heists. He had been that good. Of course, getting caught with evidence in hand? Not his finest moment.

He'd love to pick her brain, but suspected she'd be tight with that information.

Unless he started by offering up details on some of his jobs?

Maybe. His current job was to locate the missing diamond. And then... recruit Josephine Devereaux into the Elite Crimes Unit. Voluntarily. And all without getting emotionally involved.

But if his plan went the way he hoped, tapping into his emotions might be necessary.

It felt like five minutes had passed. Xavier stood, hoisted Josephine's body over his shoulder, and slipped out the back door. The taxi cab pulled up, and he hopped inside. Another comment about his date starting early. He ignored it and gave the driver an address.

Three minutes later, they reached Josephine's apartment building. Before getting out, Xavier scanned the neighborhood. It was a classic middle-class area, featuring older houses and apartment complexes. The sidewalks sported a few cracks and pitiful patches of marigolds, but the streets were clean and well lit. Best of all, they hadn't been followed. Xavier paid the cabbie and carried Josephine out.

Which unit did she live in? He scanned the front of the three-story building. She wouldn't go for the first floor. Too easy for intruders to enter. A second floor left too many escape issues. Probably a corner apartment, and something close to roof access.

"Ah." There on the far left side, in a third-floor window, stretched a familiar cat. "Thank you, Chloe."

Xavier strode inside the building foyer.

There was something about that cat. The theft of her cat had lured Josephine into leaving her freedom behind and jumping back into the life. It didn't make sense. It was just a cat.

He took the stairs and set Josephine down while he picked the lock. Standard apartment security. It took two seconds to rake the pins, and he was in. Whispering a thanks to Chloe, he wandered through the dark living room in search of the bedroom.

* * * *

"Drive!" Victor shouted at the driver as he noted the silver sedan behind them had taken the same two turns.

He reached into his suit pocket and palmed the Ruger. They drove through a residential area, so he would not use the gun unless forced. No need to attract unnecessary attention.

He'd managed to pick up the female thief's trail after missing her in Paris. He knew a woman behind the ticket desk at Charles de Gaulle, and for a certain payment she had given him flight details. He'd taken the next flight to Berlin and tracked the thief's arrival with relative ease. A woman with a cat? Yes, the man at the taxi station recalled her. Very beautiful. He looked up the drop off and had only been able to give Victor the neighborhood.

More than enough information. For the past two days, he'd staked out the area. And now that he'd found her and tranqued her, someone had managed to whisk her out of his sight. It had to be the other thief. Though Victor had not gotten a good look at him, he'd seen a glimpse. And he never forgot a face. He'd lost them in the crowd outside a nightclub, and even though he'd gotten out and asked if anyone had seen a man dragging around an unconscious woman, he hadn't gotten answers.

A bullet pierced the back tire, setting them to a swerve.

"Whoa," the driver shouted. "What the hell?"

"Don't stop!" Victor shouted. If someone was after him, he would not go down easy. In fact, he intended to be the last man standing.

Victor checked the gun magazine, then snapped it back in place and stuck his head out the window. His hand had been forced. Time to show them who they were dealing with.

* * * *

Josephine awoke with a start. She couldn't remember falling asleep. The uncomfortable thickness of a crisp new sheet glided under her stretching fingers. The soapy scent from the cheap shampoo she'd grabbed at the airport carried in through the open doorway from the bathroom. Hadn't she just been out grocery shopping?

She blinked at the daylight beaming through the window. She had slept through the night, but how? How had she made it home from the grocery store? Where was her almond milk?

Her mouth was dry, and tasted metallic. "Ugg."

"Water?"

Startled upright at sound of the male voice right above her, she pulled the sheet up and stared into Xavier Lambert's smirking green gaze. Hazel? No, definitely green. With a touch of hazel. She could stare into those eyes for days…

Wait.

"What the hell?"

"I thought you'd be thirsty." He held the glass of water to her. "It's almost noon."

"What are you doing in my home? How—where?" She eased her palm over the sore spot at the back of her neck. A memory of last night flashed before her eyes. She had been hurrying away from Xavier on the sidewalk in front of a couple of nightclubs, and then— "Did you drug me?"

"I did not." He took her hand and placed the glass in it, then stepped back and leaned an elbow on the cheap pine dresser that had come with the place. "Don't you remember? You were tranqued."

"As I was walking? But you were the only one behind me."

"I was keeping an eye on the black SUV that had followed you to the grocery store."

She gaped at him. What kind of lies had he concocted to cover the fact that he had been following her?

"I've got eggs and toast in the kitchen." He pointed to her head. "You brush your hair and teeth, then we'll talk."

Then he strolled out like he owned the place.

Josephine scrambled off the bed, prepared to shout after him that he could get the hell out, when she wobbled and caught her palms against the door frame. Whew! Still feeling some aftereffects from—someone had shot her with a tranquilizer? If not Xavier, then who? And for what reason? She didn't have—well, she did have enemies. But no one knew she'd moved to Berlin.

Except Xavier knew. Which meant anyone else could also know.

"Damn, Dmitri. That is the last time I trust you."

Leaving the water on the dresser, she made her way across the hallway and into the bathroom. No wonder he'd pointed at her head in disgust. A rat's nest tangled above her left ear. She worked the comb through the disaster, then pressed her palms to the cool porcelain vanity. Still wearing yesterday's black leggings and plain blue t-shirt, she looked a rumpled mess, but at least her hair was combed. With a wet washcloth, she wiped off the smeared eyeliner, then quickly brushed her teeth.

"He carried me home?" she asked her reflection. "But that would mean…"

Feeling steady now that she'd washed her face and gotten her bearings, Josephine marched down the hallway and into the kitchen. Xavier set a plate of steaming scrambled eggs on the counter, alongside a glass of milk. Chloe sat on one of two bar stools, flashing her a wide-eyed expectation.

She eyed the food. She'd been starving last night. Hence, the trip to the grocery store. Now? She could have eaten it all, if it hadn't been made by the creep currently drying the frying pan with a dish towel. His domesticity did not impress her. Not at all.

And besides, there was no bacon.

"How did you know where I live? And which apartment was mine? I thought that damned tracker was out of my hair." She shoved a hand into her hair and sat next to Chloe, who nudged her with her forehead. "Good morning, Chloe. Has this guy been treating you right?"

"Chloe invited me in with a wink from the window while I was standing below on the street wondering which was your place. Thanks, Chloe." He winked at the cat.

Chloe purred.

And Josephine had had enough of Mr. Charmed and Dangerous.

She grabbed a fork and it took all her resistance not to immediately dig in. The aroma was hitting her was irresistible, a testament to the guy's talents. Was there nothing the man couldn't do? "Get out."

"We need to talk."

That's exactly what he'd said to her last night. Before she'd passed out and...how the hell had he gotten her home if some SUV had been following them? Best she didn't know. If anything untoward had happened—no, she actually trusted that he'd gotten her here safely and with little effort.

"We've talked," she said as she angrily stabbed at the fluffy eggs. "We've stolen diamonds together. We've kissed. And apparently you've tossed me over your shoulder like a caveman and moved me about as you saw fit. I think we've done enough sharing. For ever."

She scooped in some steaming eggs and groaned at the savory deliciousness.

"We'll eat." He swung around the side of the counter and, nudging Chloe to jump up onto the counter, he claimed the stool and started to eat. "Then we'll get to business. I kept watch through the night. Didn't see the SUV again. My people took care of them. But somehow they found you at the grocery store. While you're eating, you might want to think about who would be after you with a tranquilizer dart."

Josephine dropped the fork onto the plate. "No one!"

Both Chloe and Xavier stared wide-eyed at her. The mutinous feline had taken up The Fox's side? Figured.

Xavier smirked, huffed out a little chuckle, then went back to eating.

Josephine decided to check her anger. Cool and calm won the game. But she was playing against the master of cool and calm. Was it time to play her ace, or should she hold it a bit longer?

Chapter 18

Josephine shoved the dishes into the dishwasher. She had only two place settings. They'd been in the cupboard when she moved in.

Xavier paced before the window that overlooked the back courtyard with the rusted swing set, hand to his jaw in thought.

She wanted to push him out the door and run off in the opposite direction.

She wanted to sit down and talk to him. To learn all the things she had wondered about over the years. How had he gotten started? Why did he always stop for coffee before a heist? How had he never known she followed him? Wasn't he curious how she had done so?

She wanted to get into his mind in a way she'd never been able to. To touch him soul-deep.

To taste his kiss again.

The clink of glasses startled her out of what was quickly becoming a daydream. She let her mind wander too often. It was helpful when plotting a heist. Not so much when she needed to stay on her toes.

Folding the dish towel and tossing it over the edge of the sink, she glanced at Chloe, who'd sat on the counter watching her. "You are on my list," she said sternly. "You let him in."

Xavier's pompous chuckle was steeped with entitlement. He was a man of privilege and class. She would not be intimidated by his superior attitude. Or by the fact that he'd just cooked her the most simple, yet tasty breakfast she'd eaten since—well, since that bacon.

Her frustration boiled over. Josephine marched up to the calm, cocky bastard and blurted out, "Why are you here?"

"In truth? For this."

His hand slid up the side of her neck and he grasped her head firmly. She saw the kiss coming, and pressed her palms to his chest to push him away, but he did not relent. The kiss landed like an arrow to the target, a deadly aim meant to claim and master. And, oh, it did.

Of all the men who had ever kissed her, this one stood above and beyond. For he did not take so much as share the heat and want that shimmered through her veins as his mouth sought to couple with hers and his tongue dashed her teeth. He didn't demand; he led. He didn't suggest; he mastered.

The caress of his tongue against hers felt like a dance she'd always dreamed of attending, but never had the right gown or shoes. No dashing away at midnight for her. This prince was hers, and she intended to entertain the fantasy of what could come next.

"We need to take care of some things between us before we talk," he murmured beside her ear. His hand slid down her arm and slipped around to curve over her derriere. "Things that don't involve talking. I know you want this, Josephine. I want this."

"I..." She couldn't make herself say "don't." Because she did. She wanted the gown and the shoes, and for the handsome prince to sweep her off her feet.

"Can we agree to this?" he asked.

"You mean sex?"

He nuzzled a kiss against her neck and she tilted her head, opening herself to him, feeling his hot tongue laving down her skin and to her collarbone. He grew insistent, grasping her chin and meeting her eyes with his solid, steady gaze. That same gaze that had seen the inside of many an impenetrable safe and had reflected the dazzle of millions of dollars of gemstones.

"Yes," she gasped, speaking against that stubborn angel on her shoulder who wished to muck up this good time. Yes, yes, and yes.

She shoved him to the wall and pushed down the arms of his suit coat, and he shook his arms until it landed in a puddle around his heels.

Before he lifted her t-shirt, Xavier glanced aside. "Don't look, Chloe."

As he peeled off her shirt to reveal her bare breasts, Josephine sucked in a breath. It was one of those breaths she always took before she stepped forward. Into the heist. That one last moment to change her mind before she jumped in and assumed the risk of losing it all.

And in that breath she surrendered to something she had wanted far too long.

Xavier lifted her and carried her to the back of the couch, where he set her down. She sat high enough that he hadn't to bow far to lash his tongue across her tight nipple. Arching her back, Josephine encouraged his explorations, from tongue twirls and slickened fingers about her nipples, to tight suckling that drew up a tingling ache in her core.

Josephine curled her fingers into his hair and pulled him down, urging his hot, wet ministrations. She squeezed her legs around his hips, which set him off-balance and toppled her backward. They fell onto the cushions, tangled up in each other. As he landed above her, he thumbed both nipples and moved up for another deep, lingering kiss. He tasted like eggs and toast and…success.

She finally had The Fox where she wanted him. Above her. Kissing her. And oh, but that was not a pistol in his pocket pressed against her thigh.

Unbuttoning his shirt, she pushed it back and over his shoulders, but the sleeves tugged on his biceps. Without breaking the kiss, Xavier shrugged it off and tossed it aside. His knee landed between her legs and nudged against her mons. One more nudge and…yes. Josephine moaned as he connected with her aching clit and a shock of delicious want echoed through her system.

His kisses moved down to her jaw and along her neck. Every millimeter of her skin felt him, even where he did not touch her. A quiet-but-insistent fire had ignited. Could he feel the burn as he skimmed her skin with his mouth?

"I had thought when we met again—if that were to ever happen—which I doubted…" he said, pressing another kiss to the top of her breast, "…that you would put up a fight. Am I winning this fight or losing it?"

"How 'bout we call it a draw?" She tried to unzip his fly, but he moved out of her grasp, so instead she raked her fingers up his rigid abs and tweaked his nipples.

He laughed a little, and it ended with a desirous moan as he met her gaze. His hand slid to her leggings, and he shoved them down, exposing her skin to the rough texture of his pants and then…the hot, hard landscape of his lower abdomen as he lay on top of her and again paid slow, leisurely attention to her breasts with licks and nips and the occasional pinch from his fingers.

Josephine sighed and moaned. "Take off your pants. I need you inside me. Now. Come on, X."

His fingers worked at his fly. "X?"

"Got a problem with it?" The heavy weight of his erection landed on her thigh. "Oh, yes."

Chloe jumped to the back of the couch, looked them over, then sprung back to the floor and fled.

"I did warn her," he said as he kicked off his pants and leaned over her. With a tempting glide of his penis over her mons, he met her gaze with a teasing, defiant glint. "You ever let a thief crack your safe?"

"That's a cheesy come-on. But effective. You think you got what it takes to penetrate the asset?"

His index finger glided over her folds and found its mark on her wet, swollen clit. Josephine moaned and nodded. "Yes, you do have what it takes."

And with that, he entered her slowly. He took his time, his eyes searching hers and smiling at her reactions. The thickness of him filled her. His heat branded her. His insistent and suddenly forceful hilting pleased her. He pumped slowly and then more rapidly, and always his finger remained at her clit, slicking and pressing and gliding across it to lure her toward the ultimate high.

Good boy, for knowing that extra detail was a necessity to get her off. Josephine stopped thinking and let her body succumb.

A trace of spice mingled with his musky salt sex. The combination was deliriously intoxicating. And when she opened her mouth to gasp, one of his fingers traced her lower lip. She sucked it in deeply as his cock pierced her just as deeply.

Xavier swore, then slammed his hips against hers. His body tremored above her. And with one last trace of his finger over her clit, Josephine, too, surrendered to the climax.

* * * *

On the way to the bedroom, Xavier stopped in the hall because Josephine put her hands to the wall and glanced over her shoulder at him. The fine hairs around her face were wet and her eyes gleamed. Her body was sleek and tight, her skin hot from their tangle on the couch.

And he foresaw no stopping any time soon.

Wrapping an arm about her chest to clasp her nipple between thumb and forefinger, he moved up behind her and dipped his head against her shoulder, kissing her neck right...there, because she squirmed so sweetly. She wiggled her ass against his cock, which was hard again even after coming five minutes earlier on the couch. He ground himself against her, fitting himself between her peach-cleft bottom. Cupping her breasts, he moved his mouth down to kiss the back of her neck over the soft hair that spilled to the center.

"We're not going to make it to the bedroom, are we?" she asked, but he knew the question was rhetorical.

Xavier lifted her with ease. She bent her knees against the wall. And he slipped inside her from behind. Completely supported by his cock and hands, she crouched there—a thief's talent—and let him take her furiously, thrusting until he felt sure he'd explode. And when he did, he caught his hands against the wall beside hers, and his body pulsed as he released within her. He let out his breath in a slow, loud groan.

She'd mentioned something about being on birth control pills earlier while on the couch. He liked having one less detail to consider.

Josephine pushed off, and his back hit the opposite wall. She laughed as he slipped out of her, but she remained with her back to his chest, her feet supporting her and pinning him to the wall.

"Is this some new sex move you're trying to teach me?" he asked.

"Maybe I'm practicing my wall-scaling skills?"

"Mm, Seph, take me with you."

She dropped her feet and turned to hug up against him. His cock was only semi-erect now, but the press of her trimmed pubic hairs against it tickled and gave him one more jolt of orgasm.

"Christ, yes."

"Thieves work best alone." She glided a finger up his chest, tripping over his hard nipple and then up higher to the bottom of his chin.

"Except when it comes to sex." He picked her up and carried her into the bedroom. "Time for round two," he announced, and tossed her onto the bed.

"I think it's round three or four now." Sitting up, she spread her legs wide and patted the space between them. "Come on, X. Want some more?"

Xavier knelt on the floor and gripped her ankles. With a tug, he pulled her to the edge of the bed. Hooking her legs over his shoulders, he kissed her lush, wet folds and tickled her with his tongue. Time to show her why this thief was a master at attention to detail.

Chapter 19

An hour later, Xavier called a time out and wandered into the kitchen. Afternoon sunlight beamed through the front window where he'd initially spied Chloe. The kitchen, toward the back of the apartment, was muted in cool shadows. He grabbed two bottles of water and returned to the bedroom. Josephine lay on the bed, stomach down, knees bent and toes toddling the air. A breeze from the open window ruffled the sheer white curtain close to her face and blew fine hair across her cheek.

He handed her a water bottle and lay on his stomach beside her, elbows propping him up.

"Ready for round six?" she asked.

"Let's talk."

She glared at him, then frowned and twisted off the cap of her water bottle. "You gotta get a new line, you know that?"

He shrugged.

"Right. Talk. Because you just used sex to soften me up."

"Really? You required that much softening?"

She swallowed a gulp of water, smiling behind the plastic rim.

"Seph," he said, "I had sex with you because I wanted to feel your body against mine and put myself inside you and taste more than just your kisses. I thought we were in agreement on that?"

"We were. We are. But you are still working for someone I'm pretty sure I'd consider the enemy."

"You have enemies?" He rolled to his side and propped a hand against his cheek. "How can someone who has left the trade still have enemies?"

Screwing the cap onto the bottle and setting it on the floor, she shook her head. "You know damn well we mark our enemies for the rest of our lives."

"Case in point. Lincoln Blackwell?"

"So we're really going to do this now? Naked?"

He nodded. "We can't hide behind clothes or pretense. All up front."

"Fine." She sat up and leaned against a pillow, slyly parting her legs and letting them fall open so he had a great view of all of her. And, yes, his cock stood up at attention. "God, your penis is remarkable."

He shrugged again.

"Now you're trying to distract me. So! Who are you working for, and why are you so concerned about me?"

"I wouldn't call this—what we just did—'concern.' I'd call it 'infatuation.' 'Lust.'" He moved up between her legs, kissed her clit—slowly, and with tongue—then rested his head on her thigh. "Desire and passion."

Josephine sighed. "Agreed."

"But as far as my job? There's the situation with the missing diamond."

"What missing diamond?"

That had either been excellent acting, or her sudden and surprised response had been genuine. She didn't know about the missing diamond. Which went a long way in assuaging the guilt Xavier felt at having fucked the suspect.

Perhaps she wasn't a suspect.

"One of the stones from the necklace was missing. The first on the left side. A five-carat stone with so many flaws you could store quantum data on the thing."

"And you consider *me* a suspect?"

"The suspect list is short. You're on it."

"Are you on that list as well? You did take the necklace from me—when I was unconscious following a car wreck, I might add—and as far as I know, you could still have it."

"I was on the list, but I've been cleared. My home and the safe house were searched."

"By your employer?"

"Yes. So that leaves you and Lincoln Blackwell."

She sat up straighter, bending her knees and crossing her legs. "Fair enough. I don't have it. Don't need something so small and worth—what?—a few grand? If flawed, much less. I have enough cash to see me through a long and happy life."

"I assumed as much. That leaves Blackwell."

Josephine shook her head. "I can't believe we didn't notice a missing stone. Seriously?"

"The entire setting was removed from the ribbon, leaving only minute holes in the fabric as a sign that something was missing. We were busy eluding the security guard. And I didn't take the time to look it over before turning it in. Just wanted that damned thing off my plate after all it took to get it."

She nudged his cock with a toe, teasing it gently up and down. "'All it took' did include meeting me."

"Which I'm still not certain was a good thing." Her glare was expected. "Sex not included. But you've put me through the wringer, Seph."

"Happy to take credit for keeping an old thief on his game."

"Digs at my not-so-old age aside, if Lincoln Blackwell does have the stone, that leads me to suspect he never wanted the whole necklace in the first place. Because why simply take out one stone? The man had to have known exactly what he wanted. What is on that stone that makes it so valuable to him?"

"I thought you said it was a recipe for a biological weapon?"

"It is. And all the ingredients have been accounted for on the remaining stones, including a location for the hit. It's impossible to infer what was etched on the missing stone. I was able to photograph the girdle at the ball, but it was the one image that was unreadable. Kierce is trying to work his magic on it."

"Sorting pixels and bytes?"

"Yes. He can work wonders." Sliding a hand across her stomach to curl about her hip, he met her gaze with searching eyes. "Tell me true, Seph. Are you and Blackwell working together?"

"No."

A quick response. Not a moment of hesitation. And she didn't nod after she'd spoken, a common tell for a lie.

"Why do you care?" She leaned forward, putting their faces a foot apart. "You're an international jewel thief. The infamous Fox. You take for yourself, give some to charity, on with the next job."

"How do you know about my charitable contributions?"

"As I've said, I've followed your career."

"You would have had to take particular steps to learn how I've distributed my funds over the years."

"I'm a particular woman."

"That you are." And more frustrating by the moment.

She'd tracked him over the years? Indeed, that would require she have intimate knowledge of his financial transactions. Or at the very least, a connection to Rutger Horst, his accountant. The man had many clients, all of them walking the wrong side of the law, but Xavier trusted Horst implicitly. He kept his finances distributed in half a dozen countries and donated seventy-five percent of all profits to charity on behalf of an anonymous benefactor. Horst guaranteed a clean ledger and no contact with any banks.

Horst was the only one who handled Xavier's money and the only one who knew where it ultimately landed. He'd kept in touch with him during his incarceration, and even now their contact was occasional but discreet. Though he no longer had new income to add to his accounts, he still required a money manager.

Did he have a reason to question that trust? Could Horst have been the one behind Xavier's arrest and ultimate incarceration?

Dimitri Rostonovich, a trusted fence, had ratted out Josephine. Of course, Rutger Horst could not be trusted. *Trust no one.* Especially in his line of work. Not even an alluring woman who had just rocked his world, and with whom he very much wanted to get back to said rocking.

Christ, what was happening? How had he missed one extremely sexy woman trailing him? For years?

That kiss. The kiss she'd accused him of forgetting. Did that hold the key to their connection?

"What's going on in that brain right now?" She nudged his knee with her leg, prompting him to move and sit up alongside her. He propped his head on the wall next to hers. "If you're trying to figure me out, stop."

"Isn't turn-around fair play?" he asked. "You've apparently figured me out."

"Never. I have no clue who you are working for. I suspect it's some kind of black-ops organization. Is it the police? Interpol? CIA? Russian mafia?"

Xavier chuckled. The movement set his hard-on bobbling, so he pulled a pillow over his lap. "I'm not allowed to detail my connections, but I can tell you we—those who work for the organization—call ourselves the Last Chance Ops. Sort of a private joke between the inmates."

"Last chance?"

"We've been given one last chance at freedom by agreeing to work for the organization for a minimal fee and offering our unique expertise on white-collar crime."

"Or?"

"Or…it's the tombstone. Thus, the last chance."

"Has to be the law. No one else could get a convicted felon out of prison. Maybe."

"Money can serve a man anything he desires. Even access to the seemingly inaccessible."

"True. So someone is basically blackmailing you to do their dirty work."

"I wouldn't call trying to stop a biological weapon from taking out the entire 8th arrondissement of Paris dirty work."

"So you're doing good now? Using your skills to save the innocent and defeat the bad guys? Sounds like a twisted superhero plot."

"I'm no one's hero. And I much preferred giving most of my take to charity. Do the math on how many charitable dollars were removed from the system when I was incarcerated. Anyway, this interacting with the public and having a boss is...trying. But I prefer the challenge to cell bars and lye soap."

"Who would have thought The Fox would be reduced to such demeaning work."

He gripped her jaw tightly, feeling his anger for a moment before softening his touch as he turned her to face him. "I am proud of the work I'm doing now. And I will find that diamond, with or without you."

"You can do it without me."

She was so quick to dismiss anything that might prove a challenge. He didn't like that about her, and yet, he could understand the innate need to protect oneself, especially when none of the players could ever be trusted. "I'd rather do it with you, Seph."

"Calling me some stupid pet name is not going to sway me."

"You know Blackwell."

"Yeah, but no one is paying me minimum wage to provide my expertise. And I don't need the feel-good pride either. I've got enough to worry about trying to go underground. Again. Blackwell found me after two years, of which, I thought I was free and clear from my past. I'm not going to be so stupid this time around."

"You shouldn't work with Dmitri Rostonovich."

"The fence was the one who ratted me, wasn't he? I thought it was him. Thanks for verifying that."

He shrugged. Would he have ever offered a competitor such information before his prison stint? No. The woman had...altered something in him. And it wasn't because of the sex, which had been great. Mind-blowing? Yes, positively. And he didn't know any more about her than he had that night she'd kissed him at the ball. But something felt different within him when he was around Josephine. And it was a hard thing to deal with, because he didn't want to begin to label it.

"So. You've gotten what you wanted from me." She trailed a finger down her breast and circled the hard nipple. "Now leave. Or I'll start thinking you've fucked me to implicate me."

"I would never do such a thing. I wanted to have sex with you, Seph. Business and pleasure are completely separate with us. And I'd like to do it again. The sex part. Hell, I'd like to sit here and talk a while, get to know you."

"How does that figure in with your job? You might think you're just here for a good time, but I know no one who works for a secret organization operates without ulterior motives. Sometimes those motives aren't even apparent until you get right down to it. And then it's too late."

Chloe jumped onto the bed and padded over the rumpled sheets to nudge against her mistress's shoulder. Xavier patted the cat's head, mining his empathy for what to say to not lose the girl. She was right. He had complicated matters with sex. But he'd truly believed he could keep business and pleasure separate.

Idiot. His job was to recruit Josephine Devereaux. Voluntarily. And he couldn't deny some forethought had gone into this seduction. He'd thought if they grew closer, she might be eager to join the Last Chance Ops. A stupid move if he had any chance of a relationship with her. And that he'd even thought that word—relationship—was proof his veneer was cracking.

Could he deal with her hating him once she had been recruited? Because she would.

He was not developing feelings for the woman. That was a fool move. He needed her to find the diamond and he needed her for the Elite Crimes Unit. And neither one of those needs required them to be in a relationship. Doctor Walters would have a heyday with this development.

The shrink would never find out about this afternoon liaison. Xavier couldn't let that happen.

"You're right." He tossed aside the pillow and looked around for his clothes. Out in the living room. Fine. So he couldn't occupy his hands with a shirt and pants while he laid it on thick. He stood before Josephine, naked, vulnerable…but never conquered. "This was probably wrong." Yet, he'd never convince himself of that. Still, he was an excellent actor. "I need you to help me find the diamond. I should have stuck to business."

The cat crawled onto Seph's stomach, finding a resting place with its paws upon her breasts, which prompted sudden jealousy in Xavier. Josephine smiled up at him, obviously sensing his struggling emotions.

"Should we forget this happened?" he asked.

"X. X," she drawled in false sweetness. "Do *you* want to forget it happened?"

He winced and turned to face the blowsy curtains. Hell no, he'd never forget. And if he did convince her to work with him, he'd spend every moment remembering the feel of her skin under his tongue or her heat caressing his steel-hard cock.

"If it'll be the thing to get you to consider working with me?" He nodded. "All's forgotten. I'm going to get dressed."

He strode out swiftly, knowing she had won that one.

And she knew it, too.

Chapter 20

"I need an assessment for Lincoln Blackwell," Xavier told Josephine.

The moon sat full and high in the sky. Xavier had not left her apartment, and Josephine was not going to offer to make him something to eat, even though they'd not eaten since breakfast and she was hungry. After he'd revealed what he wanted from her, and that he could forget about the sex, he'd taken a shower and had calmly gotten dressed. The gray designer suit wasn't even wrinkled, and he looked like a million bucks.

Make that the Dresden Green Diamond, a forty-one-carat natural green diamond currently displayed alongside the Hope Diamond. How those Dresden green eyes did glint.

And she realized he was sitting approximately as far from her now as he had been that first night she had seen him from behind the sofa in her mother's office. Lying on the floor, a book in hand, she had often tucked away in the office, away from the yelling and constant arguments, and lost herself in worlds written on pages. Until the night the thief had slipped through an open window with the prowess of...a fox.

Josephine had watched him crack the safe with an ease that had made her a fan girl from that moment on.

But even fan girls could harbor wishes for vengeance.

"Do you think I'm working for you now?" On the sofa, she crossed her legs and put her hands behind her head. She'd slipped into black leggings and a fresh white t-shirt. The urge to dress sexy for him was still there. *She* hadn't agreed to forget about the sex. And she didn't wear a bra. Her nipples peaked under the thin shirt, and his eyes strayed there. Often.

"What's it going to take?" he asked.

"I'm not sure you can offer me anything of value. As I've said, financially, I'm sound. And I'm not in the market for a gigolo or a lover."

"Everyone needs a lover."

"You seriously want me to accept sex as payment for my expertise on Lincoln Blackwell?"

"No. I want you to have sex with me because you desire me and because you desire the pleasure I can give you."

"But you've said that was all forgotten. So sex, apparently, is off the table."

At least, that's what she had to say to meet him at his own game. She would never brush that one from the table like crumbs from breakfast toast.

"It is," he asserted.

Josephine almost pouted over that reply, but she knew how to hold a poker face. "So can this organization that you work for offer me anything for the information I can give you? Clemency from my past crimes?"

"No. Uh…no."

But he'd considered it for that split second between words. Hmm… There was a chance it could happen. Probably though, he needed to get approval from some higher-ups. He did work for the law. It made little sense that he'd be on such a magnanimous mission for the bad guys.

Working with him seemed too risky. And while risk always gave her a high—she did love that "screaming no" feeling—this time the high offered an immediate drop. Most likely behind bars. She didn't want to get involved with an organization that forced criminals to do their dirty work by threatening them with death.

Yet what she could get out of partnering with Xavier was the chance to work closely with The Fox. And that had always been her dream. A dream that had clashed with her revenge fantasy, but also had been a requirement for such revenge to happen. And the little taste she'd gotten of working alongside him so far had only whetted her appetite for more.

She could be greedy; that was a flaw she'd never managed to overcome. That's why charitable contributions had been a necessity to offset such avarice. Xavier wasn't fooling anyone; the man gave his booty away to clear his conscience.

"I can't do this without you." He crossed the room and stood before the window, staring out at the setting sun. The crisp white shirt collar glowed in the beam of light and underlined his masculine profile. "That's the first time I've said that to anyone."

Bully for him. The confession didn't impress her. Much. Okay, a little. It must have been tough for him to admit such a weakness. Either that or—no, he was working her. Such a careful, painstaking admission couldn't be anything but a ruse.

And yet, she hadn't pushed him out the door and told him never to return.

Damn. She was a sucker for a bad boy with a handsome face. That "screaming no" feeling hummed at the base of her throat. And that meant—damn her!—she was in for the ride.

Josephine exhaled through her nose and squeezed her eyelids shut. "I need a promise of complete anonymity. Your organization can't know me or who you are working with. And when Blackwell is in hand, or you've got the diamond, then I'm out. This time for real. No following me. No tracking. You forget my name, my number, and all the ways I can make you come. Yes?"

He tapped his jaw, thinking. Too long.

"They already know about me, don't they?" she guessed. "Damn."

"You marched yourself into that one all by yourself. If you hadn't interfered at the ball—"

"Fine." Josephine put up a hand. She *had* stepped into that one. No need for him to admonish her. If anyone deserved the blame, she'd slap it across Lincoln's simpering smirk. "How much do they know about me? Do you have a rap sheet?"

"I do... It's not complete. Yet. Kierce is working on it."

"Good ole Kierce."

"We have your name and some info about the Phoenix ruby heist."

A fifty-carat ruby waiting for display at a small-time gemstone show. The security had been ridiculously lax. And a little flirtation with an overweight security guard had gotten her far. "It can't be proven that I actually pulled off that heist."

"Of course not." He tilted his head and winked, acknowledging that he knew because—hell, she'd just, in a roundabout way, confessed to that one. "And while I'm not required to divulge to you any information we may or may not have, I will volunteer that what they know is little."

"Why are *they* allowing you to work with me? Why not get me to do their dirty work the same way they got you to do it?"

His jaw tightened. And again he thought about the question a few seconds too long. "Because you're not sitting in a prison cell with no other options."

Josephine closed her eyes and leaned against the sofa. He lied to her. But *why* was beyond her grasp. No, it was within reach. He lied with ease. It was a criminal's best means to divert and at the same time gather intel.

She could run at any moment. Though it was difficult with Chloe. Owning a cat was like having a child. She couldn't walk out the door and leave her behind for days. And she wasn't about to abandon her in a pound just because her life had been turned upside-down.

Josephine ran her gaze over Xavier from shoes to crotch—pity, no obvious hard-on—to that firm chest beneath the clean lines of the suit, to his pretty face. Dresden green eyes lingered on her, trying to read her. But she wouldn't give him any more. She couldn't.

Could she? Why was she so conflicted about this man she didn't think she would ever see again?

Because she had seen him again. And he'd fucked her. And she'd loved it. And she wanted him again. Even with the risk and her better senses screaming "no, no, no."

The no-sex rule? She wasn't going to follow it. And really, the man had to be kept on a leash somehow. The way to a man's faith and blind trust was straight through his cock.

Curse the mystery organization and the unfortunate cons whom they forced to do their bidding. She could fall for this guy. If he didn't work for the law. Which he did. Much as he didn't want to give up the details, no other organization would be involved in recruiting ex-cons to go after biological weapons.

Unless of course, she had already fallen for him.

No.

Maybe? Argh!

"Fine. But I'm not going to have any contact with Blackwell."

"I don't believe that's necessary. He'd be suspicious if you returned, asking after a diamond of which you should have no interest. I just need intel. And while we have a dossier on Blackwell, we're not up on his current affairs. That's where you come in."

"Money laundering, investment schemes, speculative trades," she offered, because she had no alliances to Blackwell. "The man has his hands all over the foreign markets. He stays away from the United States. Too hot there. And that's where his brother lives."

Xavier turned away from the window; she'd caught his attention. "Tell me about the brother. Why does he avoid him?"

She was either in or out. And if she said one more word, she could end up regretting ever trusting this man. But really? Life wasn't worth the trip unless she toed the line.

"His stepbrother, Marcus, and he have a vicious rivalry. He never told me much, but I suspect if anyone was going to rat on Lincoln, it would be Marcus Blackwell."

Chapter 21

Xavier stood in the foyer of the apartment building, waiting for Josephine to gather her things and the cat. He'd offered to help, but she'd told him to wait downstairs. So he put in a call to Hunter Dixon and gave him Marcus Blackwell's name. Dixon said he'd put an asset in the States on him immediately.

Xavier's new orders were to bring Josephine back to Paris. For recruitment? Not until they'd used her to find Lincoln. If they were lucky, in the process she would implicate herself further and give the ECU solid blackmail material against her.

"As you wish." He tucked away the phone and rubbed his palms together. What had he just agreed to?

To keeping his ass out of prison, that was what. And be damned if Seph suffered the consequences? Apparently.

He paced between the front and back doors, glancing outside and toward the roof. Just in case she decided to make another escape.

He doubted she would this time around. They'd…well, they'd had sex. And then he'd decided his wisest move was to tell her it had been forgettable. He was kicking himself for that now. It had been the least forgettable experience in his life. But he was torn between falling for the woman and turning her over to the ECU. And he shouldn't be. His job had to come first and foremost.

"Fuck." He kicked the toe guard at the base of the wall. Job? More like prison work-release.

At the opposite end of the foyer, someone entered the building. The person's silhouette blocked the sun as Xavier turned to assess the man, who much resembled a troll in human form. Fingers of one hand curling in and out of a meaty fist, he looked...like he had come specifically for Xavier. And the knife in his other hand confirmed that suspicion loudly.

Rarely did he misjudge an invitation to defend his life. Reaching behind his waist for the cable-wire garrote that lined his belt, Xavier pulled it free and stepped back, luring the thug with a crimp of his fingers.

"You are Le Renard, the thief?" the man asked with a thick accent that Xavier couldn't quite place. He wasn't Victor Katirci—Xavier had seen that man's dossier, which had included a blurry surveillance shot of his head and shoulders. So this chunk of flesh must be one of his minions.

"Who's asking?" Xavier set back his shoulders and squared his feet below his hips. He made show of drawing the garrote tightly between his hands.

"I've come for the diamond necklace."

"Don't have it. Sorry, you made the trip for nothing."

"You will give it to me."

"Are you as thick in the head as you are in body? I can't give you what I don't have."

"Then..." The man made a show of glancing up the stairwell. "She must have it?"

Ah, hell. They must have figured out that he and Seph were working together in some manner. And the troll had to be related to the van who had followed and tranqued her—whom Xavier had assumed was Katirci. Apparently whomever the ECU had sent to take them out had failed.

Time to clean up this mess.

Xavier lunged toward the man and swung up his arm, elbowing him in the jaw. Twisting quickly, he volleyed around with his fist and connected with the man's kidney. It was enough to take the wind out of him, but he remained standing.

The hiss of the knife blade cut the air close to Xavier's face. He moved quickly, knowing he had the advantage of size in that he was leaner and could move faster than the behemoth. Swinging the garrote high and snapping it tightly, he got it around the man's neck, but there was an impediment. Thick, meaty fingers had put up a block and were already pulling the cable with incredible strength.

All he had to do was tire the man out. Before Josephine sailed down the stairs with Chloe.

"I will make you a frog, squished under my foot," the man announced as he flipped Xavier over his head and sent him tumbling against the baseboard and the wall.

Not if he could help it.

Kicking, Xavier managed a deft block, sending the knife flying from the thug's hand. A return blow hit Xavier on the bicep, sending electrical eels through his arm. It felt as if his bone had cracked. Commotion from above clued him that someone was moving about on the second floor. Not Seph's floor. He didn't need innocents witnessing this, so he lured his attacker closer to the back door.

There, Xavier spied the fire extinguisher and grabbed it. Using it as a battering ram, he lifted it overhead and smashed it onto the thug's head. The attacker collapsed with little fanfare.

Xavier set the extinguisher aside and looked over the heap on the floor. "That was much easier than expected."

Tucking the garrote back into his waist, he wandered toward the foyer. He squeezed his bicep to confirm the new bruises blooming there. Someone skipped down the stairs overhead. A cat meowed.

Seph bounced into the entryway. Her eyes landed on the sprawled thug. "Did I miss all the fun?"

Xavier laughed and took Chloe's carrier. "Come this way. We'll need to go out the back in case his friends are waiting out front."

* * * *

Lincoln Blackwell had finally gotten a good read on the five-carat stone he'd removed from the necklace. It hadn't been so much a safety measure in removing that stone immediately upon claiming the necklace as advanced knowledge. He hadn't expected Jo-Jo to come back for it, but one can never be too careful. Thieves. Couldn't trust 'em.

His tech assistant had read the information laser-etched onto the girdle and recorded it for him. The first numbers were latitude and longitude for the position where the limo was parked right now.

Smoothing a manicured hand down his silk tie, Lincoln glanced out the back window. The Bourse de Paris, the stock exchange, sat just up the street, a place he knew well but avoided for the love of freedom. Immediately before him stood a nondescript bank with an ATM machine tucked into the side of the building. It was most likely used by tourists more often than locals. Not ten feet away from the ATM, a blue tarp had been fashioned into a tent and duct-taped to the concrete by one of the many homeless that littered the area.

The finest streets in the city were frequented by the dregs of society. Wasn't as if jobs were lacking. Lincoln wagered more than half the sidewalk dwellers were intelligent and qualified to hold even the most menial of tasks. Of course, drugs tended to suck the smarts right out of a person, which is why he never touched an illicit substance. Nor did he drink alcohol. He wasn't stupid.

He eased his fingers over his right shoulder, tenderly touching the spot where he'd removed the gauze that morning. The knife wound still hurt like a mother.

But not as much as the pain of looking over his foreign bank accounts this morning. His accountant had alerted him that something terrible was up. Three accounts had been reduced from millions to zero. What. The. Hell? And while the accountant had been able to move his other funds quickly, he couldn't guarantee whomever had launched the cyber-attack on him would not be able to follow his tracks. He would keep a close eye on all accounts and report back to him.

Seventy-five percent of his wealth had been distributed amongst those foreign accounts. Lincoln had no idea who would have it out to get him. On the other hand, everyone he had ever dealt with had good reason. Including his own stepbrother. But Marcus hadn't the talent for sneaking in and removing funds via a cyber-attack. Had he?

Lincoln had dispatched a team to locate Marcus and was currently waiting for a report. He'd requested the men not do anything more than observe. For now. But if that bastard was going to fuck with him....

Suppressing the urge to punch the back of the front seat, Lincoln closed his eyes tightly. Now, more than ever, he needed one thing to go right for him.

Turning his wrist, he brought up the notes app on his iWatch and swiped to the code—the evidence from the diamond's girdle. He opened the back door and stuck out a leg. Scanning the sidewalk and streets, he verified that the foot traffic was minimal. In the distance, laughter echoed out from the city park plunked on top of Les Halles, the biggest underground mall in the city, and the entrance to its snarliest and most maddening metro station.

His bodyguard already stood near the ATM, because while gonzo financial risk was Lincoln's thing, personal risk was another arena entirely.

When he received a confirming nod from the bodyguard, Lincoln got out, tugged at the lapel of his Armani suit fashioned from needle cord cotton—hot off the runway—and approached the ATM. The bodyguard had swiped an antibacterial wipe over the keypad. One never knew. And with such elite neighbors occupying the grounds nearby....

Lincoln stifled a shudder and waggled his fingers over the keypad. He wore thin latex gloves—not because of germs, but to keep his fingerprints to himself. He entered the code into the ATM. It was an override sequence. The tiny screen flashed white, then red text scrolled across the screen.

It prompted to enter today's date, which Lincoln did. Then it paused, the date blinking.

Casting glances over each shoulder, he spied a trio of giggling girls crossing the street. They looked at him, then the tarp tent, and veered a wide curve away from the distraction on the sidewalk.

The screen scrolled a message in red LED: *Premature completion request. Task not complete. Execute assigned protocol within 36 hours.*

The screen went blank. Then it flashed the word BOOM and disintegrated into pixels, like the aftermath of a tiny bomb.

"What the...?" Lincoln slammed his palm against the screen. "Task not complete?" Of course it wasn't complete. The 8th arrondissement was still alive and very much standing. As it should be.

The screen should have prompted him for his account number and transferred five million dollars. That was the payment for setting off the biological weapon. He hadn't expected—well, yes, he should have anticipated such a warning.

"Shit."

The only way to get the cash was to ensure the task was completed. But he couldn't do that without the ingredient list on the necklace. Which he didn't have. And which he'd not the stomach to actually initiate. Take out an entire neighborhood? Not that he was averse to such an act of terrorism, but only if his hands were not in the mix.

A mix he'd inadvertently stepped into and was now trying to reverse. As a side investment his accountant wasn't aware of, he'd transferred funds to a shell company over the years. He'd trusted Ashwood—a code name; he preferred dealing with them—to invest in gold and Icelandic real estate. Thinking it was time to pull out—his assets growth had hit a stalemate— Lincoln had followed Ashwood for a few months. Tapping his phone had revealed the destination for the missing five million.

Never had he expected Ashwood would use the company's funds to kill others. That money was Lincoln's. And now, more than ever, he needed it back. Without having to shake off blood from it. He would not be dragged into an international terrorist event.

Not only had a trusted investor turned on him, but now there were the funds missing from his accounts. Bad luck had landed in spades. And he was not the man to stay in and ride it out. He had to take care of this immediately.

And yet...could his accountant somehow be involved in Lincoln's missing funds *and* the stolen shell funds? He'd sounded as surprised as Lincoln had been during their earlier phone conversation. Of course, Lincoln had not mentioned the shell debacle. But if he were involved with Ashwood in any way.... No, he would have said something over the years. Asked him about those diverted funds.

But Lincoln wasn't stupid. He'd had his share of bad luck, but never on such a monumental scale. Someone was fucking with him. The accountant was out. But first, he had to find him. And he'd suddenly dropped off the planet.

Bloody hell.

Now he had to—what? Find Katirci and get him to finish the job? Absolutely not. Walk away from five million? Again, not in hell, because his current financial status was looking dire. But how to get the cash without setting off the command to have the Turk concoct and deploy the biological weapon?

"This is all because of Jo-Jo. She is the thorn in my side." A thorn he, admittedly, loved to push in deeper. "Damn it!"

He kicked the building and strode back to the limo. Once inside, he punched the back of the front seat.

Then he recalled the entire screen message that had flashed on the ATM. Thirty-six hours? What exactly did that mean?

* * * *

The limo picked them up at Charles de Gaulle. Fortunately the ECU had not sent Alliance again. Xavier had no desire to watch Al eye Seph and make up her mind about their involvement. And comment about her suspicions. Because she would have.

He took Seph's hand and squeezed it. The seduction had started out as a ploy to gain her trust, but hell, she was a remarkable woman. He wanted more from her. And he wanted more *for* her. How could he possibly ask her to join the Elite Crimes Unit when all she wanted was freedom?

"Where will we stay?" she asked, yawning. It was early evening. Neither of them had slept much through the night and morning.

Xavier brushed the hair from her eyelashes. She leaned her head back on the seat, an elbow propped on Chloe's carrier. "My place. If that's okay with you."

"It's not. It'll be tapped and tracked."

"It is."

"And you only have one bed. How would we ever manage that?"

"I can't let you out of my sight."

"I've given you my word to help you. You'll have to trust me."

"I actually do. Not sure why. I know you now. Physically, that is. But inside here?" He tapped her forehead. "I'm curious. Tell me something about yourself."

"Like what?"

"Anything. I just want to hear you talk."

"Seriously? You are weird."

"Humor me. Let's finish the conversation we started when we staked out Blackwell's mansion."

Josephine let out a heavy sigh. "My favorite color is purple. I like cats. I hate radishes. And I miss living in the country far away from the city. I miss being free. And I crave bacon at unexpected times of any given day. Now you."

"Me?"

"Hey, you started this. That's how a conversation works. I know, it's difficult, but you can do it, X."

He smirked at the pet name. He didn't mind it. Rather liked it, actually.

"Very well. I don't think I have a favorite color. I prefer gray suits because they blend in with the crowd. When I was six, I rescued a dachshund with a broken tail and made him a splint. And I hate…hmm… Do I have to hate something?"

"You hate it when cocky jewel thieves move in on your action."

"Yes, there is that. My turn again to ask the questions?"

"Shoot."

Xavier turned toward her, resting his head on the back of the seat. "How did you get started? What compelled you to take your first piece of sparkly stuff?"

Josephine closed her eyes and, with a smirk, shook her head. He could prompt that she owed him for the information he'd given her, but that wasn't how this game was played. Patience and a certain trust was required. So he waited.

"Yeah, I suppose," she said quietly. "My mother lost everything when I was younger. A thief stole all that she had. I watched him."

"You watched him?"

She nodded. "I was lying behind the couch, reading. A favorite spot in my mother's office. I used to go there to escape the yelling. Mom and her boyfriend were always fighting. He was an asshole. A drug dealer. But none of that matters now. As for the thief, he never saw me. But I saw him. He cracked my mother's safe—a standard Moyer combo dial—in four minutes—I timed him on my Swatch watch—and took out all the diamonds and jewels inside. But they didn't belong to my mother. She was holding them for her boyfriend's boss. And that man did not forgive. She lost everything. Had to go on the run. Her boyfriend convinced her she could run best without a kid to hold her back. So, in lieu of literally kicking me to the curb, she dumped me in a foster home."

Stunned at such a confession, and feeling it was true and not a story she had invented to get his sympathy, Xavier could only listen as his heart clenched.

"I hated it," she said. "Ran away a lot. Of course, the foster home was a means to a hot meal and a bed, so I never stayed away more than a day or two. But I'd been turned on to a new drug that night I watched the thief. I started stealing. Small things. Watches, rings, money. I'd sneak into the foster home's office and read documents and take the car keys and go on joy rides. Stupid stuff. My first jewelry heist was a smash-and-grab at a family-owned corner store. Only I didn't smash. I used my wiles."

Josephine smiled, eyes closed. She was remembering. Xavier could recall his first job. He'd been much younger. Five. And the take had been a milk chocolate candy bar that he'd made last three days. It was also a memory to savor.

"I wanted to be like that thief in my mother's office, and I worked my way up to big jobs. I've always been independent, though. Didn't want to get involved with mafia or owing someone else."

"Wise move. So to learn more you…found a thief to follow?"

"That I did." She winked.

"How did you ever learn about me? It's not as if I advertise or shout it out to the world."

She shrugged. "A remarkable coincidence."

She didn't offer any more. He'd have to go more slowly if he wanted to get to her depths, to the gears that made her tick. And how, exactly, she had happened upon him.

"Seph, I'm sorry you were abandoned when you were younger. That's tough."

"How would you know? I don't think the suits and the style came after you had honed your craft. I believe your craft grew out of the entitlement, and perhaps even boredom, that comes with being one of the idle rich."

"Interesting assessment."

"But I'm correct," she said, not as a question.

"So it is confession time, yes?"

"Yes. I told you my dirty dark. Now you tell me yours."

"A dirty dark?"

"Secret," she said with an annoyed insistence.

"Right. Very well."

And he could tell her because he had always needed to tell someone. And not a shrink who liked to screw with his memories and insist he stole diamonds to piss off his father. Josephine was his mirror, and she would reflect exactly what he needed and wanted to see.

"I was due to inherit a fortune when I turned eighteen. My family is old money from Marseilles. The Lamberts have been in the tailoring business for centuries. A dull, tedious trade. But quite lucrative. My old man disowned me when I refused to take up the needle and thread. Handed the inheritance to my younger brother. I didn't mind. I've always enjoyed the thrill of challenging myself. My first job was a tidy snatch from a Persian princess."

"They've never been able to prove that wasn't an inside job."

"It was not."

All the years of secrecy and looking over his shoulder suddenly snapped Xavier upright. *Don't be a fool. Even* you *don't like what you see in the mirror every day. You take from others.* And no amount of charity could ever assuage that guilt.

He decided it wasn't necessary to give his entire life story. He was not that foolish. "We've both arrived at a similar place in our quest to survive the world. Taking things before others took them from us."

"Because we can. Because we want to."

"Because we crave that high."

"Mm…" Josephine cooed. "Better than sex. Seriously."

"I would have to agree. Not that sex with you wasn't remarkable."

"I thought it was forgettable?"

"Uh…"

"Right," she said quickly. "Sex is always good. But in the greater scheme of things? It means nothing. But to hold a cool fifty-carat flawless diamond in hand and watch the light catch in the facets?"

Xavier clasped Josephine's hand and kissed the knuckles. "How about a rare red diamond?"

"Mercy, I've never. But I also know you like the colored stuff. Have you touched a red diamond?"

"Yes, a seventy-two-carat red stone. It had such a weight to it that I could only marvel. And my heart pounded like I'd been sprinting. It was uncut and wasn't even brilliant, but still." He moaned.

"I've always wanted to snatch the Hope Diamond."

He laughed. "You and every other thief out there. You'd have to gain access to the Smithsonian vault. Not to mention getting past infra-red seismic sensors and the biometric retinal scanner. And even if you did so, there's the curse."

The curse told that bad luck or even death would come to all who owned the Hope Diamond. And in proof, the diamond boasted a historical list of victims who'd suffered such fate.

"Yes, but it's not impossible."

"Nothing is impossible." He hushed a breath over the back of her hand. "Absolutely nothing." He slid his hand between her legs and Josephine tightened her thighs, prompting him up from a place he'd slipped into. That of a certain trust when he was with her. Of desire. "Sorry. Lost myself."

"You did. You have chosen to forget about the sex. So keep your hands to yourself and jack off on your perfect heist fantasies later. Got it?"

"I guess I do." He'd failed at something just now, but he wasn't quite sure how to label it. "Thank you, Seph."

"You can thank me by letting me sleep in your bed. You take the couch."

"Whatever you ask of me, I will give you."

She opened one eyelid. "Can you give me a promise of freedom? Of never having to keep one eye peeled over my shoulder?"

"Sorry." He set her hand on her lap and turned to sit back in his seat.

Chapter 22

With Xavier shaking her shoulder, Josephine woke. She was so tired, and the few minutes she'd napped during the taxi ride was not going to cut it.

"Come on," he said. She followed him out of the car. He carried Chloe's travel cage. "I don't have cat supplies, so I ordered some online while you were sleeping. Should have food and litter waiting by the door."

The man and Chloe had definitely gotten closer. Josephine felt a twinge of jealousy, then brushed it off. What was she thinking?

He entered the code to an outer door that she guessed led into a courtyard. Had she been paying attention, she would know where she was. Or at the very least, get the code. As it was, her exhaustion level couldn't even prompt her to turn and study the street behind them. She'd acclimate later.

Inside, a tidy cobblestoned courtyard boasted a fountain and a few scraggly rose bushes long-past bloomed. On the opposite side of the courtyard, Xavier punched in another code to enter the apartment complex. When she saw the elevator that would barely fit two people, he gestured she enter it, which she did. She was functioning by rote. So when he handed her Chloe and told her to hit the button for the fourth floor, she simply followed directions. He ran up and around the twining staircase and cast her a wink when, at the second floor, she saw him through the glass elevator doors.

Smiling, she could only think that man's smile was crazy sexy. And he was hers. And…oh, what the fuck was she thinking? She really was tired if she was swooning over the thief who had forced her to return to Paris to chase after her ex-boyfriend for a five-carat diamond that neither of them would profit from and probably only end in pain, agony, or all of the above.

"Tell me why I'm doing this, Chloe?"

A peek inside the plastic cage found the cat nestled snug in the plush towel she'd laid down for the ride. Poor kitty was all tuckered out from this traveling.

Was it too much to hope she could actually return to the country home and not have to worry about Lincoln again? Maybe some deal could be struck? You stay away from me, and I won't rat you out?

No, she didn't trust that man. Ever.

The elevator stopped. Xavier opened the door, took the cat carrier, and welcomed her into a quaint, cozy apartment that was half the size of her efficiency in the 8th.

"You see?" He pointed to two bags of cat food and a huge bag of litter sitting in a new plastic litter box. "Was waiting by the door. The bathroom is on the other side of the living area, through there. I'll get Chloe situated while you do what you have to do."

She wanted to sleep. A shower would wake her up too much, but Josephine wandered into the bathroom to pee and wash her face. Five minutes later the cat box sat stationed by the front door. A bowl of cat food sat on the kitchen floor next to a bowl of water. And...the tiny bedroom set off from the foyer held a twin-size bed, with Chloe already sleeping on the pillow.

Josephine startled when she realized Xavier stood closely behind her. He smelled too good. As subtle and exotic as the bad boy thief she'd obsessed over for years. Yet it disturbed her that she hadn't noticed where he was, especially in this small apartment. "X," she said with a yawn. "I'm..."

"Tired, I know. You and Chloe take the bed. I'll sleep on the sofa."

"I'd share but...you did say..."

"It's all good, Seph."

He kissed her at the base of her neck and gave her a gentle shove. She walked like a zombie into the bedroom and collapsed onto the bed to share the pillow with her cat.

* * * *

The clatter in the bedroom alerted Xavier his guest had risen. Chloe sat beside him on the sofa. Her purrs were calming. The window, open to the courtyard, emitted a breeze and scents from the Italian restaurant below. He'd eaten breakfast and was now writing his thoughts down on a notepad. He had never ascribed to putting things in digital format. Too difficult to completely erase. And if he were hacked? So his first and only choice was always paper, that could then be burned.

Josephine wandered into the living room, yawning and blinking. He noted her trajectory with alarm. "Watch out!"

Too late. She walked into the low-hung cupboard over the dining table. She swore and crumpled onto the chair before the table.

"What the hell, X?" She rubbed her temple. "You live in a freakin' shoe box. This is ridiculous." She spied the bowl of cut peaches and strawberries he'd left for her, and popped a berry into her mouth.

He stroked Chloe's soft head. "When the only other option has bars on the window and a toilet in view of all the other residents? I believe I'm doing just fine."

"There is another option, and you know it. You could go AWOL. Get off the grid. Live on the lam."

He smirked. How many times had he considered such a thing? It wasn't as if a little surgery at the back of his neck couldn't dig out the ECU's tracker device. The idea of living on his own was too sweet. Tempting. And he had shoved away all thought of it in an attempt to rescue his very soul. Because he knew he could never manage the hard life. A life that involved some modicum of normalcy he'd never learned. Because he didn't know normal. It was either a life of privilege or, well…

Stealing was what he did best. Thievery formed the platelets in his blood. And if he couldn't do that, incorporating those skills into helping others was the only other option.

"And how did getting off the grid work for you, eh?"

Josephine flipped him the bird. Then, around a bite of peach, she said, "It was going swell until my idiot ex-boyfriend got greedy."

"Exactly. No matter how cautious we are, how clean our efforts and alliances, we can never be completely cut off. There will always be someone. Somewhere. Such as your Dmitri Rostonovich."

"The jerk. And now there's me," she said with a sly wink. "I will always know where you are, X."

"If you want to believe such nonsense, then I'll give you that." He could slip out of her life faster than raking a six-pin lock. And she'd not know the first place to begin looking for him. "Speaking of old boyfriends…" He tapped the notepad on the sofa beside him. "We've brainstorming to do. Tell me everything you know about Lincoln Blackwell, and we'll figure how best to get the missing stone from him."

"I suppose I could march right up and ask him for it."

Xavier lifted a brow, unconvinced with her confidence.

"But I'd probably have to put out, promise to marry him, and have all his children. I'm not particularly keen on that plan."

"Then we're on to plan B."

She pushed the fruit plate forward and leaned an elbow on the table, looking at him with strange admiration. And she simply stared, a little curve curling at the corner of her mouth. Bright eyes read him in a way he hadn't thought possible. So many secrets he still thought to possess. Would she learn them? Would she allow it?

"What are you looking at?" he finally asked.

"A traitor." Her glance averted lower. "Chloe, you are not supposed to cozy up to the enemy."

"Why am I the enemy? I thought we were working together now?"

"I never wanted any of this, X, and you know it. You can put any spin you want on it, and it's still going to come up that I'm the injured party. But you're cute, so I'm in."

"That's all it takes? An attraction to a man's looks? Is that how it was with Blackwell?"

"You're not going to get details on my pitiful love life, so give it up. I gave you the guy's house. I know he's a money launderer, loves his investment schemes, and never met a speculative trade he couldn't increase by two hundred percent."

"You said something about his brother? I passed his name onto my...organization."

"Marcus. Stepbrother. Jealous as hell of Lincoln. He once stole Lincoln's girlfriend by telling her about his brother's larcenist proclivities. It hurt Lincoln. His weakness is his hatred for his brother. Something about his mother loving him more because Marcus had empathy. Bunch of bullshit, if you ask me."

"We will press on that weakness. We've put a New York asset on him."

She picked up another peach slice. "I still think the quickest and easiest route is simply taking back what should have been ours in the first place."

"Another heist in the same home? You know that's 'stupid thieves' trick number one?'"

"I do. And maybe we don't have to break in. Maybe we just find Lincoln and take it off him."

"Why would he have the diamond on him?"

"He took it for a reason."

"Of which, we have no idea what that reason is."

"It can only be money. Nothing else in this world would motivate the man. You said the ingredient list was complete with all the other diamonds in the strand?"

"Yes. And one of the stones detailed a location. Are you thinking this final stone was a payment of sorts?"

"Could be. If it's as flawed as the other stones, the actual stone isn't worth any more than a few thousand, but maybe there's something etched on the girdle. A payment?"

That was an excellent theory, and one Xavier kicked himself for not considering. He scribbled "payment" on the notepad, then circled it.

"Blackwell had to have known about the Turk hired to set off the biological weapon," she said. "Because he knew the countess would be wearing that necklace at the ball. He also had to have known there would be a payment included with the necklace. All that info? The only way he could possibly know any of that was if he'd been tipped off, or had a hand in the process originally."

"Which doesn't make sense." He met her inquiring gaze with a shrug. "Why steal something if he's the planner? He had to have been tipped off."

"He probably doesn't care about the weapon part, only the cash. Asshole. He really doesn't have a care for others beyond how they can stuff his pockets. So if a few thousand die from a biological weapon? At least he gets paid."

"But the Turkish contact who was supposed to set off the weapon would be very upset if he did not get paid. He may even follow the suspected thieves who got caught in the crossfire all the way to Berlin."

"Yes. And a guy as angry as that will be hard to control." She met his gaze. "We need to get the Turk and Lincoln together."

"I believe so."

Xavier set down the pen and allowed Chloe to climb up higher on his chest. She tipped his chin with her nose and, for the first time, he decided cats were really quite special.

* * * *

"We've got some movement with Marcus Blackwell," Hunter Dixon told Xavier over the phone.

Xavier stood before the Mercedes-Benz Gallery on the Champs Elysees, waiting for Josephine, who was inside Massimo Dutti picking up some clothing. She'd insisted on feeling human and wearing something beyond the few items she'd managed to grab when she'd left her country home. As well, she said this elite shopping district was a frequent hangout of Blackwell's.

"Kierce can fill you in. And we've pinpointed a connection to the man that will also aid our efforts."

"What's the connection?"

"A financial one. We've been able to put the squeeze on him. It should force him to the surface, and soon. Devereaux is with you. You are working on her, yes?"

Working on her? In what terms, Xavier would like to ask. But he suspected the Boss had a good notion for how Xavier could convince a woman to join the ECU. Not that he'd ever use sex to persuade—ah, fuck it. He was not having this conversation with himself.

"It's coming along. I've got her close. My focus remains on the diamond."

"Quinn suspects the missing stone may be a form of payment."

"I've come to that conclusion as well. Not the actual diamond, but perhaps transfer numbers to a Swiss account. Is there any way to track something like that?"

"I'll patch you through to Quinn to handle that stuff. You stay on her, Lambert. She's ours."

He wanted to know why they needed another thief on staff, but wouldn't question. Perhaps the ECU was expanding? Of course, they always were. It was a stupid, jealous notion anyway. He didn't care. He shouldn't care.

He did care what happened to her. The woman had been abandoned by her mother because some asshole thief had taken her fortune?

"On it," he said.

Immediately, Kierce's voice came onto the connection. "You've figured it's a payment, the missing stone. Good. I've been able to sharpen a portion of the image you took the night of the charity ball. It's numbers; what I suspect might be latitude and longitude. It could be a start." The guy talked fifty miles a minute. He must be jacked up on one of those energy drinks that were always littering his desk.

"What about Marcus Blackwell? The boss says we've got him where we want him?"

"We've found him and he's talking, but remarkably he doesn't know much. Unfortunately for our intel, I think he's clean regarding this situation."

They should have shipped Gentleman Jack overseas for that one. He could get anything out of anyone.

"We did get him to make a phone call for us, though. As the boss has said, it'll bring Lincoln Blackwell to the surface."

"Have you a location on Katirci?" Xavier asked. "He may be key to snuffing the diamond out of Blackwell's hand."

"That's what the phone call was about. But putting those two near each other could prove risky. Putting the payment in the hands of the guy who was supposed to destroy the entire 8th arrondissement?"

"I would never hand over money to such a person." But he knew the ECU had no such moral qualms.

"We had Katirci in Berlin after you alerted us to him. We were only able to get him off your asses."

"I was made aware of that when one of his thugs tried to twist off my head this morning."

"Yes, and now he's gone off the grid since arriving back in Paris."

"So he is here?" Xavier glanced about the bustle of tourists crowding up and down the sidewalks of the elite shopping district. The scent of coffee lingered in the air, along with overpriced perfume. "That means he could find us before we find him. Stay with me, buddy."

"You got it. Just don't turn me off when you feel the need to make out with your girlfriend."

"Why? You get off on that stuff, Quinn?"

The man chuckled. "I mute it, trust me on that one. But if you cut me out, well…you know."

"Seph tells me the Champs Elysees is Blackwell's favorite weekend hangout. That's why we're here."

"Seph, eh?"

Ah, he had to be careful. Not only his job stood in risk but as well, his heart.

Xavier winced and clamped a palm over his heart. Had he just the ridiculous thought that his heart was getting involved in this caper?

"Talk to you later, Quinn."

He turned to spy a gorgeous woman in a sleek sky-blue sundress and strappy sandals standing not ten feet away. She pulled down the brim of a white sun hat, and her lush red lips curled into a smile as her eyes met his.

Xavier walked up to Josephine and kissed her. He hadn't taken a moment to think it a wrong move. He'd followed…well, he wasn't thinking in terms of his heart, so he wouldn't go there. He had simply been magnetically compelled to kiss her.

"You look like summer," he said against her ear. And he had the sudden hopeful thought that Kierce wouldn't take that as a compliment. "Let's walk."

He clasped her hand and took her shopping bag. They blended into the crowd. While the high-end shops catered to tourists, there was also a healthy mix of the rich and perhaps a few famous. Tourists in shorts, t-shirts and sandals rubbed shoulders with men in Armani and Zegna and women sporting an entire year's mortgage payment on their ring fingers. Such was Paris.

Kierce spoke again. "I found Katirci. He's…close."

Xavier tapped his ear. "What?"

Josephine turned to look at him, but didn't say anything.

"Wait. That's not him. Sorry. Someone else I'm tracking. But…I don't have an ID on that one. Hmm…"

Tightening his jaw, Xavier did not reply. If the guy intended to cry wolf, he did not want to be the receiver. He considered turning the earbud off, then thought better of it. He clasped Seph's hand again and led her toward the nearest shop, where they could get out of any thug's line of sight.

"Kierce?" she asked.

"He's trying to locate Katirci. The man followed us from Berlin after I showed his thug who he was dealing with."

"Peachy. I have a certain love-hate relationship with Kierce. I've never met the guy and yet he knows more about me than most, and he's always trying to nudge in on my action."

Xavier lifted her hand and kissed the back of it. "The only action you're going to get is from me." And then he realized just how possessive that sounded—and her look said the same—but instead of denying it, he simply led her into the store.

He realized too late they'd walked into a jewelry store.

Chapter 23

"Oh, darling," Josephine said as she floated into the air-conditioned comfort of the store. "Love, love, love!"

She'd assumed a persona, which, Xavier knew from experience, was impossible not to do when entering a store such as this. Why had he taken her here? He hadn't been paying attention. He'd merely sought the quickest hide-out.

In a jewelry store.

Such a place was like crack to a recovering addict. Yet Josephine had already approached the counter, tugging down the brim of her wide hat on the left side—the same side as the security camera on the ceiling. He should grab her and pull her out. But the part of the old Xavier—who'd once walked the streets a free man who held the world in his hands and had taken what he'd wanted—lifted his chin and smoothed his shirt. He wanted to watch her in action.

Accepting a goblet of champagne from the smiling clerk, Xavier nodded that he was going to stand aside and let his woman look around. *His* standard persona in a jewelry store? Quiet boyfriend. Smash and grabs or distraction had never been his thing. He preferred casing the place, noting the security cameras, and returning after closing. Right now, he stood at such an angle that none of the four cameras could get a decent fix on his face, save a side view.

Was he planning a heist? No. He just...no.

He couldn't. Because—tombstone.

Unless he took Seph's advice and went on the lam.

Could he? He could do anything he set his mind to. No challenge was too great for him. Would Seph go along with him? He wanted her to have freedom. To never again have to worry about looking over her shoulder. Could they have a life together?

When had he begun thinking of himself and Seph as a "they?" Josephine's ribald laughter alerted him. Her sudden wink and effusive good-byes came with a promise to return when she could convince her boyfriend to buy her "the ring." She grabbed his wrist and tried to pull him out the door.

Not on his watch.

"Darling." Xavier hugged Seph tightly. She cooed, her eyes flirting with his. He could fall into those bright blues. Almost.

He walked her back toward the counter where the clerk adjusted the diamond rings on the black velvet display. He clasped Josephine's hand—palming the ring she'd absconded—and leaned onto the counter, catching the clerk's heavily kohl-lined gaze and winking at her. "She wants to get married, but ah, her heart is not completely mine. You know? She has too many distractions."

"Oh, please, honey, you know you're the only one." Her hand snaked up along his, but he was too quick. Standing upright and gliding one hand along her cheek, his other moved toward the black velvet.

"Not today, lover," he said. "But we'll see about tomorrow, eh?"

Wrapping an arm across her shoulders, he steered her around and toward the door.

"*Au revoir!*" she called, waving and nodding to the doorman as they left the store.

"Really?" he said once they were ensconced within the crowd. Moving quickly, Xavier veered left and crossed the busy ten-lane street.

"What did you expect?" She skipped alongside him. "You took me into a freakin' jewelry store," she said with all the obvious accusation he deserved.

Yes, that had been a stupid mistake. But all was clear. Or was it?

Across the street, they wended their way around a hornet-yellow Maserati for rent. The crowd milling about the sports car snapped pics and teens posed by the hood. One hundred euros for a quick spin around the Arc de Triomphe? Now that was free enterprise at its finest.

Once out of the thick tourist tangle, Xavier pushed Josephine against a wall, pinning her shoulders to the cool marble of some elite department store and slamming his hips against hers. Not a hint of sexual suggestion in the moment. He was pissed.

Tugging off the oversized hat and dropping it, he said, "Do you think I will overlook that silly display in the jewelry shop?"

"I was having some fun."

"Yes? And what about that ring you've still got in your pocket? I'm not so stupid I didn't miss that one."

He gripped her forearm. The defiance in her eyes angered him, but it also made him proud of what she was, how she carried herself. The woman was exquisite. And he doubted the store would miss whatever she'd taken until inventory tonight. Yet neither had worn disguises. Not cool.

He tapped his ear, indicating to her that they were being listened to.

"You let it happen." She lifted her knee, but he defeated the oncoming defensive move with a rough clasp of his hand up under her neck.

"I lied about not knowing your rap sheet, thief. My organization has more than enough on you to have you arrested right now," he lied. "Your offenses are many. And if you don't play right—"

Josephine threw the ring at him, and he caught it. "Fuck you! This is over. I never should have trusted you!"

She took off down the sidewalk.

The stone was no more than a few carats. Not a worthy prize. But still, it had been a blatant grab. And it had served to show him of what she was capable. And that she wasn't calm and completely rational at all times.

"I need some clean up, Kierce," Xavier said.

"Got it. We've got a cleaner in the area. You should really put that one on a leash. But then again, you did take her into the candy store."

"Fuck you, Quinn."

Josephine had taken off around the corner. He didn't expect her to go far. She had nowhere to go in Paris. He was her haven. The cat was at his place. He only had to stay put a bit longer.

A black Citroen turned down the street and pulled up before Xavier. The shaded back window rolled down. He recognized the face, but didn't know the name of the elderly woman. Probably touching seventy, she wore a sleek elegant sweep of gray hair that models would kill for. He handed her the ring and walked away without a word.

Blowing out a breath, he sought a few moments of…nothing. He just wanted to be away from it all. The subterfuge. The necessary evil of working for the ECU. Of compromising his own integrity because he'd been forced to babysit a less comparable thief.

Of learning that his heart did have a function and that it could control his actions.

Last Chance Ops, indeed.

He hadn't played that one well at all. But his anger over Seph's antics had boiled over. She was not a woman a man could control, and he'd been smacked in the face with that reality.

He needed that challenge…in ways he wasn't prepared to admit right now.

Turning the corner, he paused at sight of the black limo parked half a block up the street. And struggling with two hefty thugs, Josephine's legs kicked the air. Blue skirts fluttered. They shoved her into the back seat just as Xavier took off after them. The car peeled away from the curb.

He sprinted after the vehicle for two blocks. Then it veered to the right, and he ran into a crowd lined up for a city tour bus. He shoved, but some of the tourists shoved back and told him off in angry American accents. Dodging the line he ran around it, but by that time the limo was out of sight.

"*Merde.*"

"You lost her," Kierce stated in his ear. Not a question. And a very unnecessary observation.

Bowing forward, and catching his palms against his thighs, Xavier nodded, but couldn't find the strength to mutter an agreement. Because he'd lost her in more ways than just physically. And that realization hurt his heart desperately.

* * * *

Victor Katirci had come to the conclusion that he was following the wrong people. The thieves could elude and match his minions in battle until he was blue in the face. He must go to the source. The man who had funded his delayed mission. And thanks to a surprising phone call from a stranger who had only called himself Marcus, he had a name: Lincoln Blackwell.

Chapter 24

Twenty minutes later, Xavier stood before Hunter Dixon in the Elite Crimes Unit office. Kierce had sent a car to pick him up from the last spot where he'd seen Josephine.

"Blackwell has her," Xavier said. "I'll go in after her."

"She is not the objective of this mission."

Xavier pressed his knuckles to the desktop and leaned in, meeting Dixon with a steady gaze. "I thought you wanted her recruited?"

"We do. But that's another matter. The missing diamond is what you guaranteed me you were focused on. I'm not sending you after Josephine Devereaux."

"Then send me in after the diamond."

"Jack Angelo is in position."

The Thug? "What can Angelo do? He has no experience with what is required. No finesse!"

"You are letting emotion rule your better judgment, Lambert." Dixon narrowed his gaze on Xavier. "You can't fuck her and recruit her. That's not how it works."

Xavier stabbed the desktop with a finger. "That's exactly how it works. Don't tell me that's not true. I'm not that stupid."

Dixon had no reply.

It would be foolish to argue against using sex to gain an advantage. The ECU knew fucking everything. Even when they should not. It shouldn't surprise Xavier how much they knew, but it did.

"I had her trusting me."

"And then you did not."

"She stole from the jewelry store. There's another crime to add to your dossier! I thought that's what you wanted from me?"

"Emotions, Lambert. Check 'em. Leave this to us. I'll reassign the recruitment. If she gets out of there alive."

Xavier slammed his fist on Dixon's desk. "Jack Angelo can't do what I can do."

"And what, exactly, is it that you *can* do?"

"I'm going to give Blackwell what he wants. A bigger prize than the small-time thief he's already got. Me."

"Absolutely not. You are the ECU's asset. I won't authorize such a move."

An asset. He'd heard that term so many times, he forced himself to see it as a compliment. But right now? It felt dirty.

"Then let me bring Katirci to Blackwell. That's what has to happen to get that damned stone back."

"We've activated Katirci's movement and are keeping an eye on him."

Which meant they may have already tagged the guy and were watching him to see what he did, or if he led them to Blackwell. But they already knew where Blackwell was. They could track him through Josephine now.

"What is on the stone?" Xavier asked. "Have we determined that? Maybe it's not worth the effort? We have the formula for the weapon. Paris is safe. What is it about that missing stone that you're not telling me?"

Xavier blew out a breath and straightened up. Realization washed over him. That was it, wasn't it? Dixon knew something about the missing stone. And it was more valuable in the ECU's hands than out in the wild.

"It's not what you think." Dixon stood from behind the desk, propping his hands at his hips. "Kierce managed to do something to the original shot you took of the stone—I don't know how that computer stuff works—and he was able to get a partial read of the etching."

"It's a payment."

"Exactly. Latitude and longitude led us to an ATM in the 2nd arrondissement. When an agent entered the code, he got a warning. It said that payment will not be issued until the task is completed."

"The task being, setting off the biological weapon."

"Yes. And should that task not be completed in the designated amount of time there will be repercussions. And we've been able to determine it will involve a bomb, but have no clue where it will be set off. Here in Paris? Doesn't make sense if an agent was hired to set off the biological weapon in the first place. Which leads me to believe that whomever is holding the stone will become a target."

"Meaning, death? Well, that will take care of Lincoln Blackwell for you."

Dixon winced. His eyes strayed to a stack of papers to his left. On top of that stack lay a black file. "He's been marked for recruitment as well."

"What? The bastard kidnapped Josephine—" Xavier squeezed his hands to keep himself from slipping into an emotional tirade. "This is a cluster fuck."

"That all depends on who is making such an assessment. You need to dial it down, Lambert. We need Blackwell in hand, with the stone secured before the clock runs out."

"And how much time do we have?"

"Quinn guesstimates twenty-six hours."

"Guesstimates?"

"He's running an algorithm on the ATM transactions right now. We should have an update soon."

"You have to send me in. I'm the only one who has any clue about Blackwell. Josephine has told me about him. It's obvious he's taken her as leverage. He can't actually believe she has the necklace, which must be what he ultimately wants. Do you think he'll set off the weapon?"

"Our records do not indicate that he is the type to initiate such mass destruction, but there is five million at stake."

"Shouldn't that be chump change for a man like Blackwell?"

"It would have been two days ago. But since he stepped onto the ECU's radar? He's suddenly lost almost everything he's got stashed in foreign bank accounts."

How could a man so smart as— Ah. "Recruitment tactics?"

"Exactly."

Xavier raked his fingers through his hair. The shit that had been going on behind his back was incredible. He didn't like being a pawn on the chess board. But he understood he hadn't much say about it. It was either toe the line or toe the dirt six feet under.

So this was what helpless felt like. And Seph must feel the same way. The man she hated most, who had forced her back into stealing, now held her hostage. Xavier couldn't allow her to suffer because of the intricate workings of the big bad ECU machine.

"I'm going after her," he stated firmly. "Tell Kierce to lead me to Blackwell."

Dixon sighed and crossed his arms high over his chest. The man should patent that condemning stare. "You should know, after recruitment and training she won't be stationed anywhere near you."

He expected as much. Could be good for both of them. Though it would tear him apart knowing what he'd done to her. And what they could have had, if only he'd the courage to walk away from the ECU with her at his side. Such a move could prove the greatest heist he'd ever pulled off. But the only way to garner such opportunity required he play the game.

Xavier nodded. "I'm good with that."

Dixon tapped the intercom on the desk module. "Quinn, get Lambert the last known location of Lincoln Blackwell. Let's reassign Jack Angelo to Victor Katirci. Do you have an update on the time frame?"

"Yes," Kierce said weakly.

"And?"

Both Xavier and Dixon exchanged glances as they waited for Kierce's reply.

"The initial transaction occurred a little over a day ago. That leaves eight hours, thirty-seven minutes until—well, you know."

"Go," Dixon ordered.

Chapter 25

"You've been following me," the man said.

Josephine sat ramrod straight on the wooden chair. She had no choice. Her hands had been bound together and stretched behind her, pulled down to her ankles. It wasn't an excruciating position, but it did tax her shoulders and biceps, and it wouldn't be long before fighting back—if released—was no longer an option. She regretted the dress, which lay high on her thighs, wishing she could tug it down.

"Turn about is fair play, yes?" she muttered.

Lincoln sat on the edge of a stack of wooden pallets. They were in what looked like an abandoned warehouse, with dirt floors, unpainted brick walls, and missing glass windows. He flipped back his thick black hair, which gleamed with pomade that smelled like the ocean. Dark brows wrinkled as he laughed. "I would expect nothing less from you."

"Admit it. You're obsessed with me. Following me all these years?" She shook her head. "Give it up, Lincoln. It's never going to happen again."

"I'm not so pitiful as your fantasies cast me. I'm over you, Jo-Jo."

"Don't call me that."

"Jo-Jo." He gripped her chin, tightly. "How's the cat?"

"If you took Chloe again—"

He shoved her head back and stood to pace the dirt floor. "I'm done with catnapping. Moved on to bigger and better things. But answer my question. Why are you following me? You stole the fucking necklace back. What more do you want from me? Maybe I should be the one asking why you're obsessed with me."

"You know why."

He shrugged, pouting. Then he moved closer, eyeing her with that searing gaze that had once given her the shivers—the good kind. "You are working with that thief. The Fox. I remember your obsession with *him*. I once thought you were fucking him, but then realized it was only some sort of schoolgirl crush."

Josephine sucked in her upper lip.

"But the two of you answer to someone bigger," he continued. "I'm trying to track down the puppet master, but I'm hitting a brick wall."

"Hitting bricks will only get you bruises. Slam your face against it, will you?"

The slap stung, but it hadn't been unexpected. Josephine whipped back her head, flipping the hair from her face, never breaking eye contact with Lincoln. "I guess you owed me that for the knife, eh? How's your shoulder?"

He dragged his tongue over his front teeth without opening his mouth; a move he made when he was annoyed. She hoped he'd had to get stitches.

"What's on the diamond?" she dared to ask.

His shoulders relaxed as he settled onto the pallet stack again. Stretching his legs before him, he smiled. "You don't know?"

"I've never known. I was just a pawn in your game, remember? No one gave me big-picture details. So what, exactly, did I steal?"

"I think The Fox has given you those details, so I won't waste my words."

Fair enough. She was at the end of her rope, but she had mastered the art of the precarious dangle.

"What the hell do you want with a biological weapon?"

"Eh? Hmmm…maybe you don't know all. Do you know how much I could sell such a weapon for?"

"Sure, but you don't have the ingredients list anymore."

"I don't. And I've never wanted such a horrible thing. You know it's not my style to get my hands dirty with stuff like mass murder."

"People change."

He leaned forward. "Have you changed, Jo-Jo? You tried the hard life. Look where it's gotten you. Stealing silly rings from jewelry stores."

That he'd had her watched even when she'd thought they had been the ones following him… She slipped a little further down the rope from which she dangled.

"What have you planted on me? There's some kind of tracker," she decided. "Somewhere. Something inside me? You bastard. What is it?"

"It's not so devious as that. But science is making remarkable discoveries in nano skins. Small technologies can now be worn or even passed on to others, such as by dander from a cat, and it will stick for weeks, even through the wash. I'm incredibly impressed. I've invested in the technology."

"Chloe doesn't have dander."

"But her fur is so soft, and I know cats need a little tender loving care. I gave her a massage one day when she was staying with me."

"You're an asshole."

"And I do it well. Now, about that diamond necklace. I didn't think I needed the whole thing. Just the one diamond with the payoff code. Enter the code into a secure online rendezvous point and *voila*. Five million dollars transferred to the bank account of my choice."

"So you thought you'd go straight for the money. Now that sounds more like you."

"Exactly. And yet, it's always been *my* money. You might say I made a bad investment and am now trying to recoup my losses. Little did I realize the code requires the fucking task to be completed."

"And mass murder isn't your style. Guess you haven't changed that much. But do you realize if you don't complete the task, something even worse will happen?"

She studied him intently. Those dark straight brows above his deep brown eyes made him look so intelligent. And the well-groomed stubble? Mercy, she had to look away. Bad boys. Would she ever get over them?

"Yes, but what? And with the clock ticking?" He clicked his tongue and stood up.

"You don't know what will happen?" she asked. "Neither do I. But it's going to be bad. Just hand over the diamond, and I'll make sure the good guys get it. You walk away without having bloodied your hands and mark it off as a missed paycheck. Not like you can't afford to miss a few now and then, eh?"

"Who are you working for, Jo-Jo? Tell me."

"No one but myself."

"Who is The Fox working for?"

"I honestly have no idea. He wouldn't tell me. I'm as much his pawn as yours."

"Yeah? Whoever that other thief is working for has siphoned my foreign accounts. I can't walk away from that money. I need it."

"Ha! Someone got the upper hand on you? I love it!"

Another slap to her cheek didn't even sting as she imagined Lincoln Blackwell curled up on the floor of his fancy Paris mansion crying over his empty accounts. High five to Xavier's secret club.

"You're right, you know," he said. "You're not my pawn. At least, not my only one. I've brought another piece onto the board." He leaned forward and tipped up her chin. "Of course, this whole shindig wouldn't be much fun unless I got to watch you watch him being tortured. Turnabout, wasn't that how you put it?"

That could only mean one thing. Had Xavier come after her? The fool. The gorgeous, sexy fool.

"He means nothing to me," she said firmly.

"We'll see."

Josephine swallowed and bowed her head. The asshole had won this round. Now to see how far he'd take it.

* * * *

Xavier dashed out his tongue and tasted his own blood, metallic and warm. It dripped from the cut above his eye. Blackwell's henchman wore brass knuckles. The thug landed his punches sparingly, but each one was placed in the perfect spot for optimal damage and pain. His ribs ached, but the bastard hadn't gone for his kidneys. Yet.

Xavier questioned his overzealous grab for this job. He should have let Gentleman Jack come in after all. Jack never would have gotten himself in this position. At least Xavier was sparing another man pain. He hoped that was also true for Josephine.

Arms spread wide and handcuffed to a brick wall, Xavier was still able to stand on both feet. They should have raised him so he'd be forced to stand on his toes. It would have made the torture much more effective. Yet the worst pain came from watching Seph.

Lincoln had escorted her in to the open warehouse basement fifteen minutes earlier. The man wore a four-thousand-dollar Armani suit that Xavier would have envied were he not simply trying to focus on not bleeding too much.

The floor was soft dirt, and the setting sun beamed through the top of the high windows. Seph stood fifty feet away, arms crossed, eyes on him, jaw tight. Dirt smudged her blue dress. A bruise marked her jaw. Lincoln stood beside her. She wasn't tied up or restrained in any way.

Was she trying to be strong for his sake?

Or did she simply didn't care?

The henchman's fist pummeled Xavier's left kidney. Shit. He'd been hoping that would come much later. Spitting up blood, he hung from his wrists for a few moments as he processed the exquisite pain through deep, concentrated breaths, and was finally able to support himself by tightening his quads again.

With each punch, Josephine remained silent. She didn't plead for him, which he appreciated. Theatrics would only give Blackwell more power.

Goddamn it, he loved the woman for her strength. And her stoic resolve. And for the woman she was. Not afraid to be herself, no matter the consequences.

Fuck. Did he really love her? What a time to realize it. It was a ridiculous notion. Something that could never work, at least according to Dixon's declaration that, should she be recruited into the ECU, they would never be located near each another.

There was always the chance Xavier could go on the lam. And take Seph along. Could he do that? Did he want that? Right now he had a certain amount of freedom that constantly hiding from the law could never grant him.

Xavier spat blood at the thug. The henchman bristled, but didn't wipe the spittle from his shirt sleeve. He turned to his boss for direction.

"Use the machete," Lincoln said calmly.

Xavier winced. Out of his peripheral vision, he'd noted the rusted machete tilted against the wall. Couldn't be sharp. That was not going to be a picnic. The thug tugged off the brass knuckles and dropped them. Dirt spumed up at his feet. He turned to stalk over to the weapon.

"He knows where it is!" Josephine shouted.

Xavier winced. Coppery blood swirled in his mouth. "She's lying."

"He's hidden it," she said. "Had someone do it for him. He's the only one who knows where it is. I'll go with him. We'll take it back."

That was a complete lie. And it didn't have legs, either, as far as he was concerned.

Blackwell paced over to Xavier, fingertips pressed together. Would the man take the bait? Josephine was shooting from the hip.

"You don't both need to go after it," Blackwell said. "I'll keep Seph in hand while you go after the necklace, yes?"

"Won't work," Josephine said. "He'll run the minute you set him loose. He doesn't care about me. You could keep me in a cage for years and he wouldn't do anything for you. The people he works for? They wanted him to get close to me so he could take me out."

"Is that so?" Blackwell looked to Xavier.

He forced a bloody smile. "She means nothing to me."

Lincoln grabbed Josephine by the hair and punched her hard in the gut. Knees buckling, she went down, clutching her stomach. "Perhaps I've been torturing the wrong person?"

Xavier closed his eyes. If this began, he could not endure it.

Josephine's yelp alerted him to another attack, but this time he didn't open his eyes. He heard a struggle, and Lincoln called to his man to stay put as he apparently pummeled Josephine. She was tough. She could protect herself. But for how long?

After a few rounds of exchanged punches, someone landed on the floor before Xavier's feet. He opened his eyes. Josephine lay sprawled before him; Lincoln held his foot above her neck. The bastard looked up to him. Waiting.

It was Xavier's move.

Only years of experience in keeping his emotions in check and an innate lack of empathy allowed him to do what he did next. He spat. On her.

Lincoln jumped up and gestured for his man to pull Josephine to her feet and hold her aside. She swiped a hand across her cheek and glanced at Xavier, but he couldn't read her. A bruise had already darkened one eye and her lip was split. He would kill Blackwell for that.

He's on the recruitment list.

Shit. If Xavier ended up ultimately having to work with this man.... The risk of going AWOL was looking better all the time.

"Let's do this then," Blackwell announced. He swung around and stroked Seph's face. "I want *you* to hand me my five million dollars. It's the very least you can do for old times' sake, yes?"

Lifting her chin, she remained emotionless.

"We'll put the biological weapon together, you and I," he continued. "Then you'll deliver it to the 8th. It'll be sweet. But if that guy hanging on my wall is the only one who knows where it is, I am forced to put you two out together. Sure, I could keep you in hand, but you have the impetus to keep the man in line. You'll come back to me. If you don't? You'll never be free of me. Promise."

Xavier could feel Josephine's shudder in his bones. She truly hated Blackwell.

Lincoln snapped his fingers at his lackey. "Get The Fox wired for sound and make sure the tracker is still working on the bitch. Send them out together. I'll want that necklace in hand by dawn. Yes?" He looked at Xavier.

"What's my motivation?" Xavier asked.

Blackwell shrugged. "Life?"

Xavier nodded. "Works for me."

Chapter 26

Xavier told the driver to drop them in the 1st, half a block from his home. Thanks to the microphone tightly taped around his left bicep, there was no way to keep Blackwell from learning where he lived. The apartments the ECU assigned their agents were not forever homes, so it didn't bother him. He wore a clean suit coat that had been returned to him to wear over his bloodied dress shirt and trousers, but he still got a side look from a passing tourist.

He'd left all communications with Kierce behind before he'd walked near Blackwell's hideout in an attempt to get captured. So right now the ECU was blind to his whereabouts. He'd fix that soon enough.

And Josephine, apparently, wore a tracker on her from as far back as when Blackwell had handed over the cat.

She followed him into the evening shadows of the courtyard before his apartment building. Neither spoke. They both realized words should be carefully measured and analyzed before putting them out.

Once inside his apartment, he immediately put in the earbud he'd hidden in a slit of the suit coat hem. After a snap of static, Kierce confirmed their connection. "Got you. They let you go? With the woman?"

Xavier murmured an agreeing sound.

"All right, got it. I've switched frequencies so Blackwell won't pick up on our connection, but I'm still tracking theirs. Countdown is currently at three hours, forty-two minutes."

Xavier appreciated the countdown, but wasn't sure exactly what was supposed to go down. The necklace needed to be handed over to Blackwell. But they couldn't do that until Katirci had been located. That had been Gentleman Jack's assignment. No word on the Turk from anyone yet.

He took the notepad and pen from the sofa and scribbled, then handed it to Seph. She mouthed what he'd written: "Fake necklace made. Waiting for Turk's location."

She nodded, then she tapped her wrist, asking after the time.

He led up three fingers.

"Fuck," she said out loud. "What's going to happen?"

He shrugged.

"What if the whole city...?"

He shook his head in a vehement no.

She nodded. They couldn't talk with Lincoln listening. And they had to be convincing when they did.

"I'll contact my man," he said, picking up the cell phone he'd purposely left behind before going after Blackwell. He dialed Kierce. "You got the necklace?"

Kierce affected a very unnecessary British accent. "You should have it soon, mate. We'll arrange a handoff."

Xavier wasn't sure Blackwell could hear Kierce's part of the conversation, so he'd make it easy for everyone involved. "A handoff? Where?"

"By the river. I'll call you."

Xavier hung up and looked to Seph. She shrugged. Blackwell had to have heard that. Now all they need do was wait. And not talk. So...if they were going down, he intended to do it on his terms.

He turned and pulled Seph into a kiss that was hard and brutal and steeped with the ache he'd felt when he'd had to endure listening to Lincoln brutalize her. Pulling away reluctantly, he studied her eye. The skin around it was bruised. And her lip—he touched it carefully—was split.

She touched his wrist where the handcuff had rubbed off the skin, and he flinched. She shook her head, tendering a gentle touch to his eyebrow where the cut ached.

"Worth it," he mouthed. "I got your back."

And then all the desire and want that had been building since returning to Paris from Berlin exploded within and made him reckless. He touched her breast, bent to bite through the dress right over her nipple.

She fingered the wire beneath his shirt that Blackwell's assistant had placed around his bicep.

Xavier shrugged.

And her dress was shed as quickly as his clothes. He pushed her against the wall. She slapped a hand over the microphone, perhaps muffling it a little. Parting her legs, he slid inside her hot and tight body and groaned at the sweet release that came so quickly, all he could do was tremble against her body and drop his head to her shoulder. With a gritted jaw, he held in a gasp.

Blackwell was getting a surprise performance. He didn't care. Let the man know how much Seph meant to him. He'd had some suspicion, surely. She was his, and he'd let no man think otherwise.

Of course, the villain's thugs could be on their way to his apartment at this moment.

So he had to take what he needed while he could.

He pumped inside her, his bruised ribs and kidneys screaming with pain, but it was all background noise to the pleasure that soared through him and attacked with force as he came again. Seph clutched his shoulders and cried out. He put a palm over her mouth, muffling her pleasure. She bit his finger with wanton abandon.

"They're listening," she gasped.

"Good."

"I…" She gasped again and clenched at his bicep. "…want to say things, but they're not for anyone else to hear."

Pulling out of her and zipping up, he turned and grabbed his phone. Quickly locating the music app while Seph pulled on her dress, he turned it on. Loud.

Seph took the phone and held it against his bicep as she leaned forward and whispered, "I knew you'd come for me."

"I had to get that bastard in hand." He nuzzled his nose into her hair. So sweet. So…wrong for him.

"Seriously? So you suffered the torture not to rescue me but to…" She lowered her voice even more. "…trap him?"

He'd said that wrong. He had fought to go in so he could rescue Seph. But he'd never escape the fact she was also a job. "Both."

"What's the name of this organization you work for?"

"It's…uh…" He needed her trust right now. So he picked up the notepad and wrote it down and handed it to her.

She pushed away from him, pacing the short stretch of his tiny living room. When she finally looked at him, he read the betrayal in her tearful blue eyes. "You never would have told me that unless you had plans for me."

No, he wouldn't have. And he'd just played the wrong hand when he should have instead followed his heart. But the whole world was listening. And Blackwell still needed to be convinced that Seph meant nothing to him. It was the only way to ultimately protect her from the bastard. "You're not a stupid woman."

"No, I'm not. You're going to recruit me, aren't you?"

"It's voluntary. Though I do have your list of crimes, which will be used against you. You could make it work for you."

"Loss of freedom? How's that working for you?"

"Honestly? I have much more freedom now than I had always keeping one eye over my shoulder for the law." Not entirely a lie.

"I should have figured you'd do this. I don't want to have anything to do with being a chipped monkey who works for scraps like you." Her voice raised to compete with the techno music noise. "I've always been a loner. Always will be. Do you get bonus points for bringing me in?"

"It doesn't work that way."

"No, it doesn't. Let me tell you how it works. How it has worked. And this is for everyone who is listening to know what a bastard The Fox really is. That night you broke into my mother's office and stole everything she owned?"

Xavier gaped at her confession. "That was…"

"The thief I told you about? That was you."

Now was not the time for shocked dismay, when indeed everyone was listening, but she was intent. And he wanted to hear this.

"Why didn't you report the theft?" he asked. "If you witnessed it?"

"How could I end something that I'd wanted to begin? I became infatuated that night. But also infected with the need for revenge. My mom lost everything. And I lost family."

"Family? You said your mother and her boyfriend handed you over to a foster home. What kind of family is that?"

"It was my family. The only kind I've ever known." She clutched thick handfuls of her hair, then let go with a frustrated growl. "Like I said, I'm good at being a loner. So I learned. Followed you. Honed my skills. Kept you always in sight. You say you can't remember our first kiss?"

"I do." Because it returned to him right now.

The hour before he'd moved in on the National Art Museum to grab the Hortensia Diamond, he had stopped for a coffee. It was his MO. Caffeine pumped up his adrenaline and set his senses to super-focus. That evening, a gorgeous blond woman had flirted with him while he'd stood near a high table on the sidewalk outside the café. Before walking away, she'd leaned in for a surprising connection. And he had pulled her closer for a long and lingering kiss under the moonlight. It had further fueled his adrenaline and made the snatch all the sweeter in the moment.

He grabbed Seph's hand and turned it upward to reveal her wrist. "You had only one cat tattoo that night. I do remember. You were…blond? It was the night of my arrest."

Michele Hauf

"One hour thirty-two minutes," Kierce reported in Xavier's ear.

"Exactly." Josephine shoved her feet into her sandals. "I knew your plans for that evening and had it all timed out. I'd tracked your steps for days, shadowed you like a demon. You got fifty yards away from the museum before the police shackled you with cuffs. I was the one who called the cops."

And with that, she marched out of his apartment, leaving the door open behind her. "We've located Katirci," Kierce said, "and will have him at the drop off in seventy minutes. He's gunning for Blackwell."

Seph had been responsible for his arrest.

Hell. Why all of this now? How was he expected to save the world, or one small portion of the city, when his heart had just been broken in two?

"Let her go," Kierce warned. "I'll put a man on her. If we still need her for the handoff, we'll get her in position then."

Xavier crouched to the floor, clutching at his aching ribs. His entire body ached from the beatings he'd taken over the past days, but not so much as his heart.

The woman he'd fallen in love with was the reason he was now literally owned by the ECU.

Let her go? He tightened a fist and beat the wall. The sheetrock cracked. As did his heart.

Chapter 27

Fighting tears, Josephine made her way out of the apartment building, checking the streets for black limos. She still had a tracking sensor on her—where? She had to get into a shower and scrub mercilessly. But Lincoln had said it was waterproof. Would she never get that asshole off her literal back?

She pressed her bare shoulders against the brick wall, rubbing a bit, just in case it did dislodge the unseen sensor. She was unsure where to go next. She'd just given Xavier the biggest fuck-off possible. And she hated herself for that. She loved the man. But he didn't love her. Couldn't, now that he knew the truth about his arrest.

Why had she told him? It wasn't as if she'd been an upstanding citizen who believed in truth, justice, and whatever the hell crap ended that saying.

Oh yeah, she knew why. Because she'd never been a woman to him, only a pawn. A piece to move about to get what he needed, to bring in the bad guy and hand her over to his precious organization.

He'd wanted to recruit her to something called the Elite Crimes Unit? Had he been commanded to do so only after they'd netted Lincoln in their trap, or had this always been his task? He must have used her—with sex—to get closer, to gain her trust. And she had trusted him.

She shook her head. For one moment, might he have been not working and simply loving her?

What a fucking mess she'd made of this all! Why had she turned him in two years ago, when it hadn't mattered for her mother? Xavier's incarceration had not given Judith Devereaux back the fortune she had been holding, nor had it allowed her to come out from hiding from that terrible person she'd held the booty for. It hadn't reunited daughter with mother.

It had only taken a stellar thief off the streets and forced him to work for a controlling organization that must have surely stripped him to the soul.

At the time, it had closed a door for Josephine. And had been the catalyst to going off the grid. She had completed a chapter. On to a new life.

A new life that had circled around and smacked her harder than Blackwell ever had.

"I'm sorry," she whispered. Damn her emotional weaknesses!

A tourist bus stopped four car lengths down the sidewalk. Josephine headed toward it.

* * * *

"You listen, I'll talk," Kierce told Xavier. "I've tapped into Blackwell's frequency. I'm keeping tabs on her movement. Not for your sake. She's ours."

Xavier winced. *Could she ever be his?*

"The necklace is ready to go. Dixon will be at the Place de la Concorde before the Hotel de Crillon in ten minutes. Let Blackwell know the drop off is at the Pont Mirabeau. Katirci has been alerted that the man holding the necklace looks like Lincoln Blackwell. And he knows he's also got the payment stone. He's unaware of the ticking clock, so you need to take control and make sure everyone is in position. Let Katirci grab the necklace and the payment stone and go on his merry way."

"But what happens in—"

"Forty-five minutes? Your guess is as good as mine. But I'd say whoever is left holding the payment stone is not going to be a happy camper. I think there's something in the stone. A tracker? Detonator? I can only guess."

"That is an order." Hunter Dixon's voice came over the earpiece. "We'll rendezvous in ten minutes for the handoff."

"I'm on my way." Xavier closed the apartment door behind him and took the tightly wound staircase down instead of the elevator.

They were right. He didn't need to drag Josephine into this one, even if Blackwell had insisted she stand at his side while he put together the cruel weapon. And now that Xavier knew what he did about her, he wasn't sure he ever wanted to see her again.

Striding out into the courtyard, he exhaled and spoke so Blackwell could hear. "The meeting is at the Pont Mirabeau in half an hour. Be there for the handoff."

* * * *

As the bus waited at a red light, Josephine spied Xavier hurrying down the Rue de Rivoli. Instincts kicking in, she slipped around the front of the bus and followed him, careful to keep two blocks between them. He tapped his ear. Must be listening to Kierce, who always seemed to be in his head. He and Blackwell—along with who else?—had heard Xavier push her against the wall ten minutes earlier. One final good-bye fuck?

No, he had to see her again. The man had been ordered to recruit her. He'd said the recruitment was voluntary. Never going to happen. But if he rambled off her list of offenses, would she have no choice but to volunteer? The amount of time she'd have to spend in prison for her crimes would kill her. But did the secret organization really have that information, or was it all a bluff? She couldn't know until she heard what they had against her.

But she wasn't going to walk up to him and let him think he had a chance with her. The man had spoiled everything by putting his job before her. Even if that had been his only option, and prison was the fallback, she still hated him.

Logically, anyway.

Emotionally? It took all her strength not to rush up to him and beg him to hold her and kiss her until she forgot the world and how nasty it could be. With him, she'd found a brief spark of happiness. Working alongside him had rocked. And the sex hadn't been anything to complain about either.

How had she turned into her mother? How had she become a woman who'd do almost anything for the bad boy?

But Xavier worked for the good guys now. His bad cred had taken a beating, surely. She didn't want to walk away from the man. And she regretted having turned him in two years earlier.

Xavier turned toward the river. He still had Blackwell and the necklace to deal with. She should stand back and let the handoff happen. Blackwell would be arrested. Maybe. And the ECU would accomplish its mission. She would then be free of Lincoln, but never from the ECU.

Could she allow Xavier to walk out her life so easily?

"No," she said. "If we have one last chance to escape, we've got to take it."

Picking up her pace, she intended to get as close to Xavier as possible without giving away her location. She knew Lincoln had a bead on her location. The world was watching; she would linger behind the curtain until it was time to appear on stage.

* * * *

In the limo's back seat, Hunter Dixon handed Xavier the fake necklace. Knowing Xavier was wired, he spoke plainly. "Blackwell should come alone and meet at the landing below the Pont Mirabeau. *Rive Droite*."

"I'm sure he got those instructions." Xavier studied the fake necklace. It was a good imitation; the diamonds less valuable, but real. Worth about twenty grand, he estimated.

Dixon held up a notecard: "She followed you."

He nodded. He'd known Seph had been following him, for Kierce had tracked her all the way. If she knew what was best for her, she'd turn and walk the other way. He was in too deep to pull her out now. He prayed she got smart. And fast.

Dixon gestured he exit the back of the car. He'd said all that was necessary. A team would be placed nearby to take Lincoln Blackwell in hand. He wasn't sure what was planned for the Turk, but he'd leave it to the ECU.

Now it was Xavier's play.

Tucking the beribboned diamond necklace, missing one stone, into his suit pocket, he strolled the sidewalk hugging the river, gliding his fingers over the stone balustrade. At the end of the stone, he turned a sharp right and skipped down the stairs to the cobblestone walk fronting the cool waters. The moon was at half crest and it was late, so the tourist-stuffed *bateaux-mouches* no longer traced the waters. A dark barge was moored a hundred yards ahead. Scents of gasoline and stale water filled the night.

It was difficult not to look around, hoping to spy Seph. She wouldn't come close. If she stepped into the fray, she risked fucking up the whole mission. On the other hand, Blackwell would expect her presence because he intended to take her into hand. Xavier hoped she stayed away.

And yet he wasn't sure how he'd react to the woman who had turned his life upside down and fucked it up forever.

He checked his cell phone. Sixteen minutes to the final count.

This would be the most torture he had endured. Ever.

Chapter 28

He must know she followed him. Even though The Fox did not give out any clues— he hadn't once looked over his shoulder as he strode alongside the river and began down the stairs that paralleled the river Seine— but it was in the way he carried his head.

From all the times she'd followed him, she knew that he saw everything, but not with his eyes. His senses were attuned, just as they should be when he crouched alone in a room before an uncrackable safe, or when he hung suspended from a cable while he sought a valuable jewel without setting off the infrared sensors. He could smell the changes in the air. Touch the heat or cold. His body was truly of the universe and that universe suspected Josephine was near.

She didn't try to distract him, staying as hidden as possible. He must have the necklace. A fake?

The ECU must have set a trap for Blackwell. Josephine wanted to be there to see it go down. She deserved that much.

As did Xavier. She noticed the hitch in his step. His left leg was injured; perhaps the bone fractured by Lincoln's thug. Not enough to keep him from walking, but more than enough to be painful. He was a class act.

Pity someone had taken him off the streets and turned him into a performing monkey.

Sighing, Josephine shook her head. It wasn't her fault. And she wouldn't be blamed for it. Yes, she had tipped off the police, but what had happened after his arrest had nothing to do with her. He was a big boy. The man had life in his grasp and knew how to survive.

If she could take back that call to the police station to report The Fox was going to steal the Marie Antoinette diamond, she would. Now. But then? She'd been tainted with the blind and ridiculous need for revenge. She'd gotten it. And it had boomeranged to knock her off her feet. She'd never thought to see the man again after that night she had kissed him *adieu*. Never even hoped to work alongside him. And to have his trust.

Or to make love with him.

"You've been a fool, Seph," she whispered, loving the nickname he had given her. Would she have a chance to hear him call her that again?

A limo pulled up to the curb before the river. Lincoln Blackwell got out, along with one of the thugs Josephine recognized. Surprisingly, he gestured the bodyguard remain by the car, then walked alone down the stairs to the riverside. The bodyguard leaned over the stone balustrade to watch.

It was a stupid move on Lincoln's part. But then again, Xavier was also alone. In theory. He had a voice in his ear and likely a whole cavalry waiting to take Lincoln in hand when the moment was right.

And when would that right moment occur? Lincoln wanted the whole necklace, but he'd also want to keep the single stone if it had a payment code on it. Or would he attempt to trade it? No. The five-carat stone was his cash cow. He might, however, tease it as a trade. Because Xavier wouldn't hand over the necklace without asking for something in return.

And what about her? Had Lincoln given up on his plans to include her in his dastardly dealings? Unlikely. Which is why she kept a three-sixty degree scan of her surroundings.

Xavier had said something about arranging for the Turk to show up. Where was the terrorist who had been hired to take out an entire neighborhood? How had they gotten him on their side? *Had* they?

So many unknown factors. Yet she felt that "screaming no" rise in her throat, and the thrill of the game made her smile.

Slinking up to the top of the stairs and squatting on the top step, Josephine hid herself in the night shadows that shrouded the inner half of the stairway. From this angle, she couldn't see the bodyguard, which meant he couldn't see her either. Xavier's gaze swept the staircase, but he didn't pick her out. Or he didn't indicate that he had, as Lincoln left the bottom stair and walked up to him.

In the river, a barge wobbled. There was someone on it. Many people lived on barges along the Seine. But if someone were walking around at night, wouldn't they turn on a light?

Creeping down a few steps, Josephine kept one eye on the barge, which was out of Xavier's range of view.

* * * *

Victor Katirci was supposed to be positioned nearby. Xavier hadn't seen any suspicious figures—beyond the henchman who leaned over the balustrade keeping watch over his boss—and the guy he'd tortured a few hours ago.

The adrenaline racing through his body reduced the pain in his thigh to a minimal throb, yet Xavier felt sure the crack in his heart would kill him.

He'd let himself get involved…and fall in love.

"Fool," he muttered to himself as Lincoln approached.

"Who's the fool?" Kierce asked.

He wouldn't answer. He didn't want to tip off Blackwell. What he really wanted to do was punch the asshole to the next country for hurting Seph. But he'd curb that anger.

Dressed in black and looking more villainous now that Xavier associated him with the rusty machete, Lincoln Blackwell stopped ten feet away from him.

"Where is Jo-Jo?"

"Jo-Jo?"

"Your current fuck," Blackwell said. "She's part of this deal." He tugged something out of his pocket.

Xavier glanced above, scanning the stone balustrade. Where was the backup that Dixon had promised? He couldn't hand over the necklace until he knew all players were in position.

"I got your back, Lambert," Kierce said. "Katirci is close. And we've got a team waiting to take Blackwell once he receives the necklace. But there's something weird on your GPS…"

Great. Leave him hanging with that ominous statement?

Something glinted in Blackwell's hand. The missing diamond. On which, the girdle sported a code to pay the terrorist who decimated Paris five million dollars.

"No diamond until I get both the necklace and Jo-Jo," Lincoln said.

"You try to get around the work and just go for the payday?" Xavier asked.

"Always take the easiest option. Remember that," Blackwell said. He made show of looking over Xavier's shoulder. "So where is she? I've tracked her here."

"I thought I made it clear she means nothing to me." He wasn't going to lie. But the man didn't need to know that Xavier had no clue what the hell Josephine was up to either.

And then he noticed the shadow glide closer on the stairs. Why had she come down here? He didn't need her…

Maybe.

"I believed you right until you fucked her."

Xavier smirked. He'd hoped that act would stab the man right in the balls. Suck it, Blackwell.

"You got the necklace?" Blackwell asked.

Xavier pulled out the necklace and dangled it between them. Perhaps it would be enough to keep him from demanding Josephine. Xavier scanned the cobblestone sidewalk and up the wall to the henchman, who now wielded a pistol in plain view. No tourists, thankfully. But no backup that he could see. Of course, he shouldn't be able to sight them with ease, or their cover would be blown.

"That is mine!"

Xavier's shoulders tightened, and it took all his courage not to turn around to see who had shouted in a gruff accent. Had to be Turkish. Please, let it be Turkish and not some random homeless person. He had to keep an eye on Blackwell. And Josephine—ah hell. She rushed up behind Blackwell, stopping four feet from him. Blackwell didn't notice.

"Boss!" the bodyguard shouted.

Shit. Xavier couldn't control four people who each had their own agenda. But he did know who had to walk away with the evidence.

Xavier held up the necklace and swung it so the moonlight reflected off the stones.

Kierce crackled in his ear. "Code Emergency, Lambert. It's a missile."

What? He touched his ear, pretending to rub it. From behind, a gun barrel stabbed into his shoulder blade.

"A missile is tracking the diamond—the single stone. It's going to make contact in two minutes!"

To swear would only waste precious time.

Xavier tossed the necklace to Blackwell. The man lunged forward and caught it with a crooked finger. The man behind Xavier swore and moved the gun to point over Xavier's shoulder. Xavier put up his hands in surrender. He glanced up to the bodyguard at the railing. He'd moved, swinging around at the top of the stairs.

"This is real?" Blackwell asked.

"You've got less than a minute," Kierce barked. "Blackwell, we need. Everyone else is expendable. Go!"

"Now, Seph!" Xavier shouted.

Josephine moved before Xavier got the words out. She hit the hand in which Blackwell clutched the single stone. His fingers let loose and the diamond flew, arcing twenty feet in the air. It flashed brilliantly at the apex, then fell in a sweet curve that brought it close...so close...

Xavier swept out his hand and caught the diamond.

Blackwell swore. The thug grabbed Josephine by her hair, but she managed a roundhouse kick that took him off guard and toppled him backward to land on the hard limestone steps.

"That is mine!" Victor Katirci dashed beside Xavier, gun in his right hand, left palm awaiting the diamond.

"Fifteen seconds, Lambert!"

"You bet it is." Xavier slapped the diamond onto Katirci's outstretched hand. "Run, Seph!"

He saw movement, but couldn't be sure if it was Seph or Blackwell racing up the stairs. Someone swore revenge in a most villainous tone.

But Xavier's seconds were almost up. And Josephine was in the range of danger. He turned and threw his body against the hefty Turk, setting them both airborne.

The Seine splashed around them. The Turk's body briefly broke the surface, then he and Xavier disappeared together into the watery depths.

Chapter 29

Josephine rushed to the river's edge. Lincoln swore behind her. "What was that?"

Wind rushed over her head. Why? Something crashed into the water. The wake splashed in her face as the whole sidewalk shook. A sonic boom? The entire world seemed to shift. The Seine burped up a massive spray of river, then rippled out in high waves.

"Was that a missile?" Lincoln said from the bottom step. "Holy... I did not sign up for this."

He kicked his bodyguard in the shin, then helped him up. They dashed up the stairs and into the night.

Josephine clung to the edge of the wet stones, searching the dark waters that rippled madly with moonlight with the aftershocks of what must have been some kind of bomb. Had it been a missile?

No, it couldn't be. "X?"

Had he known what was headed their way when he'd shouted for her to move? She'd instinctually known what he'd needed her to do, and in that moment, had congratulated herself for being stubborn and following him to the drop-off site. But now...

The waves receded and the wake grew more distant. The water's surface calmed. He'd been under for a long time.

Leaning forward, desperate to spy her lover—the man she respected and had learned from over the years—she almost toppled forward and caught herself just before she hit the river. She didn't know how to swim. But she had to. Someone had to locate his body.

His body?

"No!" she shouted. "This is not how it ends. X, please." The last word came out as a sobbing whimper.

She stretched her arm, hand sinking into the cool waters. Tears fell on her wrist, splashing the cat tattoos. She'd failed not only Xavier, but herself.

"I'm sorry."

The man hadn't deserved this kind of ending. He was too good. And so what if *good* was all in the perspective. He'd chosen his path and had walked away from a family fortune, only to put so many millions back into the world through charity. Others could argue he could have done the same through a legal, legitimate business like tailoring, but Josephine knew that some people were simply cut from a different cloth. The life of a criminal had been Xavier's only option. Because he'd had no other training... What had he told her about that sport when she'd been trying to get information out of him? He'd once been...a competition swimmer.

"Yes! Oh, yes, come on!" She slapped the water's surface. "You've got this. You can't go down this way, X."

A gush of water roiled toward her and Josephine looked up. A body floated closer. Face up and arms extended, the body...kicked.

"X!"

A few more kicks, and he was close enough for her to reach out, grab his collar, and pull him to the stone ledge. Xavier clung to the edge and slapped an arm across the sidewalk. He spat up the river and shook his head, spattering her with more water. With one tremendous guttural heave, he landed on the sidewalk and sprawled, eyes closed and spitting out more water.

"You're alive," she said tearfully. "What the hell was that?"

"Missile," he managed.

She touched his face; swept the hair from his forehead. Bruises darkened his skin and his shirt hung in shreds.

"Hit...Katirci," he said. "Blasted him out of my arms. Detonated... one second later. Seph...."

"Yes? I'm here. I'm so sorry for what I said to you. But you had to know."

He opened his eyes to look into hers. "Truth?"

He wasn't asking if she was truthful about being sorry, but rather if she was really the one who had had him arrested.

She nodded.

He closed his eyes. Coughed. Groaned. "Blackwell?"

"He took off."

"ECU...waiting. Lost...Kierce."

She checked his ear, but didn't see the earbud.

"Let me call you an ambulance," she said. "You've been through so much."

"ECU...will handle. Seph..."

She leaned over him, wishing to lie on his shoulder but not wanting to cause him more pain. "Yes?"

"I..." He coughed, and more water sluiced from his mouth. He took a deep breath and closed his eyes. "I had fallen in love with you."

Had fallen in love with her? Meaning he didn't love her anymore?

Well, of course not. She'd confessed to him. How could a man possibly love someone who could do such a terrible thing to him?

"Need...time," he managed. "You...go."

Her breath left her lungs in a huff. She bowed her head to his shoulder and sniffed back the tears that threatened to become a wail. But she wouldn't. She couldn't.

"ECU...wants you. Go!" he managed, and then coughed repeatedly, his body pulsing on the ground.

She kissed his mouth, tasted the river and her own regret, then nodded. "I love you, too. Sorry. We did this all wrong."

And she stood. Feeling the pull of freedom drawing her away from her lover's prone body, she struggled not to turn and walk away from him. But he was right. The ECU wanted her, and they were likely in the area.

Instead of heading up the stairs, Josephine rushed forward, past the docked barge and to the next bridge, where she took the stairs up to the street. Nothing. No headlights from passing cars, no muffled laughter from lovebirds in the nearby park.

Heartbeat thundering, she had nowhere to go.

Chapter 30

Xavier woke in the dark, on the most uncomfortable bed he'd ever slept in. Something crackled beneath him. Plastic. There was a plastic sheet under his body. He moved his arm and something tugged sharply inside his elbow crease. Looking at the dull gray walls and gold plaid draperies surrounding him, he realized he was in the hospital.

He was too exhausted to feel anything more than mild annoyance. The ECU actually allowed their asset to be hospitalized? Under what name? Or had they cut him loose, and his next trip was back to prison? He didn't wear cuffs. Though there could be a guard posted outside the door.

But he'd accomplished the mission. He had stopped the biological weapon from being created, and the payment stone was at the bottom of the Seine, along with an expended missile and the Turk's bones. The ECU would clean up that mess with little difficulty.

And Lincoln Blackwell must be in hand, either by the Paris police or Interpol.

Sitting up, he rubbed his brow. The worn blue hospital gown went to his knees. To the left, folded on a chair, were his pants, but no shirt.

Then he remembered his dive into the Seine and finally managing to surface. The explosion had pushed his body away from Katirci and probably shredded his shirt in the process. And he'd pulled himself up out of the water to land...

Beneath her tearful gaze. She'd been waiting for him like some kind of angel come to bless his not-quite-dead soul. Seph. He'd told her he loved her. But that had been before she'd confessed she was the reason for his arrest.

She'd taken his livelihood away from him. She had castrated The Fox and stuffed him into a windowless prison cell. She had...

...told him she loved him. He remembered that part. He'd been coughing and spitting up the nasty river water, but he did recall those words leaving her mouth.

He hated her for that. He loved her for that. He...didn't know how to feel, actually. In all his years, he'd never loved a woman. He'd never once considered running away with her, despite the risk to his freedom.

I called the police and told them you planned to steal the Hortensia diamond.

Bitch. He had underestimated her. Again.

And yet, all he wanted right now was to see her. To look into her blue eyes. To smooth his thumb over the tattoos on her wrist. To taste her kiss. To see if he could forgive. Because if he could, he'd have her in his arms again.

Was he crazy? Was he on drugs?

He turned and studied the label on the IV drip plugged into his arm. Just saline. He tore off the tape from over the needle and pulled it out with a hiss. Then he swung his legs over the side of the bed and assessed his condition. Not so dizzy. And the only pain he felt was in his ribs from the beating he'd taken. Yes, his leg hurt. It wasn't broken, but probably deeply bruised. All in all? He was good to go.

And if he were to be sent back to prison, or worse, the grave, he wanted to steal as much freedom as possible before that happened.

Pulling on his pants, he bent over and read the chart at the end of his bed. His eyes wandered over the date entry. "Two days?"

Had he been asleep this whole time? Crazy. Now he really did need to escape.

Tugging at the gown, he decided to leave it on until he got outside. Good cover. And with hope, he could snag a shirt on the way out. No shoes that he could see, but he'd worked under worse conditions.

He probably wasn't allowed to simply walk out without signing forms, or even the ECU's permission. Xavier popped his head out the doorway. No guard. The nurse's station loomed down the end of a long hallway. Looked like only one nurse, facing away from him and staring at a computer screen.

The elevators were on his right. Nice.

The first floor was practically deserted. It must be well after midnight. Xavier marched toward the front. There was a gift shop, but a gate barred the door. T-shirts hung on display inside, but it wasn't worth the effort of picking the lock when the doors to the outside loomed just ahead.

Walking swiftly, Xavier made it outside, pulling off the gown and tossing it behind a shrub. The cool night breeze hardened his nipples and rippled goosebumps across his skin. He recognized the area. He'd been inside *le Hôtel Dieu*, the city hospital on the main island. The streets were dark, and the streetlights were overwhelmed by the tree canopy. Limping, he quickly crossed the street. He was still standing, and that was all that mattered.

He didn't get far before he sensed someone behind him. He didn't hear footsteps or breathing, but his thief senses knew. The ECU? Or one of Blackwell's thugs? Dodging left around the end of a long stretch of greenhouses, he waited for someone to swing around the corner.

And waited.

Moonlight glistened on the river. Had his senses gone haywire while lying on the plastic sheet for two days? He *had* heard someone.

He edged closer to the corner of the building, weighing the risk of glancing around the side, when she spoke. "It's me."

Shoulders dropping in relief, Xavier tilted his head against the wall. He didn't need to look around the corner. Seph was there.

And he wasn't sure how he felt about that.

"I've had the hospital staked out since they took you there the night you almost drowned," she said.

She stayed on her side of the building. He was grateful. Facing her would bring up too much stuff he wasn't ready to deal with.

"I befriended a fence a couple years after you robbed my mother's home," she said. "One who liked to talk. I showed him the drawing of the fox you'd made on my mother's safe, and he told me about you. That you liked the colored stuff. That you were the best."

Xavier closed his eyes and bowed his head.

"He tipped me off that your next hit was Venice. I followed you there. Watched from a distance, taking pictures, studying your movements, your reactions. Your style. I managed to follow you on four jobs. A few other times, you pulled back like you thought someone was watching you. You're always aware of your surroundings. So I never got close to you. Didn't want to spook you. I admired you so much."

He winced. She should not have. A jewel thief as her hero? That was wrong. So wrong.

"But I still wanted revenge. At the time, I wasn't so good at controlling my feelings. So you became the scapegoat for my terrible life; my uncaring drug-addict mother, her ruthless boyfriend. But when I saw them slap the cuffs on you? My heart broke. All I could do was walk away from it all. It was over. I had no reason to continue what I was doing. The heists."

He had been her inspiration and her downfall. As she had been his. Because yes, she had inspired him these past few days.

"I'm sorry, X. I had to tell you. I had to do it. At the time it was the stupidest thing I've ever done. It was revenge. It was twisted attraction. It was me triumphing over the greatest jewel thief I'd ever known. It was..."

"Enough," he said. "I get it."

And, oddly, he did. If she had witnessed him stealing from her mother's safe, and that callous theft had left her destitute? The catalyst to her mother dumping her in a foster home? Of course Seph would seek revenge. He would have done the same thing, had he witnessed someone robbing his family home when he was a kid.

But the facts didn't make him hate her any less. She'd stolen a part of him. His reason for being. His career. His...excuse for not trying harder to live in the real world.

And that realization didn't make him love her any less.

"You still need to recruit me, don't you?"

Did he? He wasn't sure if he were even an active Elite Crimes Unit agent. Had he used up his last chance?

"I went to your place. Had to feed Chloe. I was going to get a hotel room, but, well, I left her there because like I said: stakeout duty. Uh... that means I'll have to return to get her. You can tell me a time tomorrow when you won't be around and I'll stop by."

He wasn't sure what tomorrow would bring for him. He needed to sort out things. Everything. And he didn't know if he could do that if she peeked around the corner and he looked into her devastatingly gorgeous eyes.

"Eleven," he said. "I'll make a point of not being there."

"Right. X?"

The wobble in her tone cut through his cracked heart. He hated to hear her hurting. "Yes?"

"We could have been great together."

Probably.

She sniffed a tear. "I love you."

He waited for more, but wasn't sure why. That's all he needed to know. Should he return the same endearment? He wanted to. But not without looking at her.

His heart pulsed with anticipation and he tossed aside his reluctance. He swung around the corner, his arms open for the woman he loved. But instead of Seph, Xavier saw only the steel-and-glass greenhouse wall and the bare sidewalk. Not a shadow betrayed her presence.

The thief had slipped away in the night.

With his heart.

* * * *

Chloe greeted him with a meow. And Xavier's cell phone rang the moment he entered his apartment. Par for the course.

It was Kierce, reporting that a car would pick him up in the morning. With the recruit.

Right. The recruit he was supposed to bring in to the ECU. Xavier muttered a *thanks*, then tossed the phone onto the bed. He stripped off his pants and headed for the shower.

The pick-up was scheduled for after eleven o'clock. How to play this one?

* * * *

"Sorry, X, I had to break in." Josephine leaned over the man lying on the bed. His eyes blinked open. "You've been through a lot. You needed the sleep. It's past eleven. I'll take Chloe and leave."

But she couldn't force herself to move from Xavier's bed. It might be the last time she saw him. Would she remember his face? That sexy midnight stubble? The piercing Dresden green gaze and tousled hair? Looks didn't matter; it was the way he'd made her feel that she hoped to never lose. Imbued in her veins, Xavier flowed through her.

She touched the corner of his eye where a cut had scabbed. The skin around his left eye was maroon, but it wasn't swollen. He wore no shirt, and bruises lashed his ribs and over his kidney. He'd suffered for her. And she couldn't begin to imagine the emotional suffering he endured.

Check that. Of course she could, because her heart hurt. Desperately.

"You said you loved me the night by the river," she said. "You don't have to love me. I mean, it was just cool that you once did."

"Yes, well…" He reached for the cell phone on the nightstand and wobbled it in display. "Got the order last night before I dozed off. I'm to bring you in for recruitment."

"I thought that was supposed to be voluntary?"

"Apparently, they've changed their minds."

So she'd take that as a warning that she should get the hell out of here. Instead Josephine stayed on the bed. And when Xavier sat up and leaned against the headboard, apparently in no rush to shackle her and drag her off to some secretive pseudo-prison filled with ex-cons, her heart only beat faster.

"Did you mean it?" She searched his gaze.

"Did I mean what?"

"That you loved me? At least once?"

He nodded, raking his fingers through his hair, and looked away. A sure sign that he was struggling, too. "I thought about taking off with you. Leaving the grid. Going under."

"We can do it."

He shook his head.

No, he couldn't betray his organization. The risk was too great. And she'd learned that no matter what he did, the man did it well and to the highest and most satisfying completion. He took pride in his work. Even if that meant his actions benefitted the very law he once stood against.

So she touched his jaw, turning his face toward hers, and waited for him to look at her. "Then maybe I could live with the kind of freedom you deem so tolerable to an ex-thief?"

"Don't say that, Seph," he snapped. "All you've ever wanted is freedom. I know that. Get out of here. Walk away from me. Have a life. Because you won't have one working for the ECU."

"I'd be doing something I enjoy. Something I have a talent for. It could be a life with you."

"Why do you believe that?" He forced himself to meet her gaze. She stared at him so intently, it hurt to look at her.

Josephine took a deep breath. "You're saying what you need to make me leave," she declared. "I thought it was your job to bring me in."

"I love you too much to do that."

"Oh, you bastard." She kissed him, hard and long and deep.

He pulled her tightly against his body. His hands clutched her derriere and glided up her back and along her thighs. And in her kiss, she gave him all that she could. More than she had ever given another person. Trust, respect. Truth. A promise that she was his. Always.

"Go," he whispered. "I'll never stop thinking about you, Seph. But when I do think about you, I want to picture you as a free woman."

"You can't force me to do anything, X."

"No. But the car to take me in to the ECU will be here in twenty minutes. Don't force me to hurt you this way. Please?" His jaw tightened as he tried not to let the pain taint his voice. "Josephine. Take the damn cat and go."

She touched his cheek where the bruising didn't show, but she suspected it hurt like a mother. He shook his head, knocking away her touch. She didn't know what she'd do without him. So much of her past had been about him. Following him, learning from him, hating him. And now, loving him.

Of course, she had loved him since that first night she'd watched him rob her mother. He hadn't destroyed her life then. He'd only welcomed her into a new and exciting way to survive.

But now he was giving her an opportunity to walk away. From sacrificing her to his Last Chance Ops.

From ever being happy again.

She nodded and stood, turning to hurry out of the bedroom. Picking up Chloe's carrier, she opened the front door and walked out. Without a look back. Without a goodbye.

As it should be.

Taking the elevator down, she clutched the plastic carrier like it was a life vest. "What should I do, Chloe?"

The cat meowed.

Exactly.

It was time to take control of her life. And live it in the manner that would make her most happy. Outside, she hailed a cab and promised the driver a big tip if he'd chill for a while.

Chapter 31

Xavier entered the underground headquarters for the Elite Crimes Unit. He wasn't sure what to expect when he faced the Boss and told him he had failed the recruitment. By now, he hoped Seph was well on her way out of the country. Destination? Somewhere. Anywhere he didn't know about.

He missed her already. He could find her if he utilized all of the ECU's resources. But he wouldn't. He'd have to fight the urge to find her every day for the rest of his life, but it was in Seph's best interest.

He had to stop thinking of her as Seph. She was Josephine Devereaux. Jewel thief. The woman who had put him behind bars. The woman who had nearly gotten him killed because she didn't know how to drive. The woman for whom he'd suffered torture to secure her freedom. The woman…

…who would never vacate his heart.

Get your act together, man.

He needed to play this right for Dixon to buy his story about losing her trail. But no matter what he said, it would go over like a steaming pile of bullshit. Kierce could follow the tracker Blackwell had planted on her, which could still be on her. And the ECU knew he'd had the cat and she would have come back for it.

How to play this?

Kierce nodded to him, then went right back to whatever he was doing behind the computer monitor. Xavier hadn't been connected to the guy since the night of the handoff. The communications device had literally been blown out of his ear when he'd hit the Seine with Katirci.

Kierce's head went up at the alarm bell that indicated another agent had entered.

Xavier didn't care who walked in. He strode past Kierce's desk without a word.

Prison or the tombstone? No matter how he was punished, it would suck. Would he get credit for the year he had been out and working for the ECU? Doubtful. He'd only done it under the threat of death.

Hunter Dixon strolled down the hallway, bent over a file. He didn't notice Xavier until he stood right before him. "The handoff went well. Katirci was expendable. Smart move, Lambert. The Paris police have taken Lincoln Blackwell into custody. We'll be letting him stew in prison for a few months before we move in. Escaped from the hospital, eh? To be expected. And you have…"

Hunter looked over Xavier's shoulder. Just as he summoned his courage to confess, someone behind him reached around to shake Dixon's hand.

"Josephine Devereaux," she offered, balancing the cat carrier in her left hand. "I'm here voluntarily on behalf of Monsieur Lambert's suggestion." Chloe meowed. "Sorry, my cat and I are currently homeless. She goes where I go. Just so you know. That's a deal breaker."

Dixon's eyes glittered as he exchanged a smiling glance with Xavier. "Mademoiselle Devereaux. And…Chloe. We have a lot to talk about. This way." Dixon gestured for her to follow him down the hallway to his office.

Xavier grabbed Josephine's hand. "Don't do this."

"I have to. It wouldn't be a life if you weren't in it." She kissed him quickly. Too quickly. Then sauntered down the hallway after the boss.

Xavier touched his cheek where her kiss warmed his skin. He hated her for making such a sacrifice.

And he loved her for following her heart.

* * * *

Four months later…

Josephine dashed through the streets of Paris. Her heartbeat thundered, and her skin glistened with sweat. Her thighs ached, but she smiled. The exertion always gave her a high. So did the thrill of running loose and free, not being watched twenty-four/seven. Every day at the end of her martial arts training for the ECU, she went for a run and ended up at the little apartment she'd been granted temporary custody of in the 4th arrondissement. No one from the ECU physically tracked her because they didn't have to. She wore a chip at the base of her skull.

So far? She did not regret walking into the ECU headquarters and turning herself in. And while the organization seemed to go out of their way to keep her and Xavier apart—lately he was only assigned jobs out of the country—he did have downtime. And they'd developed a code so he could let her know when he was in town.

Today the red chalk marks on the curb opposite the ECU's gym had advertised a sale at a trendy clothing shop.

Josephine veered off the main street, slowing her pace and blowing out her breath to cool down. The clothing shop she entered was air conditioned, but even in her running shorts and tank top, she wasn't cold. She said *bonjour* to the hipster clerk texting on her iPhone and made a show of looking over the racks as she headed toward the dressing rooms.

The dressing room attendant recognized her, grabbed the black tag from the wall, and handed it to her with a wink. Josephine strolled to the back stall, which was the only one with a full-sized door—used for more upscale clients—and plunged into Xavier's arms.

He kissed her neck and licked at the salty sweat dripping down to her breasts. The man quickly tugged up her shirt as she unzipped his fly. Clothing was shed amidst frantic kisses and dangerously teasing touches. Standing before her naked, his cock full mast and ready for action, The Fox winked. "You here to try something on for size?"

Josephine's gaze dropped to his erection. "It looks a little large. But I think I can make it fit."

* * * *

Hunter Dixon led Michael Walters down the hallway toward the small cafeteria, where the smell of brownies had lured them both. The frosted treats had been left by an asset who always cooked after a long few weeks on an intense job.

"You do a work-up on Lincoln Blackwell yet?" Dixon asked.

"In the process. Horst keeps providing incredible information. Blackwell has a long list of crimes. How long will he be locked up before the ECU takes him?"

"Not sure. The Commander thinks a few years behind bars might serve him well. I'm gunning for one year. We can use someone like him out in the field. So are you meeting with Horst tomorrow?"

"Yes, my flight to Italy leaves this evening. Keeping that man as a double agent was brilliant on the Commander's part. He helped put Blackwell out in the open by cleaning out his accounts."

"Just don't ever let Xavier Lambert know his accountant works for us."

"Lambert has kept his accounts clean since he's been with us. The man is smart. He's not going to fuck up his last chance. Case in point. He didn't take off with Josephine Devereaux when he had the opportunity."

"How is Devereaux working out?" Dixon asked around a bite of brownie.

"She's adjusting to the program nicely. We won't have a problem with her."

"Is that so? I just watched the GPS track her into a clothing store, and I know she's not much of a clothes hound."

Walters smirked as he poured a cup of coffee.

"You know Lambert is in town on hiatus for a few days as well," Dixon added.

"We both know what's going on between then. And I suggest we turn a blind eye. It's best for both of them. And, ultimately, for the success of their missions. A happy asset is a valuable asset."

"Is that your professional opinion?"

"You know I've turned my eye from others who engage in the same sort of liaisons."

Walters tilted his head, giving Dixon a message that was plainly understood. He didn't have to mention the Commander's name. It was implied.

"Right," Hunter said. "All's well in the Elite Crimes Unit."

"Indeed."

Meet the Author

Michele Hauf has been writing romance, action-adventure and fantasy stories for over twenty years. Her first published novel was *Dark Rapture* (Zebra). France, musketeers, vampires and faeries populate her stories. And if she followed the adage "write what you know," all her stories would have snow in them. Fortunately, she steps beyond her comfort zone and writes about countries she has never visited and of creatures she has never seen.

CPSIA information can be obtained
at www.ICGtesting.com
Printed in the USA
LVOW11s1545280317
528762LV00001B/168/P